My Favourite
Rabindrana

CW00458611

My Favourite Stories of Rabindranath Tagore

Translated from Bangla

by

Ratna Jha

Vij Books
New Delhi (India)

Published by

Vij Books

(An imprint of Vij Books India Pvt Ltd)

(Publishers, Distributors & Importers)
4836/24, Ansari Road
Delhi – 110 002
Phones: 91-11-43596460, Mob: 98110 94883
e-mail: contact@vijpublishing.com
web : www.vijbooks.in

Contents

Introduction

The idea of translating Gurudev Rabindranath's short stories was not something that came to me all of a sudden. I toyed with it for a very long time, for nearly ten years, before finally getting down to it. I had to muster a lot of courage to venture into such a challenging task. Gurudev was fond of using puns. Trying to explain the deeper meaning of certain sentences, while maintaining the tempo of the story was a daunting task. I got around it by attaching a glossary with explanatory notes.

I spent most of my school days in Santiniketan's Patha-Bhavan, which Tagore founded in 1901. The misery that he had felt during his short stint in a school had led Tagore to set up this wonderful 'open' school where classes were held under trees. He felt mother nature was a great teacher, so children should never be far from her. Having felt caged in cold, forbidding classrooms, where walls stood guard over children like sentries, he wanted children to be free. So, in his school, teachers sat under the shade of trees waiting for their students, while children walked from one teacher to another. I remember how we would tell our teachers about our discoveries – a bird's nest hidden among the leaves, fruit ripening on some tree, a rare butterfly, and so on. And our teachers never thought we were wasting time. They encouraged us to feel enchanted by the ever-changing moods of nature. Class eight was the first time that we started having classes indoors. This was because our science teacher wanted to show us zoology specimens and working models of other science subjects.

Everyone in school referred to Rabindranath as Gurudev. Even today I refer to him by that name; he will be my Gurudev always. This book is my way of paying homage to the great man whose writings have shaped my thinking. His songs – he composed more than two thousand – have become a part of my existence, an expression of myself. They have been my inspiration in difficult times, my refuge in sorrow, my companion in loneliness.

Gurudev wrote nearly ninety short stories, creating a new wave in Bengali literature. His first story, Bhikharini (The Beggar Woman) was written in 1877, when he was just sixteen years old. It was published in a magazine called *Bharati*. 'Ghater Kotha' (Story of the quay), another of his earlier stories inspired by a quay in Chandan Nagar, was written in 1884. But his career as a short story writer really started in 1891, when he went to East Bengal (now Bangladesh) to look after the family estate.

I chose to translate seventeen stories from *Golpo Guchcho*, the collection of Gurudev's short stories, because of my childhood association with them and also because they relate to women of substance. Our Bangla teacher, Umadi used to read out parts from these short stories and then ask us to read the rest of them on our own. She had a beautiful voice, and a perfect diction and she used to hold us spellbound when she read out the stories to us. Most of us went to the library to read them – being appreciated by one's favourite teacher was indeed a big temptation!

Gurudev felt that a society or a nation could progress only if women were given the opportunity to develop their personality to the fullest extent. This, we must remember, was at a time when the emancipation of women was frowned upon by the vast majority of people in our country. He was way ahead of his time in his thinking about women, which becomes very obvious in stories like 'Mahamaya', 'The wife's letter' and 'Laboratory', to name only a few.

Mahamaya, who is forced to become a 'sati', manages to leave her husband's funeral pyre stealthily and walk away with her lover. They do not marry; they live together – something that was unheard of those days.

Mrinal, in the story 'Wife's Letter' breaks away from an inert relationship and opts for an independent existence far away from the suffocating atmosphere of a joint family, in which she had spent fifteen years of her life. In her last letter, which is also her first letter to her husband, she writes about severing ties with him. She says 'I will never return to your house in 27, Makhan Baral Lane. Do you think, I am going to kill myself? Have no fear. I will live.'

'Laboratory' is one of Gurudev's last short stories. Sohini, the main protagonist, is   independent in her thinking. Her primary aim is to safeguard her husband Nandakishore's laboratory, which she treats as a surrogate for Nandakishore. She is willing to go to any extent for this, including using her feminine charm. When she realizes that her daughter,

Nila, is consulting her lawyers to claim her share of Nandakishore's money, Sohini doesn't hesitate to declare boldly in public that Nila is not Nandakishore's daughter, that she was born out of wedlock. In 1930, when this story was written, Sohini's admission of her own waywardness in public was unimaginable.

Gurudev wrote 'Musalmanir Golpo' (The Story of a Muslim Woman) a little before his death. Kamala, the main character, was an ordinary woman before being married off to a wealthy man. She and the bridal party are waylaid by dacoits and the entire entourage, including her husband, deserts her. That night is a night of transformation for Kamala. She is saved by Habir Khan, who takes her home and gives her shelter for the night. When he takes her back to her house the next morning, her relatives don't accept her because she had spent a night in a Muslim household. Habir Khan takes her back to his house, where she is treated with respect and allowed to practice her own religion. Later, she marries Habir Khan's second son of her own accord and becomes a Muslim. Her experience in Habir Khan's house changes her vision of religion. She says, 'The person who has given me shelter is my God – he is neither Hindu, nor Muslim. I worship him.'

Both 'Postmaster' and 'Shubha' are about unrequited love. In the first, a young man from Kolkata is posted to a remote village to run a post office. He employs Ratan, an orphan girl, to assist him with household chores. She cleans and cooks for him, fills water from the river, lights his hookah, and so on. When he falls ill, she nurses him. Slowly, an undefinable relationship grows between them. When the time comes for the postmaster to leave, Ratan hopes that he will take her along with him; though she doesn't know how and in what capacity. The poor girl is heartbroken when he leaves.

Shubha is a young girl who cannot speak. She is like the little mermaid in Hans Christian Anderson's story. The mermaid loses her voice and cannot tell the prince that she loves him. Shubha, too, cannot tell Pratap about her feelings towards him. Pratap sits beside Shubha on the river bank with his fishing rod for long hours. Shubha desperately wants to become a water nymph and dive into the river to bring the jewel on the legendary serpent's head for Pratap. So that he can dive into the river with the jewel in his hand and reach the underwater kingdom to discover that Shubha is actually a princess. But, alas, Shubha is married off and the groom does not know of her disability. When he gets to know, he dumps Shubha and remarries.

Hindu revivalism started in the late nineteenth century in Bengal. The aim of this movement was to prop up religious and social orthodoxy through the so-called scientific defence of old customs and superstitions. The Age of Consent bill was passed shortly before 'Khata' (Notebook) was published. The object was to stop child marriages. Naturally, conservative Hindus reacted sharply. In the story, Uma is married off to Pyarimohan at the tender age of nine. Her father had allowed her to attend school, but she is forbidden to read or write in her husband's house. There are three notebooks in the story – the first one belongs to Uma, the second, to her brother and the third, to her husband. The notebooks of her brother and husband are full of erudite essays in support of Hindu revivalism. Uma's notebook, on the other hand, is a collection of observations made by a child. Someone discovers Uma's notebook and her husband confiscates it. The author comments, 'Priyamohan too has a notebook, but unfortunately, there is no benefactor of the human race to seize and destroy it'.

Many of Gurudev's short stories have been adapted into films. 'Samapti' (conclusion) is one of the three stories of Satyajit Ray's movie called *Teen Kanya*. The others were 'Postmaster' and 'Monihara'. In Samapti, Apurva gets drawn to Mrinmoyee, the naughtiest girl of the village who doesn't hesitate to play pranks on anybody. He marries her against his mother's wishes. Apurva's patient and mature handling of the 'shrew' transforms her into a beautiful woman, who begins to understand the meaning of love.

In 'Shasti', Chandara is sentenced for a murder that she did not commit. Her husband implicates her to protect his elder brother, who is the actual murderer. He justifies his action by saying, 'If I lose my wife, I can get another, but if my brother is hanged, I will never get another one.' Chandara is shocked when she hears this. She doesn't defend herself in the court. When she is asked about her last wish the day before she is to be hanged, she says that she wants to see her mother. The kind jailor tells her that her husband wants to meet her. She refuses to see him and says, '*Moron!*' (a mild rebuke which means go to hell).

Tarapada, the leading character of 'Atithi' (The Guest) is a wanderer He has been a wanderer by choice since he was eight years old. He meets Motilal babu and his family in a boat. For the first time he becomes interested in family life. He spends almost two years with Motilal babu and his family. Then one day he leaves without informing them. He goes back to his nomadic existence.

Kabuliwala explores a father's love for his child. Rahamet, Kabuliwala, is an Afghan trader and moneylender. At the time when the story was written, Kabuliwalas (Afghan traders were known by this name) were feared by the Bengali middle class. Notwithstanding this, Rahamet conquers little Mini's heart with his funny tales and bribes of dry fruits. He is later convicted in a case of assault. When he returns after serving his sentence, he is astounded to find that Mini is about to get married. The narrator, Mini's father, realizes that Rahamet sees an image of his own daughter in Mini – the infinite love of a father separated from his daughter had found expression in the bond between a Kabuliwala and a little Bengali girl.

In Khokababur Protyaborton, the servant's devotion to his master's son and his guilt about inadvertently causing his death is so great that when his son is born, he is convinced that khokababu has come back to him. He spoils his son more than is good for him, but the son doesn't reciprocate his love. Later, he takes his son to his master's house and presents him as the khokababu who had gone missing. Unfortunately, his confession is taken at face value and his master's wife is convinced that he had kidnapped their son. What is heart rending is that his son, too, is convinced that he is Khokababu and dismisses his father haughtily.

Gurudev was influenced by the lives of the common people around him. He felt for their trials and tribulations. The children in his short stories make you feel that he must have come across them somewhere.

I have tried my best to stick to the text so that not much is 'lost in translation'. I do hope that I have managed to make a peep hole through which the reader can get a glimpse of the great man's work.

My sincere thanks to my sisters Medha and Chandana for their assistance. I owe my gratitude to Vij Books for taking out this book.

1

Kabuliwala

My five-year-old daughter, Mini, can't stop talking even for a moment. She was a year old when she started talking and she hasn't wasted a moment since then. She talks all through her waking hours. Her mother scolds her very often and asks her to keep quiet. But I don't. Things don't seem normal when Mini is quiet. So I encourage her to talk, and that is why she talks to me freely.

I had just started writing the seventeenth chapter of my novel when Mini came in and started off, "*Baba*, Ramdayal *darowan* calls crows 'kauwa'! He just doesn't know anything! Don't you think so?'

Even before I could tell her that the same thing is denoted by different words in different languages, she started talking about something which was totally different; she said, "You know Baba, Bhola was telling me that it rains because elephants spray water with their trunks from the sky. I think he talks rubbish."

Before I could give my opinion about Bhola, she suddenly asked me, "Baba, how is *Ma* related to you?"

I smiled and said to myself, 'My *shali*.' To her, I said, "Okay, now go and play with Bhola. I have a lot of work to do."

She didn't go. Instead, she sat cross-legged at my feet, near my desk, and started reciting a rhyme at high speed, beating the rhythm on her knees. '*Aagdum baagdum*'. In the seventeenth chapter of my novel, Pratap Singh was holding Kanchanmala in his arms and was about to jump into the river along with her from the window of their prison. Mini suddenly stopped her game, went running to the window overlooking the road in front and shouted, "Kabuliwala, O Kabuliwala!"

A tall turbaned Kabuliwala with a big *jhola* slung over his shoulder was walking down the road. Every year, Afghans came to Kolkata with their wares, of dry fruits and woollen shawls, and they were known as Kabuliwalas in local parlance. I wonder what crossed my little daughter's mind for her to start calling the Kabuliwala at the top of her voice. I was a little apprehensive, as I did not want anything to hold up the completion of my seventeenth chapter.

But Mini's call attracted the attention of the Kabuliwala and he started walking towards our house, smiling. As soon as she saw him coming, Mini ran inside the house at top speed. Mini strongly believed that Kabuliwalas were child lifters and one would certainly find a child or two like her inside a Kabuliwala's *jhola*.

The Kabuliwala came in and said 'salaam' with a smile. Though Pratap Singh and Kanchanmala were in a 'do or die situation', I could not ignore the Kabuliwala's presence in my study so I decided to buy something from him.

I bought some of his wares and then we started talking. We discussed many things, like Abdur Rehman, Russia, the security policy of the British at the border, and so on.

Before leaving, he asked me, "Babu, where is your daughter?"

I sent for her as I wanted to dispel her false notions about Kabuliwalas in general. Mini came and stood very close to me. She kept looking at the Kabuliwala's *jhola* suspiciously. The Kabuliwala took out some raisins and apricots from his *jhola* and offered them to her. But Mini refused to take them; she moved closer to me. That is how they met for the first time.

A few days later, I was going out for some work one morning; what I saw surprised me no end. My daughter was sitting on a bench near the front door and chatting with the Kabuliwala. She was talking incessantly and the Kabuliwala, who was sitting at her feet, was listening to her prattle with rapt attention. He joined in occasionally in his pidgin Bengali. In all the five years of her life, Mini never had such an attentive listener, other than her father. I noticed that her *anchal* was full of raisins and nuts.

I said, "Why have you given her all this? Please don't give her these in the future." I took out an eight-*anna* coin from my pocket and gave it to him. The Kabuliwala took the coin from me and put it inside his *jhola*.

When I came back in the evening, I found a big uproar in my house. It centred around the same eight-*anna* coin which I had given to the Kabuliwala. I heard Mini's mother, who was holding the shining round white object in her hand, say, "Where did you get the coin from?"

"The Kabuliwala gave it to me," replied Mini.

"Why did you take the coin from the Kabuliwala?" Was her mother's next question.

 Mini was on the verge of tears now. She said, "I didn't ask him; he gave it to me on his own."

 It was at this point that I intervened and rescued Mini from the impending danger of being severely reprimanded, and took her out with me.

I discovered that this was not just the second time that Mini had met the Kabuliwala. They had been meeting nearly every day. The Kabuliwala had already conquered a large part of Mini's greedy little heart by bribing her with dry fruits. I learnt that these two friends had a few favourite dialogues and jokes. For example, the moment Mini saw him, she would laugh and ask him, "Kabuliwala O Kabuliwala, what is inside your *jhola*?"

Rahmat (that was the Kabuliwala's name) would laugh and reply in a put-on nasal tone and say, "*Hanthi*." He meant that there was an elephant in his bag – not a very subtle joke, though – but the two of them would have a hearty laugh after that. I enjoyed listening to them laugh happily and freely.

They shared yet another dialogue which was repeated very often. Rahmat would say, "Khonkhi (Kabuliwala called Mini by this name),*tumi sasur bari kakkhono jabe na* (you must never go to your father-in-law's house)."

 Most girls of Mini's age were quite well-versed with the term *sasurbari*, but since ours was a modern family, Mini had no idea about it. That is why Mini could not understand the significance. But she was not the one to remain silent. She would ask him instead, "Are you going there?"

Brandishing his raised fist, Rahmat would say, "*Hami sasurke marbay* (I will beat him up)."

She would burst into peals of laughter, imagining the plight of the poor father-in-law.

It was autumn; in the olden days, this was the time when kings would set off from their kingdoms to conquer other kingdoms. All my life, I had never been outside Kolkata, and I longed to go out and roam all over the world. Whenever I heard about some foreign country or met a foreigner, a beautiful picture of a small cottage nestled in a forest, surrounded by hills close to a river, would appear in my mind's eye. It would make me yearn for a carefree, independent existence; a life full of happiness and free from the boredom of a daily routine.

But I had got used to my humdrum existence. I was accustomed to staying in one place and the thought of leaving this cosy nook and going elsewhere filled me with apprehension. That is why I enjoyed talking to the Kabuliwala. I was transported to his native land as he spoke. I could see the red-hued inaccessible and barren mountains, burnt by the scorching sun, rising on either side of narrow mountainous paths. I could see camels laden with merchandise walking in a line. I could see turbaned travellers and tradesmen riding on their camels or walking next to their camels, with spears and flint rifles in their hands. The Kabuliwala's deep and sonorous voice unfurled before my eyes a beautiful canvas showing scenes from his motherland.

Mini's mother was suspicious and nervous by nature. So much so that if she heard someone shouting loudly on the road, she would think that it was some drunkard who was walking towards our house. She believed that the world was infested with things that cause harm to human beings, like thieves, robbers, drunkards, snakes, tigers, caterpillars, cockroaches and *Goras*.

Her mind was not free of doubts about Rahmat either. She kept asking me to keep an eye on him. When I tried to laugh it off, she bombarded me with questions like, "Don't children get kidnapped? Isn't slavery still prevalent in Afghanistan? Is it very difficult for a Kabuliwala of Rahmat's dimensions to carry away a small child quietly?"

Even I had to agree that such a possibility existed, but it was unlikely in the present scenario. Actually, everybody is not trusting. Thus my wife was never comfortable about Rahmat's proximity with Mini. And I could not ask him to stop coming to our house, for no fault of his.

Every year, Rahmat went back to his country during the month of *Magh*. Before leaving, he went from door to door collecting money from the people who owed him. This kept him very busy, but despite his busy schedule, he found time to see Mini at least once a day.

When I watched them from a distance, I felt as though the two of them were hatching a plan in utmost secrecy. When he could not come in the morning, he would come in the evening and spend some time with her. On days when I saw Kabuliwala, dressed in a loose long shirt and *shalwar* and with a big *jhola* slung over his shoulder, sitting with Mini in a quiet and dark corner of the house, I would get a bit worried. But when I saw Mini run out to meet Kabuliwala, shouting, "Kabuliwala O Kabuliwala," and I heard the two friends of unequal age repeat the same questions and answers and laugh, joy would fill my heart.

One morning, I was sitting in my room, correcting proofs. Winter was almost gone, but during the last few days of its stay, the temperature had suddenly plummeted and we were chilled to the bone. I was enjoying the sun rays which were creeping in through my window and warming my feet. It must have been eight in the morning and people were returning from their morning walk, bundled in their woolen garments, when I heard a commotion.

I saw Rahmat walking between two guards. He was tied up with a rope. A group of curious boys was following them at a distance. Rahmat's shirt was bloodstained. One of the guards was holding a knife. I went up to the gate and stopped the guards and said, "What's the matter?"

What I heard from the guards and from Rahmat was, that one of our neighbours had bought a Rampuri shawl on loan from Rahmat. When Rahmat went to his house to collect his money in the morning, he denied that he owed Rahmat any money. An argument ensued between the two of them. It ended in fisticuffs and Rahmat stabbed him with his knife.

Rahmat was still very angry and was uttering unspeakable abuses aimed at the liar. Mini's attention was drawn by the hullabaloo, she came out, shouting, "Kabuliwala O Kabuliwala!"

Rahmat's face brightened the moment he saw her and he smiled genially.

Kabuliwala did not have a *jhola,* so the conversation about the *jhola* was omitted; she straight away started with, "Will you go to your father-in-law's house?"

He said, "That's exactly where I am going." (In local parlance jail is also called father-in-law's house).

But Mini did not look amused and Kabuliwala noticed it. He raised his tied hands and said, "I would have beaten him, but my hands are tied up."

Kabuliwala was sentenced to a few years of imprisonment for causing grievous injury.

We had forgotten about him. We were so immersed in our daily routine that we never thought of how a man like Rahmat, used to living freely in the hills, was spending his days in a prison cell.

Though I am her father, I have to admit Mini's behaviour was very disgraceful. She had forgotten her old friend! The next person she got friendly with was Nabi, the groom. As she grew up, she added more girls to her list of friends than boys. She even stopped coming to my study! It was like an *aari* with me.

Many years went by. It was autumn again. The date of my Mini's marriage had been fixed. The ceremony would take place during the Puja vacations. Like the goddess of the Kailash mountains, Mini, the source of our happiness, would leave her father's house in darkness and go to her husband's house.

It was a beautiful autumn morning. The sunshine was like molten gold after the rains. Even the dilapidated houses in the congested alleys of Kolkata sparkled as the sun shone on them. There was a mood of festivity in my house. The *shehnai* players had been playing raga Bhairavi since early morning. The raga has an element of pathos in it, and it reminded me of the forthcoming parting. My Mini was getting married today.

My house had been bustling with intense activity since the morning. People went in and out endlessly, without a break. Tall bamboo poles were being dug into the yard to put up a *shamiana*. The tinkle of the decorative chandeliers put up in every room and verandah could be heard all over; there was not a moment of silence in the house.

I was sitting in my study, doing the accounts, when Rahmat walked in. I could not recognize him at first glance. He was a shadow of his former self. His hair was short and his hallmark –the *jhola* – was missing. I recognized him only when he smiled.

I said, "Rahmat, when did you come back?"

He said, "I was released from jail last evening."

The word jail had a jarring effect on me. I had never seen a convict from such close quarters. My mind turned bitter. I did not want him to be present on an occasion as auspicious as Mini's wedding. I said, "I am a bit busy today as I have a lot of work. Please go today."

On hearing this, he got up to go and walked up to the door, then he stopped. After a bit of hesitation, he said, "Can I see Khonkhi for a minute?"

Maybe he thought that Mini was just the same as, he had seen her last. He must have expected that Mini would come running, shouting "Kabuliwala O Kabuliwala!" And they would start their pet dialogue once again, like always.

I said, "There is a lot of work today, so it will not be possible."

Rahmat looked disappointed. He looked steadily into my eyes and said, "Babu, salaam," and went out of the door.

I felt bad when he left and was seriously thinking about calling him back, but he came back even before I could get up from my seat. He came in and said, "Babu, I got these for Khonkhi–please give them to her." Having said this, he placed a box of grapes and a packet of dry fruits on my table; he had probably borrowed them from a friend. I took out some money to pay him. Kabuliwala refused to accept it. He held my hand and said, "Babu, you have been very kind to me. I will remember your kindness forever, but please don't give me any money…

"Babu, I too have a daughter at home. I am reminded of her when I see your daughter and that is why I bring dry fruits when I come to see her. I don't come here to sell my wares."

Then he took out a folded piece of paper from the inner pocket of his loose shirt. He unfolded the paper very carefully and spread it out on my table. What I saw moved me. It was the print of a small hand. Not a photograph or a painting; just a simple imprint made with the help of lamp black. Kabuliwala came from his country every year to sell dry fruits on the streets of Kolkata, holding this piece of paper close to his heart –the paper with an imprint of his daughter's hand comforted him and helped him to bear the pain of being separated from her.

Tears welled up in my eyes. I forgot that he was just a Kabuli dry fruits seller and I was a Bengali gentleman belonging to the elite class. Just like me, he was a father; the father of a girl. The impression of the hand of his Parvati (girl who lives in the hills, another name of goddess Durga) reminded me of my daughter. I sent for Mini. The ladies of the house raised many objections, but I did not pay them any heed. Mini walked into my room bashfully, dressed in bridal attire, with a red veil covering her head. She stood close to me.

Kabuliwala couldn't believe his eyes when he saw her. It took him some time to recover. He did not know what to say. After sometime, he said, "*Khonkhi tumi sasur bari jabis* (are you going to your father-in-law's house)?"

Mini understood the meaning of *sasur bari* now. She blushed deeply and turned her face away. I was reminded of the day when they had met for the first time. It made me feel sad.

After Mini left, Rahmat sat down on the floor with a deep sigh. It must have occurred to him that his daughter too must have grown up, like Mini, in his absence, and like Mini, she too must have changed a great deal in the last eight years. Maybe he realized that it was not going to be like earlier; he would have to renew his friendship with her. His mind must also have been assailed by doubts about what might have happened to his daughter in his absence. The sound of *shahnai* floated in the morning breeze – serene, soothing and sun-drenched. Rahmat's mind must have travelled to the barren hills of Afghanistan as he sat in my home in Kolkata.

I gave him a currency note and said, "Rahmat, go back to your country, to your daughter. The happiness you will feel on reuniting with your daughter after so many years will bestow blessings on my child."

After giving Rahmat the money, I had to readjust the budget and cancel a few things planned for the celebration. The decorative electric lights were not as elaborate as planned and the wedding band was cancelled. It made the ladies of the household unhappy, but I did not care. The blessings of a father in a faraway land made my daughter's wedding celebrations appear brighter.

Glossary

Darowan — Gate keeper

Shali — Sister–in-law (wife's sister)

Aagedum bagedum — Bengali nursery rhyme

Jhola — Kind of capacious bag slung from the shoulder

Anchal — Free end of a saree that hangs down from the shoulder

Hanthi — Elephant

Sasurbari — In-law's place

Gora — British soldier

Magh — Tenth month of the Bengali calendar (Jan—Feb)

Aari — To stop talking with someone.

Shehnai — A wind instrument played during auspicious occasions

Shamiana — A kind of canopy

2

Khoka Babu Comes Back

(Khokababur Protyaborton)

Raicharan was twelve years old when he came to work in the house of his master. He was from the district of Jessore and like his master, he was a *Kayasth* (a caste among Hindus) by birth. He was dark, slim and long-haired. His eyes were large. Raicharan was given the responsibility of looking after the master's one-year-old son.

By and by, the little child grew up. He left Raicharan's lap, went to school and then to college, after which he entered the judicial service. Raicharan continued to serve him as his personal servant.

A new person entered the household after some time – the mistress. Her arrival restricted Raicharan's right over Anukul babu as, the new mistress took over most of the tasks performed by him.

Raicharan's right over Anukul babu became considerably limited, but this state of affairs did not last long. Soon, Anukul babu was blessed with a son. And Raicharan, with his endeavour and love, captured the heart of the new member.

He would swing the child with great enthusiasm, throw him up and catch him expertly, bring his head close to the child and shake it vigorously, and babble meaninglessly to him without waiting for an answer. As a result, the baby would squeal with delight at the sight of Raicharan.

When, with a bit of effort, the baby started crawling over the *choucath* (lower portion of the door frame, embedded into the floor) and hide himself, giggling, when someone came close to him, Raicharan's happiness knew no bounds. He was thrilled by the child's cleverness and skill, and went to his mistress and declared, "*Ma* (the mistress of the house is addressed as Ma), your son will become a judge one day and earn five thousand rupees a month."

It was beyond Raicharan's imagination that a child so small could achieve a feat as difficult as crossing the *choucath*. He felt that such intelligence and cleverness were reserved for babies who would become judges in the future.

It was a matter of great wonder when the baby started walking on his unsteady legs. When the baby began calling his mother "Ma", his *pishi* (aunt) "Pichi", and Raicharan "Chnno", Raicharan passed on the good news to whoever he met.

What struck him as extraordinary was the fact that the baby called his mother "Ma" and his aunt "Pichi", whereas he called Raicharan "Chnno". He was in awe of the baby's intelligence. He believed that even an adult couldn't have thought of this name.

After some time, Raicharan had to pretend to be a horse for the child's amusement, holding a rope in his mouth as if it were a rein. There were times when they wrestled and pandemonium would ensue if Raicharan did not fall after he was defeated.

At this juncture, Anukul was transferred to a district on the river Padma's bank. He brought a perambulator for the child from Kolkata. Raicharan would dress up the child in a satin coat and a cap embroidered with *zari* (golden thread) gold bangles and ankle bells, and then take him out in the perambulator, both in the morning and evening.

The monsoon arrived. The Padma River, swollen by the rain, became hungry; it swallowed crop-laden fields, forests and villages as it flowed past them. Huge chunks of the coastline broke and fell into the turbulent water of the river, accompanied by a loud splashing sound.

Though the sky was cloudy that afternoon, there was very little chance of rain. Raicharan's whimsical little master did not want to stay at home. He went to his perambulator and sat in it, making it very obvious that he wanted to go out. Raicharan got up and started pushing the perambulator slowly. In a while, they went past the paddy fields and reached the riverbank. No boats were visible on the river. No one was to be seen in the paddy fields. It was becoming dark. Some light peeped out through a gap in the clouds. The sky was preparing for a sunset on the opposite bank of

11

the sea-like river. The silence was broken by the baby, who pointed towards a *kadamba* (burflower) tree and said, "Chnno foo." He pronounced *phool*, which means flower, as foo.

A kadamba tree stood at a small distance from them. A few flowers on the high branches of the tree had attracted the attention of the little master. He wanted those flowers. A few days earlier, Raicharan had made a small cart out of sticks for the child, using the ball-shaped kadamba flowers as wheels. Raicharan had tied a string to the cart and dragged it. The child had been thrilled to see it move. After that, Raicharan had promptly been promoted from a horse to the exalted position of a groom.

Raicharan was reluctant to wade through the gluey mud to reach the tree. So he tried to distract the child. He pointed towards an imaginary bird in the opposite direction and said, "Look, look at that bird there. Call him – 'come little birdie, come, come, come.'" He made a lot of unintelligible sounds and started pushing the perambulator in the opposite direction. But it is not so easy to distract a child who is intent on getting something; the imaginary bird turned out to be a poor substitute. There was nothing else in the vicinity with which to divert his attention.

Raicharan had no option, so he pulled up his dhoti in order to wade through the the slush and said, "Khoka babu, sit quietly in the *gari* (vehicle; he meant perambulator). I will quickly bring some flowers for you. Be careful, don't get off the *gari* and go to the river's edge."

That was a grave mistake. Raicharan should not have told the child not to go to the river's edge. The river's edge became a greater attraction for the child than the flowers. The turbulent water of the river invited him. The swift flowing water was like hundreds of small children laughing and running away from some superhuman Raicharan.

Those naughty children beckoned to him and the urge to join them made him restless. Raicharan's little master climbed down from the perambulator slowly. He picked up a long blade of grass and walked to the water's edge. He sat there holding the blade of grass as though he was fishing. And the gurgling water of the river invited him to its playroom.

There was a loud splash, but the sound of such splashes was common when the river was in spate. It didn't bother Raicharan much. He climbed down the tree, smiling, with his arms full of flowers. His heart sank when he reached the perambulator. The child was not there.

12

Within minutes, the whole world turned dark and dismal, shrouded by a haze. Poor Raicharan called his little master over and over again: "Khokababu o Khokababu!" His voice broke with the effort, but no one appeared and said "Chnno!" mischievously.

The turbulent river rushed past him – unconcerned – too busy to pay attention to such small things.

In the evening, the worried mother sent people all over to search for the two. They went to the riverside, holding lanterns, and found a distraught Raicharan running across the fields like a madman, shouting over and over in a broken voice, "Khokababu, my darling, please come back!"

Raicharan came back home at last and fell at the feet of his mistress. Every time he was asked about the child, he would answer through tears, "I do not know."

The people were in no doubt that the river had taken the child away. A few suspected that it was the gypsies' doing. Some gypsies had pitched their tents a slight distance away from the village. But his mistress was of the firm belief that Raicharan had taken away her child. She called him aside and pleaded with him with folded hands to return her child, and promised to give him as much money as he wanted. Raicharan said nothing in reply; he just struck his forehead in despair. His mistress threw him out of the house.

Anukul babu wanted his wife to rid her mind of this unjust suspicion, so he asked her, "Why would Raicharan commit such a heinous crime? What could be his motive?"

She retorted, "Why wouldn't he? Wasn't our child wearing gold ornaments!"

2

Raicharan went back to his village. He still did not have any children, and there was very little chance of begetting any. But within a year of his arrival, his elderly wife gave birth to a son and died.

Raicharan developed a grudge against the newborn. He felt that the little baby had come with the intention of taking Khokababu's place. He was disturbed because how could he rejoice at the arrival of a son when his master had lost his son because of him? This made him feel like a sinner. Had it not been for Raicharan's widowed sister, the child wouldn't have remained on this earth for long.

The child grew up under the care of his sister. After some time, even this child crawled over the door frame. He giggled like Khokababu when he did something which he had been told not to do. When Raicharan heard the child laugh, he noticed an uncanny resemblance between the laughter of his son and that of Khokababu. His heart would miss a beat when the child cried. It made him feel as though his Khokababu was crying for him.

Phelna was the name that Raicharan's sister had given the child. Phelna means a person unworthy of attention. Soon, Phelna started calling Raicharan's sister "Pichi". And when Raicharan heard what the child said, he was in no doubt that Khokababu had come back to him because he couldn't stay away from his Chnno.

He had a few irrefutable arguments to support this. First, the child was born soon after he had come back to the village; his wife had never conceived before this. Moreover, the child crawled, walked unsteadily and called his aunt "pichi", just like his little master. Raicharan was certain that the child would become a judge in the future.

He remembered his mistress' suspicion regarding him. He sympathized with her and said to himself, 'The mother's suspicion was right. It is I who took the child away from her.' The fact that he had neglected the child for so long filled him with remorse. He became a slave of his child.

Raicharan decided to bring him up like a child from a well- to-do family. He bought him a satin coat and a cap embroidered with *zari* (gold thread). He melted his wife's gold ornament and got a bracelet and bangles made for the child. He never allowed his child to play with the children of the village. He became the child's constant companion and his only playmate. His neighbours found it very amusing and made fun of him. They started calling the child 'prince'. Soon, Raicharan became the laughing stock of the village.

When it was time for Phelna to start going to school, Raicharan sold his property and took him to Kolkata. After a great deal of effort, he managed to find himself a job and sent Phelna to school. Despite his hand-to-mouth existence, he never compromised on Phelna's upbringing. He sent Phelna to a good school, fed him good food and clothed him like a child from a well-to-do family. He would say, "Little one, you have come to me because you love me. I will make sure that you never lack in anything."

Twelve years went by. The child turned out to be a good student. He was good-looking and healthy. He had a whitish complexion and was a bit fastidious about his hair. His tastes were like those of the high-born. Unfortunately, he never treated Raicharan like a father. Raicharan loved him like a father, but he served him like a servant. It was Raicharan's fault that he never told anybody that he was Phelna's father. The children in Phelna's hostel used to make fun of Raicharan and one can't say if Phelna, too, joined them when they made fun of the poor man behind his back. But Raicharan's nature was such that the children in the hostel loved him all the same; even Phelna loved him, though this love was tinged with condescension.

Raicharan was getting old. He had become weak and his master had started finding fault with his work. Because of his age, he had become forgetful and could not concentrate on his work. But a person who pays his servant will not turn a blind eye when he makes mistakes because of his advancing age. The money that Raicharan had got from the sale of his property had almost run out. Phelna, on his part, started complaining about his clothes.

3

Raicharan left his job. The decision was sudden. He gave Phelna some money and said, "I am going to the village for a few days, on some urgent business."

Raicharan didn't go to his village; he went to Barasat instead. Anukul babu was posted as a *munsif* (judge of the lower court) in Barasat. Anukul babu had not had a second child and his wife had not been able to overcome the sorrow of losing her child.

One evening, Anukul babu was resting after coming back from the court and his wife was talking to a *sadhu* (holy man). The sadhu was trying to sell some roots to her at a very high price, with the assurance that they would help her to conceive. They heard someone calling. There was someone in the courtyard.

"Who is it?" Anukul babu wanted to know.

Raicharan walked into the room. He touched Anukul babu's feet and said, "It's me, Raicharan."

Anukul babu's heart melted at the sight of the old man. He asked Raicharan many questions about his well-being and then offered to employ him once again.

Raicharan smiled wanly. He said, "I want to meet *Ma thakrun* (mistress) and pay her my respects."

Anukul babu took him inside to meet his wife. Unlike her husband, she did not seem happy to meet him. Raicharan was unperturbed. He touched her feet and said with folded hands, "It was not the river that took your child away; it was me – this lowly, ungrateful…."

"What are you saying? Where is he?" cried Anukul babu incredulously.

"Master, he is with me. I will bring him the day after tomorrow."

That was a Sunday. The court was closed. Anukul babu and his wife waited eagerly for Raicharan. Raicharan and Phelna came at ten o'clock in the morning. Anukul babu's wife was beside herself with happiness when she saw him. She sat him down on her lap and hugged him and gazed at his face; she laughed and cried at the same time and went berserk with joy. Phelna was a good-looking child and was well-mannered. His attire was just right. The manner in which he was dressed betrayed no sign of poverty. The sight of the child moved Anukul babu too, but he did not show any emotion. He asked Raicharan calmly, "Do you have any proof?"

Raicharan said, "How can there be any proof? Only God knows that I had stolen your child. No one else in this world knows."

Anukul babu thought for a while and decided not to investigate the matter any further and to accept Raicharan's confession. His wife had already accepted the child, so he felt that further investigation would not be worthwhile. Moreover, why would Raicharan tell him a lie and lastly, how would Raicharan have so perfect a child?

Anukul babu spoke to Phelna and learnt that he had always been with Raicharan, and knew him as his father. According to Phelna, Raicharan had never behaved like a father with him; he had always acted like a servant.

The talk with the child left Ankul babu's mind free of all doubts. He told Raicharan, "You must leave this place and don't try to contact us after this."

Raicharan folded his hands and said, "Master, where will I go now in this old age?"

The mistress said, "Let him stay here. I have forgiven him. God will bless my child for this good deed."

Anukul babu's righteousness prompted him to say, "He has committed an unpardonable crime. He cannot be pardoned."

Raicharan held Anukul babu's feet and said, "It was God who did it; I did not do it."

This made Anukul babu angry – how can anybody blame God for his own misdeeds? He said, "I can't trust a person who has betrayed me."

Raicharan said, "It wasn't me who betrayed you."

"Then who?"

"My fate."

This answer did not satisfy an educated person like Anukul babu.

Raicharan tried again. He said, "I have no one in this world."

Phelna was there all along. He gathered from the conversation that was going on that, he was a munsif's son, and Raicharan had stolen him from his real parents and kept him all this while. Even though he was angry with Raicharan, he told Anukul babu magnanimously, "Father, please pardon him. Even if you do not let him stay with us, please send him some stipend every month."

Raicharan did not utter a word after this. He gazed at his son's face for a few seconds, then touched the feet of his master and mistress and left his master's house.

He got lost in the crowd of the multitudes that inhabit this earth.

At the end of the month, Anukul babu sent Raicharan some money at his village address. The money came back undelivered because no one lived there.

Glossary

Kayasth — A caste among the Hindus

Choucath — Lower portion of the door frame embedded into the floor.

Ma — Mother, often the mistress of the house is addressed by this name by the domestic helpers

Pishi — Aunt, father's sister

Zari — Golden thread

Kadamba — Burflower

Phool — Flower

Munsif — Judge of the lower court

Ma Thakrun — Mistress

3

Bolai

It is believed that 'the story of man' appears as an epilogue in the history of the animal kingdom. Quite often we see characteristics of different animals in human beings around us. At times we find qualities of animals which are polar opposites in the same human being for instance, the characteristics of a cow and a tiger can be seen in the same person again characteristics of a snake and a mongoose can be found in some other person and so on. While singing a raga we weave various notes together. The notes mingle with each other so well that the end product is a harmonious melody. While singing a raga, certain notes are given more importance than the others and that becomes the distinctive feature of that particular raga. Something similar happens in humans too.

In my nephew Bolai, the notes related to the plant kingdom superseded all other notes. Right from the beginning, he was a quiet child who preferred watching things around him more than moving around. When layers of dark clouds gathered in the eastern sky. He would stand and watch the sky as the clouds heaped up. He would inhale deeply the fragrant, moist breeze that came in from the forests after touching the trees. When it rained in torrents, he listened to the sound of the falling rain with his entire being. A little before sunset when he walked on the terrace bare bodied to absorb the last rays of the setting sun, he made me feel as though he was collecting something from the sky above. At the end the month of Magh (December-January) when the mango flowers bloomed waves of happiness ran through him as though he was being reminded of some long forgotten happy memory. In spring when the *Sal* flowers bloomed his mind would stretch out like the branches of the *Sal* trees and acquire a hue of its own. At that time, he would talk to himself and tell stories —a patchwork of stories that he had heard before. The story of *Bangoma* and *Bangomi* (mythical birds) who live in the hollow of a Banyan tree was his favourite. He had huge eyes which captured everything around him. He was not much of a speaker, may be that is why he thought a great deal. Once I took him to a hill station. There was a grassy slope in front of our house. It started from the highest point of a hill and ended at the base of the hill. He was thrilled when he saw it. To him the slope was not stationary. For him the green layer of grass was like a green river, moving all the time. He would reach the top and come rolling down like a bundle of grass. And when the tips of the grass tickled his ears, he would burst into peals of laughter.

After a shower at night when the first rays of sun fell on the trees of Deodar forest like molten gold, he would get out of the house quietly and sit under a tree. The forest gave him an eerie feeling. He used to say that he could see the tree people who lived inside the trees. According to him they did not speak, but they knew everything. They were very ancient, belonging to the time when our great great grandfathers were alive – when 'there was a king once upon a time'.

His huge eyes did not look up into the sky always, there were times when I have seen him walking in my garden searching for new saplings on the ground.   It would excite him no end when he found new saplings raising their curly heads from the earth. He would bend down and talk to them and say, 'so friend what's next?' There was a bond between them. He felt that even they wanted to talk to him and ask him questions. Maybe they asked him, 'what is your name?' Or maybe, 'where is your mother?' To which he might have said, 'I don't have a mother.'

He felt very bad when people plucked flowers. He knew that his feelings were of no importance to others, that is why he hid his feelings. When boys of his age threw stones at *amloki* (amla) trees to bring down the fruits, he just turned his face away as he couldn't see them hurting the trees. While walking through our garden his friends would hit the trees with sticks, as they passed by or they would break a branch of the *bakul* (tanjong tree) tree while walking past it just to tease him. Bolai wanted to cry, but he didn't. He feared that they would think that he was mad. What tormented him the most was when the grass cutters came. He had seen many seedlings pushing their heads out of the soil. He had discovered blue flowers with a tiny gold dot in the Centre hiding in the grass. Next to the hedge there were *kalmegh* creepers (*Androgrphis paniculata*) and *ananta mool* (Indian sarsaparilla) he had seen them grow. He loved the shining new leaves of Neem seedings which geminated from the seeds discarded by birds. It pained him to think that all those and more would come under the cruel scythes of the merciless grass cutters. They were not ornamental plants—very ordinary plants, maybe that is why no one paid attention to his complaints.

On some days he would sit on his aunt's lap, hug her and say, "Aunty please, tell the grass cutters not to cut down the plants."

His aunt would say, "Bolai don't be foolish, those are weeds if they are not cleared from time to time this place will become like a jungle."

Bolai had understood from a very early age that his sorrows were his alone no one else could perceive them.

Bolai belonged to the time, millions of years back, when the forests were being born in the marshlands rising up from the sea bed. It was very quiet other than the birth cry of the newborn forests. There were no animals and birds, so there was no din or noise. The plants were the first among all living beings to appear on the earth. They folded their hands and prayed to the Sun, they said "We want to live. We are perpetual travellers. We will travel in the day as well as at night we will travel in sun and in rain. We will travel onwards through our deaths and march towards our goal which is 'life that never ends.'" This was their anthem, and the plants have never stopped singing since then. They can be heard in the woods, in the hills, in the meadows everywhere.... The mother earth speaks through their leaves and branches she says, "I want to stay and I will stay." Since time immemorial plants, the mother of life on this earth have drawn food from the earth to feed her children. She sent the message of endangered life to the skies above, which said, "We want to live, we want to thrive." Bolai could hear this message, it ran in his blood stream. We made fun of him because of this at times.

One morning, I was deeply engrossed in reading the newspaper, Bolai came and insisted that I must go to the garden with him. I went along with him. Bolai showed me a seedling and asked, "What is its name?"

It was a tiny Silk cotton sapling, in the middle of the gravelled garden path.

Poor Bolai, he made a mistake by showing the plant to me. Bolai had noticed the plant when it had germinated, he was thrilled like a mother who hears her child's first babble. He had watered it and looked after it diligently and had kept a close watch on the plant. Silk cotton trees grow very fast, but it could not match Bolai's enthusiasm. Bolai wanted it to grow faster. When it grew up to a height of two feet Bolai was thrilled. He was amazed when he saw new leaves on the tree. He thought that it must be an extraordinary plant. His reaction was like a mother who notices the first hint of intelligence in her child. Bolai must have thought that he would impress me. And that is why he dragged me to the garden that morning.

I said, "I will tell the gardener to up-root the plant."

Bolai was shocked by what he heard he said, "Please do not tell him to do so. I beg of you." What a terrible thing to say! He must have thought.

I said, "You must have gone out of your mind, can't you see that the plant is growing in the middle of the garden path. It will be a big nuisance when it grows up and becomes a tree. The garden will be in a mess with cotton flying all over the place."

When he could not convince me, the motherless child went to his aunt to plead his case, he sat on her lap, encircled her neck with his arms, wept and said, "Aunty please tell uncle not to up-root the plant"

He had appealed to the right person. She called me immediately and said, "Please dear, do not uproot the plant let it grow."

Had Bolai not shown the plant to me I wouldn't have noticed it. But now the dumb plant drew my attention to it every day. It grew shamelessly and stood there like an eye-sore. Within a year or so it became huge and Bolai grew very attached to it.

The tree stood stubbornly on a spot in the garden where it shouldn't have been, and it grew at a fast pace. Nearly every one pointed out that the tree was not in the right place. I tried to convince Bolai to allow me to get rid of it. I even tried to bribe him by promising to plant rose bushes if he lets me chop off the plant.

As a last resort I said, "As you like silk cotton trees so much, I will get a silk cotton sap ling and plant it next to the hedge. But please let me get rid of this."

Bolai would get rattled every time I spoke of getting rid of the tree. And his aunt would say, "Come on, the tree is not looking so bad."

Bolai was just a toddler when my sister-in-law died. My elder brother was devastated by her death. Maybe to get over it he went abroad to study engineering. Bolai grew up in our child-less home looked after by his aunt, my wife.

My brother came back from England after ten years. He decided to give Bolai a British style of education, so he took him away to Shimla along with him. With the intention of preparing him for further education in England. In those days there were many residential English medium schools in hill stations which gave the students anglicized education.

Bolai left crying, and our home became a desolate place without him.

Two years went by. Bolai's aunt missed him a lot and quietly shed tears. She spent a lot of time in Bolai's bedroom tidying it. She would wipe Bolai's discarded shoes and his torn rubber ball, she would arrange his picture books and story books which were mostly about animals. Bolai's aunt would sit in his room and try to imagine how Bolai must have out grown all the things that he had left behind.

One day I noticed that the silk cotton plant had become a full-grown tree, I was shocked by its audacity, so I decided to end its impertinence once and for all by getting it felled.

Just after the tree was felled Bolai wrote a letter to his aunt from Shimla asking her to send a photograph of the silk cotton tree."

He was supposed to come to us before going abroad, but that did not materialize. That is why he wanted to carry a photograph of his friend with him.

 His aunt made a request to me she said, "Please ask a photographer to come."

"Why?" I asked.

She showed me the letter that Bolai had written in his unformed childish handwriting.

I said, "But I have got the tree felled."

She did not eat anything for two days. She didn't speak to me for a very long time after that.

When Bolai's father took him away it was as though a part of her was severed. And when Bolai's uncle chopped down the tree— it broke her heart.

The tree was her Bolai's best friend—his image.

Glossary

Bangoma and Bangomi — Mythical birds who live in the hollow of Banyan tree.

Sal — A north Indian Tree Which yields teak like timber.

4

The Unwanted (Aapod)

The storm picked up by evening. Rain lashed the earth, thunder rumbled and lightning leapt across the sky. The gods and the demons were at war. The clouds, flew from one side of the sky to the other like black flags. The waves of the river Ganges rose and crashed on the banks with deafening sound. The wind became so strong that it made the branches of the huge trees bend and touch the ground, helplessly.

While mother nature was playing havoc outside, inside a *bagan bari* (a mansion surrounded by sprawling gardens) in Chadannagar, a conversation was going on between a couple in the safety of a room with closed doors, its windows glowed in the lamplight.

Sharat *babu* (mister) said, "If you stay here for a few more days, you will be fully cured and then we can go back home."

Kiranmayee did not agree. She said, "I am absolutely all right. It will not harm me one bit if we go back now."

I am sure nearly all married people can understand what I have described to you in just a few words did not get resolved so fast; it was not all that complicated, but still, it was not proceeding towards a logical conclusion. The situation could be compared to a boat without a boatman. It was going round and round and was about to drown in a flood of tears.

Sharat tried again. "The doctor was saying that it would do you good if you stayed here for some more time."

Kiranmayee retorted, "As though your doctor knows everything."

Sharat tried to scare her and said, "Do you know people in the villages get afflicted by all kinds of diseases at this time of the year?"

"You mean to say no one falls sick here!" said Kiran impatiently.

Kiran's history was somewhat like this. Nearly everybody, including her mother-in-law, loved her very much so, when she fell ill her family members and the villagers got very worried. The doctors advised her to leave the village and live in a place where the climate was healthier than what it was in the village. Her husband and mother-in-law had no objection; in fact, they readily accepted the suggestion. They left their home and work in order to be with her. The older villagers did not think it was prudent to be so hopeful that her health would improve merely by shifting to a place where the climate was supposed to be better. They looked upon it as an example of being henpecked. Didn't other women from the village fall ill, did they all opt for a 'change of place', they contended. And didn't the people living in the place where they were planning to take Kiran fall ill? Was there any place on earth where fate could be kept at bay? Kiran's husband and mother-in-law did not pay heed to this criticism and the advice offered by the wise people of the village. They loved Kiran dearly and Kiran's life was very precious to them. When the mother and son did not listen to the villagers' advice, they concluded that people often lose their heads when their near and dear ones face a life-and-death situation.

Sharat and his wife had been living in a mansion in Chandannagar for quite some time. Kiran was free from her ailment, but had not regained her strength. There were telltale signs around her eyes and on the rest of her face that reminded her relatives of the agony she had gone through, and at the same time, made them feel thankful that the worst was over.

Kiran was a fun-loving person who loved company. She missed her friends and this lonely existence was making her feel terribly bored. Moreover, she had no work to do; all she was expected to do was to take her medicines on time, follow a strict diet and apply a warm compress from time to time. She was tired of it and longed to go back home, and this was the reason for the domestic revolt behind the closed door that evening.

The fight continued for as long as Kiran could retaliate verbally, but after a while, she stopped talking and turned her face away from her husband. The poor man was left with no alternative but to accept her demand. He was about to give in, when he heard his servant's loud voice outside the closed door, trying to attract his attention.

Sharat opened the door. He was told that a boat had capsized in the Ganges and a *Brahmin* boy from the boat had swum across and landed in their garden.

When Kiran heard about it, she forgot about the fight she had been having, and got busy. She pulled some clothes and a towel off the *alna* (clothes stand) and gave them to the servant, so that the boy could change out of his wet clothes. After that, she heated a bowl of milk and sent it across for him.

After some time, she sent for the boy. He was young, with huge eyes and long hair. The telltale signs of adolescence were not visible on his upper lip; he was apparently a small boy. Kiran served him food personally and supervised as he ate. After he had finished eating, she asked him his name and enquired about other details.

He told her that his name was Neelkanta and he was a part of a *jatra dal* (folk-theatre troupe). They were going to Singha *babu*'s house to perform when the storm rose and their boat capsized. He was a good swimmer, which is what saved him, but he was not sure as to what had happened to the others.

The fact that the boy could have died evoked Kiran's sympathy; thus he stayed back in the house on her insistence. Sharat felt the arrangement was good. He thought that at least there would be something to keep his wife busy. Kiran's mother-in-law, too, was happy because giving shelter to a *Brahmin* boy was an act of piety. For the boy, the benefits were twofold. First, he had managed to slip out of the clutches of two fear-inducing characters – *Yama* and the *adhikari*. Yama is the god of death and the *adhikari* was the owner of the *jatra* party, who made him slog. Second, he had landed up with a rich family.

But very soon, Sharat and his mother changed their mind about the boy's presence in the house. They wanted him to leave the house as early as possible, and that was because of his behaviour.

There were many complaints about him. Many people had caught him taking drags from Sharat's hookah on the quiet. On rainy days, he would pick up Sharat's silk umbrella without any qualms and set off for a stroll in the neighbourhood in search of friends. He had befriended a stray dog of the locality and because of his pampering, the dog had become so bold as to make frequent visits to Sharat's spick and span room, leaving paw marks on the immaculately clean carpet. By and by, Neelkanta's fan following grew, as a result of which the small unripe mangoes in the local orchards never got a chance to reach maturity.

There was no doubt about the fact that Kiran pampered the boy beyond measure. Sharat and his mother had told her many times not to do so, but she didn't pay heed to their advice. She enjoyed dressing him up nattily in Sharat's old clothes and shoes and watching him strut around like a *babu* (an educated person). Very often, she would call him to her room in the afternoon and ask him to recite the parts that he had enacted in the *jatra* . He would sit on the floor and recite from '*Nala Damyanti pala*' (a play about the undying love between Nala and Damayanti), his words would be accompanied by actions. And Kiran would sit on her bed with a box full of *paan* (betel leaves, used as a mouth freshener) and listen to him while her maid dried her hair with a towel. The long, tedious hours of the afternoon would pass quickly this way. There were times when Kiran tried to rope Sharat into becoming a part of the audience. Though he joined them after a lot of coaxing, he did not find it amusing; in fact, it irritated him. Moreover, his presence inhibited Neelkanta. Often, Kiran's mother-in-law joined them, especially when the play was about gods, but her urge to take a siesta would overtake her religious fervour and she would fall asleep.

Being slapped by Sharat or getting his ears pulled was a routine affair for Neelkanta. He did not feel bad about it at all because he was used to tougher punishments. He was of the opinion that like the earth, which consisted of land and water, human life too consisted of two things – punishment and nourishment. In some cases, punishment got the upper hand over nourishment.

It was difficult to guess Neelkanta's age. His face appeared to be more mature than that of a boy of fourteen or fifteen, but one could not say that he was seventeen or eighteen either because he looked younger than that. There were two possibilities: either he was immature for his age or maybe he looked more mature because of the company that he kept.

Actually, Neelkanta had joined the *jatra* troupe at a very young age and from then on, he had been enacting female roles, like Sita, Radhika and Damayanti. Much to the *adhikari's* (owner and director of the troupe) delight his growth had stopped after some time. This suited the *adhikari's* requirement as he could go on playing female roles for quite some time.

People in the troupe treated him as a small boy and he, too, felt the same. There were no signs of early adulthood on his face, not even a downy growth on his upper lip, as a result of which he continued to look like a boy of fourteen even at the age of seventeen. But his habit of smoking and the adult manner of talking that he had picked up from his associates told a different story. His large eyes gave an impression of innocence and simplicity, but his association with grown-up people in the troupe had made him mature in certain superficial aspects.

After receiving shelter in Sharat *babu*'s *bagan bari*, he went through a growth spurt. Soon, he crossed the boundary at which his physical growth had got arrested and started looking like a boy of seventeen or eighteen.

No one noticed this outward change in him, but the first sign of this change was that he started finding Kiran's attitude towards him embarrassing and painful. He felt very hurt one day when Kiran requested him to dress up as a woman and enact the role of some female character. Though he couldn't figure out why he felt so bad, but from that day onwards, he would disappear whenever she made such a request. Unfortunately, he failed to understand that his position was no better than that of an entertainer from a *jatra* troupe.

He even tried to take tuitions from the *bazar sarkar* (person who does all the shopping for the household and keeps a daily account). But the man did not like Neelkanta because the mistress of the house was fond of him. So he was not of much help to Neelkanta. Till then, Neelkanta had never studied seriously, so whenever he sat down to read he could not concentrate. The letters would just float in front of his eyes. He would often sit under a *champak* (magnolia)tree by the Ganges with an open book on his lap, trying to concentrate; the river rippled by, boats floated on the river, birds chirped in the branches overhead and Neelkanta sat there with his head bent over a book. His mind drifted from one thought to another, but the fact that he was sitting with a book made him feel very important. Whenever someone walked by, he would promptly lift the book from his lap and start reading loudly; once the spectator left, he would go back to day-dreaming.

Earlier, it was in a mechanical fashion that he would sing the songs he had learnt, but now the tune of the songs touched him. There was a lot of alliteration in the lyrics that he could not comprehend, but when he sang:

Oray rajhansa, janmi dwija bongshay

Emon nreeshrigsha keno holi ray

Bol ki jonnay, a aranay

Rajkanyar pranshangshay korili ray

[Oh swan, in spite of being born in a *brahmin* family

how could you be so cruel?

Tell me why you endangered the life of the princess in this forest

fraught with danger.]

The song took on a different meaning when he sang it all by himself. The images of the swan and the princess would appear in his mind's eye, though one cannot be certain about the role played by him. At that time, he would generally forget about the fact that he was a young boy from a *jatra* troupe – an orphan of no social standing whatsoever.

When a poor boy lying in bed in his tumbledown cottage hears stories about the jewels and immeasurable wealth of kings, when he hears about handsome princes and their beautiful consorts, his imagination takes wings and flies him to a land of fairytales. The fetters of his impoverished existence break and he acquires a new identity. Similarly, the songs that Neelkanta sang in solitude, amidst chirping birds, rustling leaves and the sound of the flowing river, created a beautiful world around him. The mellow and affectionate face of the woman who had given him shelter would appear before him. Her hands would beckon him with her wrists full of tinkling bangles. Her white and soft feet, like the petals of a lotus, would appear in his mind's eye, but all of a sudden everything would disappear like a mirage.

Soon, Neelkant would gather his band of young plunderers and invade the neighbouring orchard. The aggrieved party would come and lodge a complaint with Sharat. A few resounding slaps would land on Neelkant's cheeks. But the punishment would not deter him; he would set off again with his friends to plunder some other garden with redoubled vigour.

Around this time, Sharat's younger brother, Satish, who was studying in Kolkata, came over to spend his vacation with his brother and sister-in-law. This made Kiran very happy as it gave her something to do. Kiran and Satish were of the same age, so the two of them would engage in friendly banter the entire day. She enjoyed teasing him and devised many ways of doing this. She would smear vermillion powder on her hands and standing behind him, would cover his eyes with her hands. She would quietly write *bandor* (monkey) on his shirt. She would lock his room from outside and run away, giggling. Satish was not one to be outdone. He, too, would devise various ways of bothering Kiran. He would hide her bunch of keys, put red chilli powder in her *paan*, tie her *aanchal* (free end of the sari which hangs from the shoulder) to one of the legs of the cot on which she would be sitting and many such things. At times, they would fight and stop talking to each other. Kiran would cry, but very soon, they would say sorry and make up to each other.

Neelkanta was not a part of all this, and that made him very angry. He wanted to take it out on someone, but he did not know who. So the first thing he did was to mistreat his followers. Then he kicked his dog hard; the poor animal ran away, howling in pain. After that, he picked up a stick and slashed the weeds and undergrowth with it as he walked through the garden.

Kiran enjoyed feeding people, especially those who were food lovers. Neelkanta fell in that category so Kiran loved feeding him. She would call him to eat and look over him as he ate. She would request him to take extra helpings of the special dishes and Neelkant would gladly oblige. There were times when Kiran could not be present when Neelkanta was served food because of some prior engagement. Her absence would not perturb him; he would eat heartily even though she was not there and polish off everything. So much so that after drinking milk, he would pour water in the bowl and drink it up so that not a drop of milk was wasted. But after the arrival of Satish, he would barely touch his food if Kiran did not call him to eat. He would tell the maid that he was not hungry and leave, hoping that the maid would inform Kiran and she would call him. But that never happened because the maid would eat the leftover food and keep it to herself. Neelkanta would go back to his room, blow out the lamp and cry into his pillow.

He was very confused, as he didn't know exactly why he was feeling hurt and who would listen to his complaint. He half expected that someone would come and console him. When no one came, the goddess of sleep came and calmed his frayed nerves with her magic touch.

Neelkanta firmly believed that Satish must be tattling about him to Kiran, so on certain days when he saw her looking quiet and preoccupied, he would conclude that she was angry with him because of what Satish had told her about him.

Neelkanta believed that the gods were partial to Brahmins. Being a Brahmin lad, he had no doubt that the gods would listen to him. He prayed every day that the tables would turn and in the next birth, he would be born in a rich family and Satish in a poor family like his. He also believed that an angry Brahmin's curse never fails. So he would mentally try to burn Satish with his *bramha tez* (when angered, a true Brahmin is supposed to have this divine power of being able to reduce a person to ashes by just looking at him). But instead of burning Satish, he himself would burn with anger when sounds of laughter would reach his ears from the second storey of the house. This left him in no doubt that Satish and Kiran must be making fun of him behind his back.

Neelkanta did not dare to cause any direct injury or harm to Satish, but he would trouble Satish whenever he got a chance. He would steal Satish's soap from the steps of the quay when he stepped into the river for a bath. Once, Neelkanta came up quietly and threw Satish's favourite shirt into the river while he was bathing. But Satish didn't guess that it was Neelkanta who had thrown his shirt into the water. He thought that the wind had blown away the shirt, though there was hardly any breeze blowing at that time.

One day, Kiran called Neelkanta to her room and requested him to sing one of his *jatra* songs with the intention of entertaining Satish. Neelkanta did not oblige. This surprised Kiran no end. She said, "Now what is the matter with you?"

When he didn't reply, she said, "Why don't you sing that favourite song of yours?"

He said, "I have forgotten the song," and walked out of the room.

It was time for the family to move back to their village as Kiran had recovered considerably. The staff started making arrangements. Satish, too, was going back with them, but no one was bothered about Neelkanta. It didn't strike anyone that he must be told whether he was going with the family or staying behind.

Kiran proposed to take Neelkanta along with them, but her husband and mother-in-law opposed this vehemently. So Kiran had to abandon the idea. Finally, two days before their departure, Kiran called Neelkanta and advised him to go back to his village. She spoke to him very affectionately.

Kiran had been ignoring him for a few days before this, but when Neelkanta heard her speak so affectionately, he could not control himself and started weeping. Seeing him cry, tears welled up in Kiran's eyes. She was full of remorse for having given Neelkanta so much attention and liberty.

Satish was standing nearby. He felt disgusted when he saw Neelkanta crying. He said, "Oh god, why is he crying like a baby when there is no reason for him to cry!"

Kiran scolded Satish for his rudeness.

Satish tried to reason with her and said, "You don't know these kind of people. You tend to believe everybody. Just look at him – he came like a beggar and now he lives like a prince. He doesn't want to go back to his family because he has got so used to living a good life and will miss all this. He knows that a few tears are good enough to melt your heart…."

Neelkanta got up and walked out of the room.

He was very angry with Satish. He created an imaginary Satish in his mind and tried to torture him with needles, with fire, with sharp knives and many other injurious things, but nothing happened to Satish; it was only he who bled internally.

Satish had brought a beautiful pen stand from Kolkata. On it were two boats, fashioned from seashells, each of which had an inkwell in it. A swan made of German silver sat between the boats, its wings outstretched. Satish was very attached to the pen stand. He wiped it every day to keep it gleaming. Kiran would pull his leg about his attachment to the swan. She would come to his room and sing the song about a swan that Neelkanta had once sung. She would tap on the beak of the swan and sing, "*Oray rajhansa* ." And after that, they would laugh loudly and engage in friendly banter.

The pen stand disappeared from Satish's table on the day before their journey back home. Kiran teased Satish and said, "Your swan must have flown off in search of princess Damayanti."

But Satish was in a towering rage. He was absolutely sure that Neelakanta had stolen it. Some of the servants had even told him that they had seen Neelkanta snooping around his room in the evening.

The suspect was brought before Satish. Kiran was also present. Satish did not mince words. The moment Neelkanta stood in front of him, he said, "Where have you hidden my pen stand? Please give it back to me."

Neelkanta had been punished and beaten up many times. Sometimes he had been guilty and deserved to be punished, but there were times when it had been no fault of his. He had taken all this in a light-hearted fashion. But now that he was being accused in front of Kiran, he could no longer remain nonchalant. His eyes turned red with anger. He felt as though his chest would burst with all the anger which he had kept bottled up inside. Given a chance, he would have sprung on Satish and clawed him like an angry cat.

Kiran took him to the next room and said, "Nilu, if you have taken the pen stand, come and give it to me quietly. No one will say anything to you."

Neelkanta didn't say a word. Tears streamed down his face and he covered his face with his hands.

Kiran came out of the room and said, "I am very sure that Neelkanta has not stolen it."

Satish and Sharat were not convinced. Both of them were of the opinion that it had to be Neelkanta and no one else.

Kirant was firm. She stuck to her opinion and said, "It can't be him."

Sharat said, "Call him. I will talk to him."

Kiran said, "Go ahead, but please don't ask him about the missing pen stand."

Satish said, "We must search his box."

Kiran said, "I swear that I will never talk to you in my life if you do so. No one should cast aspersions on a person who is not guilty."

Tears welled up in her eyes as she spoke. This brought an end to the whole thing as no one wanted her to cry.

Her family members attitude towards him evoked compassion in Kiran. She took two new shirts, two good *dhotis*, a pair of new shoes and a ten-rupee note and entered Neelkanta's room. Her intention was to put the gifts inside Neelkanta's trunk and leave the room. She found the trunk locked.

There was a duplicate key of the lock in the bunch of keys that was always tied to her *aachal*. She unlocked the trunk. The trunk was full. The things inside lay in a haphazard fashion. Kiran decided to take all the things out and arrange them properly, thinking that it would make some space for her gifts. The things that came out were a spool for flying kites, a stick, a top, a knife, some dirty clothes and a few clean ones, and the last thing that came out was the pen stand with the flying swan. Kiran took it out and held it for some time, crestfallen. She was deep in thought as she didn't know what to do.

Meanwhile, Neelkanta had entered the room through the door behind her. Kiran was not aware that he had come in. Neelkanta saw everything. He believed that Kiran had come to his room without telling him to search his trunk and find out if he had stolen the pen stand. Ironically, she herself had got caught in the act. He wanted to tell her desperately that he was not a thief; he had stolen it just because he wanted to take revenge. It was his weakness for the beautiful thing that had made him put it into his trunk; he had every intention of throwing the stuff into the river. There was no doubt left in his mind that Kiran thought he was a thief. And that was a terrible burden to bear.

Kiran sighed deeply and put the pen stand back into the trunk. She put the rest of the things in and arranged them, placed her gifts inside the trunk, and closed the lid and locked the trunk again.

The next day, the boy was missing. The neighbours said that they hadn't seen him since the evening. The Police was informed, but even they couldn't trace him. Sharat said, "Let us examine his trunk."

Kiran said, "No." She was emphatic.

When none of the family members was around, Kiran asked one of the servants to bring the trunk to her room. She took the pen stand out of the trunk, walked to the river and threw it into the water. No one got to know about it.

They went back to their village. No one stayed back. The *bagan bari* became a desolate place. Only Neelkanta's pet dog kept searching for his master for days.

Glossary

Bagan bari — A mansion surrounded by garden

Alna — Clothes stand

Jatra dal — An itinerant folk theatre troupe

Yama — God of death

Adhikari — Owner of a troupe

Babu — Gentleman

Paan — Beetle leaves used as mouth freshener

Bazar Sarkar — A person who does all the shopping for the household and keeps a daily account.

Brahmin — A person belonging to the highest cast among Hindus

Bandor — Monkey

Aanchal — The free end of the saree that hangs from the shoulder

Bramhatez — When angered a true Bramhin is supposed have this divine power of being able to reduce a person to ashes by just looking at him.

Dhoti — Long loin cloth traditionally worn by Hindu men

5

Holidays (Chooti)

Photik Chakrabarty, the leader of the village boys, hit upon a new idea of amusement. A massive log of *Sal* (a north Indian tree that yields teak-like timber) was lying on the river bank. The owner had left it there with the intention of making a mast out of it. Photik decided that he and his team would roll it and leave it somewhere else. The thought of how surprised and irritated the owner would be on finding the log missing when he came to work on it made the rest of the gang accept the proposal with glee.

So, they all got down to it with zeal, but just as they were about to start, Photik's younger brother Makhonlal came and sat on the log solemnly. The boys were put off by his arrival and the disdain that he exhibited toward them.

One of the boys tried to dislodge him from his seat. He pushed him a bit, but that had no effect on the young philosopher, who continued to meditate on the futility of such games played by lesser mortals like his brother and his friends.

Photik got angry and threatened to beat him up if he did not get up.

It fell on deaf ears, Makhon settled down more comfortably on his seat.

Photik's honour was at stake, he should have slapped his younger brother nice and hard to show his worthiness, but he didn't do so, because he did not have the courage. In front of his friends, he pretended that could set his brother right, if he wanted to, but he didn't do so because he had a better plan. He proposed that they should roll the log along with Makhon sitting on it.

Makhon, on the other hand felt, that his persistence would earn him great honour, what he did not realize was that like all other feats involving guts and honour this act too was fraught with danger.

The boys started pushing. "Heave-ho, heave-ho" they cried together. The heavy log moved slowly and took a turn, bringing down Makhan along with his philosophical ruminations on the lap of mother earth.

The boys were thrilled by this unexpected outcome. But Photik was not happy in fact he appeared worried. Makhon promptly got up and sprang on Photik and rained blows on him. He scratched his brother's face and ran back home crying. The game came to an end after this.

Photik sat quietly on a half-submerged boat and chewed the juicy lower ends of some reeds which he had pulled up from the bank. It was then that a boat from some faraway place pulled into the quay. A middle-aged man got down from the boat. He was gray haired though his moustache was dark.

"Where do the Chakrabartys live?" the stranger asked Photik.

Photik continued chewing and pointed vaguely towards a certain direction, "Over there, he said."

The man repeated the question and asked, "Where?"

"I don't know," answered Photik insolently and continued extracting the last bit of juice from the reed. The man found someone else and took directions from him and proceeded.

Very soon Bagha Bagdi the servant arrived. He said, "Photik your mother is calling you."

"I will not go," replied Photik arrogantly.

Bagha Bagdi had no option but to use force, he lifted up Photik bodily and started walking towards home. Photik made all efforts to extricate himself from Bagha's arms, but he couldn't.

His mother flared up the moment she saw him. "You hit Makhon again?" She wanted to know.

"No, I didn't," replied Photik.

"You are lying again."

"I did not hit him, you can ask Makhon."

Makhon repeated his complaint when she asked him to confirm, he said, "Yes ma, Photik did hit me."

Photik could not tolerate this false allegation against him, he got up, gave a resounding slap to Makhon and said, "You liar!"

The mother took Makhon's side, she caught Photik and shook him up and landed a few blows on his back. Photik pushed his mother in defense.

"How dare you!" she screamed.

At this point the same gray-haired man entered the room, amidst the hullabaloo.

He said, "Hello what's happening!"

Photik's mother was surprised and happy beyond measure to see her elder brother after such a long time. She couldn't believe her eyes. She said, "Oh my god! *dada* (elder brother) It's you! When did you come back?" Then she touched his feet as a mark of respect.

Her elder brother had gone to work in the western part of the country quite some time back. While he was away, she had borne two sons and she had lost her husband. All these years she hadn't met her brother even once. This was the first time that Bishambhar *babu* (mister) had come to see his sister after coming back from his place of work.

Arrival of Bishambhar *babu* became a cause for celebration in the household, which continued for quite some days. Two-three days before leaving, Bishambher *babu* asked his sister about the boys' education. In reply she said that Makhan, her younger child, was doing quite well in studies, but unfortunately the same could not be said about Photik. Photik was unruly, disobedient and had no interest in studies. She also added that Photik bothered her a lot.

Bhishambhar proposed to take Photik with him to Kolkata. So that he could stay with him and study. Photk's mother agreed to the proposal willingly.

"Would you like to go with *mama* (maternal uncle) and study there?" She asked Photik.

Photik Jumped with joy and said, "Yes I will go."

Photik's mother was more than willing to let him go because she was perpetually plagued with the fear that Photik might harm her younger son by his pranks—drown him or may cause him some severe injury. But even then, she was a bit disappointed by the enthusiasm exhibited by Photik.

Photik was so excited that he could hardly sleep at night for the next few days.

"When are we going?" "At what time are we leaving?" Were the questions that he kept asking his uncle over and over again.

He was so happy that he gave away his fishing rod, kite and spool magnanimously to his younger brother for keeps.

The first person that he met on reaching Kolkata was his *mami* (maternal uncle's wife). One can't say that she was happy about the unnecessary increase in the size of the family. So far, she had been managing her household satisfactorily with her three sons, the sudden addition of a thirteen-year-old boy fresh from the village who she hadn't met before, to the family filled her with apprehension, she could not help being critical about her husband's lack of common sense.

A thirteen-fourteen-year-old boy is a big misfit in society, at this stage his company is not desirable, he is not attractive, he does not evoke any feeling of affection in the mind of the on looker, moreover he is not good at anything. He is frowned upon when he talks like a child and he is admonished when he talks like an adult. He out -grows his clothes quickly which is treated as an offense by the provider. He is even blamed for the loss of sweet cherubic looks of his childhood and for the hoarseness of his voice. Mistakes made by a child and even by an adult are forgiven, but not so in the case of a fourteen-year-old. Even unavoidable mistakes made by them become a cause for irritation. He feels that he is a misfit, and that makes him apologetic about his existence in the society. But on the other hand, his need for affection is maximum at this time; he can be enslaved by a person by being affectionate towards him. Unfortunately, no one takes the risk of being affectionate, lest it is considered as pampering. His situation is like a stray dog that has no master. Staying in a place away from home makes him miserable. He feels hurt by the affectionless treatment of the residents. Generally, boys of this age have a high regard for the fair sex. Indifference from them hurts them.

Photik was like an ill-boding star in the eyes of his mami and that made Photik miserable. But it made him very happy whenever his *mami* asked him to do something; he would do the work so enthusiastically to please her that very often he would overdo it. This would irritate his *mami*, she would say, "That will be enough. Please go and concentrate on your studies." His *mami's* sudden interest in his education would surprise him, his enthusiasm would go plummeting down and he would feel down in the dumps.

The indifference and neglect in his uncle's house and the lack of freedom made him yearn for the carefree days that he enjoyed in his village. He missed his huge kite. He remembered how he flew it over the meadows of his village. He missed the river into which he could jump and swim whenever he felt like. He missed his friends with whom he would play pranks on unsuspecting people. He missed those long aimless walks in the village when, he would sing his self-composed songs loudly and tunelessly. But the person whom he missed the most was his mother; apparently the same person who he once thought was a tormentor and unjust. Like an animal that loves without any reason and wants to be as close as possible to the one he loves, like a calf who seeks his lost mother at dusk lowing loudly, this shy, nervous, lean and unattractive boy's mind too was assailed by similar feelings.

He could not concentrate on his work in school. His teachers considered him to be a block-head. When they asked him anything he would gape at them silently. When the teacher caned him, he would bear it unflinchingly like a beast of burden. During break he would stand near the window of his class room and look at the terrace of the neighbouring house. On some days when the children came out to play on the terrace, he would watch them and his heart would long to join them.

One day he mustered some courage and asked his *mama,* "When will I go home to my mother?"

His *mama* said, "You will have to wait for the *Puja* (Durga puja) vacations to start, that will be in the month of *Kartik* (October-November). Quite some time to go."

One day Photik lost a book. As it is he found it difficult to do his lessons and complete his homework, the loss of the book made it all the more difficult. His teacher thrashed him and insulted him almost daily for his incomplete work. His cousins avoided him in school. They even poked fun at him like the others whenever he got punished.

There came a time when he found the situation unbearable, so he went to his *mami* and confessed about the loss of book. His *mami* curled up her lips in derision and said, "Very good, you've done a good thing, but don't expect me to keep buying books for you every month."

Photik left the place quietly. He felt ashamed that he was wasting money. It made him feel small in his own eyes. He felt angry with his mother for sending him to his *mama's* place, where he was being treated like an unwanted person.

That evening after coming back from school he felt cold and had a headache, he knew that he was going to have a fever. But he kept it to himself as he did not want to trouble his *mama* and *mami*, moreover he was not sure about his *mami's* reaction. He had no idea if anyone in this world other than his mother would look after a good for nothing boy like him.

Photik went missing from home the next morning. They looked around in all likely places where he could have gone including the neighbours' houses, but Photik was not found.

It had been raining heavily since the night before, thus they all got drenched in the rain while looking for him. Finally, Bishambhar *babu* went to the police and lodged a complaint about the missing boy.

After waiting for the entire day, a police vehicle stopped in front of Bishambhar *babu's* house in the evening. It was still raining. The road in front of the house was water logged. Two police men got down from the car holding Photik in between them. They took him inside the house. His clothes were wet and smeared with mud, his face was flushed, eyes were red and he was shivering. Bishambhar *babu* took him in his arms and walked inside the house.

The moment his *mami* saw him she said, "Why don't you send him home instead of getting into such a lot of hassles."

Photik's *mami* was beside herself with worry. She had hardly eaten anything that day and she had scolded her own children unnecessarily.

When he heard his *mami* he cried and said, "I was going home, but these people forced me to come back."

Photik's temperature shot up later in the evening and he became delirious. He kept talking throughout the night. Bishambhar *babu* brought a physician home next morning to see Photik. When they entered the room, they found Photik staring at the ceiling. His blood shot eyes were widely open. He looked at his *mama* and asked, "*Mama* have my holidays begun?"

Bishambher *babu* wiped Photiks eyes with his handkerchief and took Photik's burning hand into his and sat close to him.

Photik went into a delirium once again, he muttered in a hoarse voice repeating the same thing over and over again, "Oh mother please don't hit me believe me it is not my fault. I have not done anything."

Next day, Photik became a bit better for a short while. He looked all around the room as though he was searching for someone. He looked disappointed when he didn't see the person, and after a while he turned towards the wall and closed his eyes.

Bishambher *babu* understood who he wanted to see, so he whispered into Photik's ear and said, "Photik I have sent someone to bring your mother."

Another day went by. The doctor looked worried when he said, "The patient is in a very bad shape."

Bhishshambher *babu* sat next to Photik's bed, in the subdued light of a single lamp as he waited for Photik's mother.

Photik's delirium continued. While coming to Kolkata he had heard the *khalasis* (sailors) of the steamer measuring the depth of water with a plumb-line. In his delirium he imitated the *khalasis* and cried out in a sing-song fashion, "*Ek bao mele na, do bao mele na......*" (deeper than first mark, deeper than second mark........). It seemed as though Photik had embarked on a long voyage and his plumb line could not measure the depth of the water.

Photik's mother arrived. She entered the room like a storm crying loudly. Bishambher tried to hold her back, but she fell on the bed howling, "Photik my darling my dearest child!"

Photik responded normally and said, "Yes."

His mother cried again, "Oh Photik my child!"

Photik turned slowly on the bed and said very calmly, "Ma my holidays have begun I am going home."

Glossary

Sal- A north Indian tree which yields teak like timber

Dada- Elder brother

*Babu-*Mister

Mama- Maternal uncle

Mami- Wife of maternal uncle

Puja- Annual festival of worshipping goddess Durga

Kartik – Mid - October to mid - November

Khalasi- Sailor

6

The Guest (Atithi)

1

The *zamindar* (landlord) of Kanthaliya, Motilal *babu* (mister) was coming back home by boat with his family. One afternoon when the boat was anchored close to a *gaunj* (market) for cooking lunch, a *brahmin* (member of the highest Hindu caste) lad walked up to Motilal babu and asked him, "Where are you going to *Babu*?" He appeared to be around fifteen or sixteen.

Motilal *babu* said, "We are going to Kanthaliya."

The boy said, "Can I come with you till Nandigram? It comes on the way"

Motilal *babu* nodded his head and asked him, "What is your name?"

The boy said, "Tarapada."

The boy was good looking and fair. His eyes were large and there was a smile on his lips. He was wearing a not too clean a *dhoti* (a piece of cotton material tied around the waist extending up to the ankles. The upper part of his body which was exposed was well formed, as though a sculptor had taken great pains to carve it. There was a brahmin- like aura about him which made Motilal *babu* feel that the boy must have led a life of a *tapaswi* (religious ascetic) in his last birth.

He said, "Son you can come with us, and please join us for lunch."

The boy accepted the invitation happily and said, "Please wait for me." Then he joined the attendants who were preparing lunch.

Motilal babu's cook was from North India, he was not very good at cooking fish. Tarapada was a better cook than him. He helped him to cook fish and

45

a couple of other vegetables. After the food was ready he took a bath in the river, took out a clean *dhoti* from his bundle and wore it. He combed his long hair which reached his neck with a wooden comb. Then he cleaned his *janeu* (sacred thread worn by brahmins) and wore it across his chest. After that he went to Motilal *babu*.

Motilal babu took him inside. His wife Annapurna and his nine-year-old daughter were sitting there. Annapurna, was very impressed by Tarapada's appearance, the moment she saw him affection welled up inside her and she wondered, how Tarapada's mother could stay away from a son like him.

During lunch Motilal babu and Tarpada sat next to each other. Annapurna noticed that the boy was a sparse eater. She thought that the boy was feeling shy so she kept requesting him to take more, but he did not take more than what he felt was necessary. She deduced from his behaviour that he was a self -willed person and he did exactly what he felt was right, without offending anyone or without being called stubborn. And there was no element of diffidence in his behaviour.

After everybody finished lunch Annapurna sat next to him and asked many questions mostly about his home and family, but what she learnt was not much. When he told her that he had run away from home when he was around seven to eight years of age; She asked, "Don't you have a mother?"

He said, "I have."

"Doesn't she love you?" asked Annapurna.

Tarapada found the question funny; he laughed loudly and said, "Why wouldn't she?"

"Then why did you leave her?"

"Well other than me she has four sons and three daughters."

Annapurna felt sad when she heard the answer. She said, "What kind of argument is that! Just because you have five fingers can you cut off one finger?"

Tarapada's history was short and unique. He was the fourth son of his parents. He lost his father when he was very small. Though there were many brothers and sisters, but Tarapada was the favourite child of the household. His mother, brothers and sisters loved him dearly; even his neighbours loved him. His teacher never scolded him or punished him, and if he ever got punished by his teacher, people of the village felt sad when they came to know about it. There was no reason for him to leave home. There were boys in the village who got beaten up regularly for stealing fruits from trees of their neighbours and even got beaten up very often by their parents, when they came do know about their misdeeds, but they never thought of running away, but why did Tarapada, who was loved by everyone in the village run away with a *yatra party* (itinerant opera) without a second thought, was a mystery.

When he ran away for the first-time people searched for him and when they found him, they brought him back to his village. His mother held him and cried till he got soaked with her tears. His sisters cried and cried. His elder brother scolded him because it was his duty as a responsible guardian to do so. But afterwards, he felt bad and he pampered Tarapada with many gifts. The women of the village called him home and tried to persuade him not to run away again, but nothing could hold him back, not even a bond as strong as love. The star under which he was born had made him footloose, nothing could make him stay in one place for long. Whenever he saw a boat from some faraway place, or he saw a *sannyasi* (religious Hindu mendicant) from some distant land resting under the huge *Ashwath* (ficus) tree of his village or may be when he saw a group of gypsies building a temporary camp next to the river his heart would pine for freedom. He would long to set off for an unknown destination where no one would try to bind him with their love and affection. He ran away from home thrice. After the third time his relatives and the people of his village gave up, they stopped looking for him.

He joined a *yatra party* after leaving home. During his stay he became very close to the *Adhikari* (owner and director of *Yatra* party) who started treating him like a son. The other members too became fond of him. Whenever they performed in a rich man's house, the ladies of the house would take an instant liking for him. They would call him inside the house and talk to him and treat him well. But one day, he just left the group without telling anybody. No one knew where he went.

Tarapada was very fond of music. It was music that he had heard in a *Yatra* recital which pulled him out of home. As a kid he would listen to songs in musical soirees with such rapt attention and sway with it, that the people around him found it difficult to control their laughter. Not only music, all kinds of sounds made him happy. When a flurry of rain pattered on leaves, when thunder rumbled in the sky, when the wind howled like a motherless baby giant during a storm, he would lose control over himself with happiness. The high-pitched call of a kite flying high up in the sky in a silent afternoon, the croaking of frogs in unison on a rainy evening and the howling of jackals late at night excited him. These sounds were like music to his ears. This love of music attracted him to a group of *Panchali* (Bengali poems based on mythology set to tune by renowned singers.) He became a member of the group. The leader of the group took pains to teach him the verses and the songs, he was a quick learner. The man grew fond of him. But one day Tarapada broke away from the bond and flew away like a bird who finds the door of its cage open.

His last sojourn was with a group of gymnasts. Many fairs are held in rural Bengal during the months of *Jaishtha* and *Ashadh* (second and third month of the Bengali calendar). Entertainment is a major attraction of these fairs, *yatra* parties, dancing girls and *panchali* singers entertain the crowd in these fairs. The entire fair moves around in boats like a flotilla on the rivers and their tributaries. To begin with Tarapada joined the shopkeeper's group and became an assistant to a *paan* (betel nut and condiments wrapped in a betel leaf, works as a mouth freshener) shop owner. He roamed around in the fair and sold pan to the visitors who came to the fair. While roaming around his natural curiosity led him to a group of gymnasts from Kolkata, he watched them practice and perform. They impressed him and he joined the group. Tarapada could play the flute well, which he had learnt by himself and had improved his skill by practicing regularly. This was useful for the gymnasts. Tarapada was given the job of playing the flute in the background as the group displayed their skills to the audience.

After sometime he came to know that zamindars of Nandigram were starting an amateur *yatra* group, so he picked up his small bundle and set off for Nandigram, and that is how he met Motilal *babu.*

After leaving home Tarapada had associated with different groups of people, but none had left any deep impression on his mind. He continued to be the same, like he was when he left home simple, natural and imaginative. He must have seen and heard many ugly incidents, but fortunately none of them had influenced him in any way. He was like a white swan that swims in muddy water, but remains untouched - even after diving into dirty water out of curiosity, it manages to remain white. The boy's youthful looks and his natural behavior had impressed Motilal babu. He was an experienced business man and a good judge of people. He accepted Tarpada amidst his family happily.

2

The boat started after lunch. Annapurna continued to ask questions to Tarapada about his home, his mother and his family. He tried to satisfy her curiosity with short and precise answers. Tarapada felt relieved when the session got over. He came out on the deck, and what he saw filled him with happiness. The river swollen by rains was full to its brim. The turbulent water of the river was flowing at a great speed. The sun was very bright as there were no clouds. The half-submerged reeds, and their white flowers, the green and dense sugar cane fields, and the forest beyond were glowing by the magical touch of the sun. The blue sky above was looking down with great admiration at the earth which was beautiful, and youthful. Tarapada sat down under the shade of the sail. Sloping meadows, half submerged jute fields, undulating paddy fields, narrow paths from the quays going into the villages, small villages shaded by trees ......his eyes took in everything as the boat went by. The water land and sky, the clamorous lively and moving surroundings and the quiet earth which didn't sleep for a moment were his old friends, who never tried to tie him down. A calf running along the bank with his raised tail, a hobbling pony with his front legs tied trying to reach grass, a kingfisher's sudden dive into water from a bamboo pole, little boys playing in the water, women laughing and chatting as they bathed in the river, fisher women buying fish from the fishing boats, Tarapada's insatiable eyes saw everything from the place where he was sitting and hungered for more.

He climbed on the roof of the boat and got friendly with the oarsmen and the helmsmen. Soon he was chatting with them. He volunteered to help them. He propelled the boat with a long pole. When the helmsman wanted to take a break for a smoke Tarapada offered to hold the helm for him. He even knew how to adjust the sail when the direction of the wind changed, this he did quite deftly.

In the evening Annapurna called him and asked, "What do you eat in dinner?"

He said, "I eat whatever I get and at times I eat nothing."

Annapurna was upset by his indifference to her hospitality. She wanted to look after this 'runaway' *brahmin* boy, but she didn't know how. She sent her servants to the villages to buy milk and sweets for him. At dinner Tarapada ate everything, but milk. Even Motilal *babu* who was a man of few words requested him to take milk, but he refused. He said, "I don't like milk."

Two days went by after Tarapada's arrival he willingly gave a helping hand in everything, cooking, buying vegetables from the local village, rowing and steering the boat.....

Any interesting scene drew his attention, and whenever a work needed to be done, he would invariably give a hand. His hands were always busy and so were his eyes and mind they registered everything. Like the perpetually active Mother Nature he was carefree and indifferent, but always busy. Nearly every human being has a place to which he belongs which he calls his own, but Tarapada was like a wave of happiness, which had no connection with past and future—the only thing that he knew was to keep going ahead.

He had learnt the art of entertainment, during his association with many groups of folk artists. Being a carefree person, his mind was not burdened with any worries and that was a boon for him. His mind was like a clean slate. He could memorize and remember songs and verses without any difficulty.

Like every other evening, one evening Motilal *babu* was reading out from *Ramayana* (Hindu epic based on the life of Lord Rama) to his daughter and wife. He had just reached the chapter about Lav and Kush (sons of Lord Rama), when Tarapada could not hold himself, he came down from the roof of the boat where he was sitting and said, "*Babu* please keep your book aside, let me sing out this bit for you." He started singing *Panchali* based on Lav and Kush. Verses written by Dashu Roy and sung by Tarapada in his melodious voice attracted many listeners. All those who were sitting on the roof of the boat came down and sat near the door. His sweet voice attracted quite a few other boats that were passing by; they stopped and listened to him for a while. Music flowed in the evening air and along the banks of the river. People living on the bank of the river came out and heard him. They stood silently–listening. The listeners were disappointed when the narration got over as they wanted it to continue for some more time.

Annapurna's eyes were full of tears when it ended. She wished fervently that she could hold the boy close to her. Motilal *babu* wished that the boy would stay with them, and fulfill his desire for a son. But their daughter Charushashi was not happy. She felt jealous.

3

Charu (abbreviated) was the only child; thus, she was the only claimant of her parents' love. She was a stubborn child and there was no end to her whims. She had an independent opinion about things concerning her, which were her clothes, her food and her hair style. But there was no permanence; her opinion could change at a very short notice. Her mother felt very apprehensive on the days when they were invited out, lest she created a shindig about her hair and clothes. There were times when she would make her attendant re-do her hair many times and at the end cry and throw a tantrum saying that the hair style was not up to her liking, but she was an entirely different person on the days she was happy; she became easy to please with no objection to anything. On such days she hugged and kissed her mother umpteen times to express her love. It was very difficult to understand her, she was like an enigma.

She disliked Tarapada, and hated him with all her heart, her hatred for Tarapada had become a cause of concern for her parents. While eating she would suddenly start crying and push her plate aside saying that she did not like the food, she would beat her attendant at the slightest pretext, she would complain about nearly everything without any reason. These were the ways in which she expressed her dislike for Tarapada indirectly.

Within a few   days Tarapada's musical talent made him very popular and this angered Charu. She just refused to accept that Tarapada was talented. And when it was proved beyond doubt that Tarapada was indeed very talented it angered her all the more. The day Tarapada sang the *Panchali* about Lav and Kush, Annapurna thought Tarapada's sweet and melodious voice must have impressed her daughter, because she believed that even a wild animal could be tamed by music. So, she asked her daughter, "Charu, he sang well, didn't he?" Charu did not say anything, she just shook his head vigorously, indicating, "I did not like it one bit and I am not going to like it ever."

Charu's mother understood that her daughter was jealous so she tried to restrain herself, she stopped demonstrating her affection towards Tarapada in front of Charu. When Charu went to bed after an early dinner in the evening, Annapurna would come out and sit next to the door of their room. Tarapada and Motilal babu would be sitting on the deck of the boat close by. Annapurna would ask Tarapada to sing. His sweet and melodious voice would rise and go beyond the boat, it would skim over the surface of the river and reach the sleepy villages on either side of the river. Annapurna's heart would well up with love for the boy. Sometimes Charu would wake up and come there, she would complain about the noise and say, "Oh mother why are you people making so much noise, I can't sleep." The fact that her parents had sent her to bed and were sitting with Tarapada and enjoying his songs was something that did not go well with her. Charu's reaction would amuse Tarapada.

Tarapada tried quite hard to get friendly with Charu. He sang songs, played the flute and even told stories to her but he did not succeed. The only time that she paid any attention to Tarapada was when he swam in the river in the afternoons. She enjoyed watching him swim, his easy movements in the water, his fair skin and beautifully proportioned body made her feel as though some water god was swimming. Charu would wait for a glimpse, though she never let anybody know about her interest. She would sit with her knitting and pretend to knit as she watched him from the corner of her eyes. At times she would watch him directly, but pretend to be indifferent.

4

When they went past Nandigram, Tarapada didn't show any intention of leaving the boat and going ashore. The boat continued its journey towards Kanthaliya. It moved slowly through the distributaries, propelled by sail and towed by men at times. The life of the passengers on the boat became slow and peaceful like the small rivers that they were sailing on. No one seemed to be in any hurry. Meals in the afternoon got delayed on most of the days. In the evenings the boat was usually anchored close to a big village near a quay, where there would be thousands of fireflies twinkling on the trees of the forest nearby and the cicadas would sing in unison for them.

It took them ten days to reach Kathaliya . Palanquins and ponies were already there to take the party home. Guards holding guns and lathis were waiting to receive the master. They fired the guns to welcome the *zamindar*. The guns not only announced the arrival of the master to the village, but also scared the crows away that flew away cawing loudly.

Tarapada realized that the fanfare would take a long time to end so he decided to skip it and explore the village himself. He got down from the boat and went around the village on his own and made many friends and in a short time established relations with them. Some he called *dada* (elder brother) some *Khura* (uncle) some *didi* (elder sister) and some *mashi* (aunty) in a matter of two to three hours he became a relative of almost every inhabitant of the village. This- was easy for him because he had no permanent ties. With in no time Tarapada managed to win the hearts of the villagers.

Tarapada had no airs and so the villagers accepted him as one of them. He had no prejudices thus he could mix with everybody. He was just like any other boy, when he interacted with a group of boys, though he stood out among them because of his qualities. In the company of old men, he was neither immature nor too worldly wise. When he roamed around with a shepherd, he was a shepherd, but a brahmin too. He was always ready to give a helping hand to anybody who needed it. While sitting and chatting with a sweet meat seller, if the owner said, "I have some urgent work, will you sit in my shop and look after my shop for a while?" Tarapada would willingly sit in the shop with a *Sal* (a North India tree with broad leaves which yields timber like teak) leaf in his hand and drive away the flies by swaying it like a fan.   He knew a bit about weaving and he could work on a loom, he could even handle a potter's wheel and he had a fair knowledge of making sweets. His knowledge came in very handy whenever he volunteered to help. Tarapada conquered the heart of every villager except one, and that was Charu. Charu continued to be jealous of him. Maybe it was this reason that made him stay back.

Though Charu was still a girl, but she proved beyond doubt that women are indeed very difficult to understand. Shonamoni was a good friend of Charu. She had become a widow at a tender age of five, she lived with her mother. She was not well when Charu came back, so she could not meet her. She came to meet Charu after she became alright. And on that very day Charu had a fight with her and that too for no rhyme or reason.

Charu wanted to surprise Shonamoni by telling her about Trapada, whom she considered to be the newly acquired gem of the family, she wanted to tell Shonamoni about how he joined them and travelled with them in great details. But even before she could complete the story Shonamoni told her that she already knew Tarapada. She told Charu that Tarapada calls her mother *mashi* (aunty) and she calls Tarapada, *dada* (elder brother)--- he comes to their house quite often and entertains them by playing his flute--- not only that he has made a flute for her on her request---he plucks flowers for Shonamoni from thorny bushes and   plucks fruits for her from high branches which she cannot reach. The information was like a blow to Charu. Charu was very possessive about Tarapada— apparently

Charu considered Tarapada to be an exquisite gem which should be seen and appreciated from a distance and that too after taking permission from the family. And the ordinary folks of the village should be thankful to them for bringing such a unique person to the village. What she learnt from Shonamoni made her very angry. She could not understand how Tarapada could become so friendly with Shonamoni that Shonamoni calls him *dada*! Charu used to dislike Tarapada, so much that there was a time when she had wanted him to leave the village as early as possible, but now suddenly she had become so possessive about him that she could not tolerate anybody becoming close to Tarapada! This was indeed very perplexing.

This brought an end to Charu's friendship with Shonamoni, for some time as and they declared *aari* (not on talking terms). After this she went to Tarapada's room, he was not there then. She got hold of his flute, placed it on the floor, stamped on it and jumped on it mercilessly till it broke. Tarapada entered the room when Charu was destroying the flute. He was very surprised to see Charu in his room. He said, "Charu, why are you breaking my flute?"

Charu's eyes flashed with anger and she turned her flushed face towards him and said, "Because I felt like it, and I will do it again." She kicked the broken flute a few more times and ran out of the room crying loudly. Tarapada picked up the flute and examined it. It was in a bad shape—beyond repair. He found the whole thing very funny, he wondered why his poor flute had to bear the brunt of her anger. Charu's behavior awakened curiosity in his mind—why would someone behave like that?

There was another thing that made him very curious and that was the English books in Motilal *babu*'s library and the pictures inside them. He had a fair knowledge of the world outside, but however much he tried he could not enter the world of pictures in those books; though his power of imagination helped him to interpret many of them, but that did not satisfy him entirely.

Motilal babu noted Tarapada's interest in the books and said, "You will understand the meaning of those pictures only if you learn English. Would you like to learn the language?"

He said, "Yes I want to."

Motilal babu was glad. He promptly employed the head master of the village school to teach Tarapada English every evening.

5

Tarapada started learning English, his good memory and power to concentrate were of big help. It was like exploring a new world, he immersed himself in it and he severed his ties with his friends in the village. The villagers didn't see him for a while. His play mates would watch him from a distance as he walked up and down on the bank of the river trying to memorize his lesson, but they never disturbed him. They just observed him and felt bad that Tarapada didn't play with them anymore. Even Charu didn't get to see him, usually Tarapada had lunch with the rest of the family in the inner quarters of the house. Annapurna presided over the meals and served him food with a lot of love and attention. The whole process used to take a long time. Tarapada wanted to finish his meals and get back to his studies as early as   possible. So, he requested Motilal babu to permit him to have meals in his own room. Annapurna felt hurt, because that was the only time when she got to see Tarapada, so she objected, but Motilal babu said 'yes'--he was impressed by the boy's enthusiasm.

Suddenly Charu decided that even she would take English lessons along with Tarapada. Initially her parents did not take it seriously, thinking it to be one of her whims they laughed it off. But after a while they had to give in because of her tears and tantrums; and also because of their   affection for her. Charu started attending English lesson along with Tarapada. But Charu was one of those people who could not sit quietly and concentrate. Learning something seriously was beyond her capacity. Not only that she caused a lot of disturbance during the tuitions and   she kept hindering Tarapada's progress. She never completed the tasks given to her. When Tarapada progressed far ahead of her, she got upset and insisted that she must be taught the same lesson as Tarapada. When Tarapada finished the 'first' book a 'second' book was bought for him, Charu got very upset and insisted that she too wanted to study the same book. During his free time Tarapada would revise his lessons sitting in his room and complete the task given by the tutor, even this was unbearable for Charu. She would enter his room in his absence and pour ink on his note book, she would steal his pen, even tear up the page of the book which he was supposed to learn. All this used to amuse Tarapada and he tolerated without getting angry or raising his hand. But there were times when it went beyond the limit of his tolerance it was then, that he scolded her, or even gave her a whack or two, but even then, he couldn't make her change her ways.

Finally, he found a way to stop it. One day after tearing up his ink smeared note book in disgust Tarapada was sitting quietly in his room. Charu came and stood near the door, she thought Tarapada would fight with her, but he didn't say a word; he ignored her. Charu entered the room, and walked around him, went out of the room and came back again, even then there was no reaction from him. She came so close to him that if Tarapada wanted he could have given her a nice hiding for what she had done, but there was no response from him. Charu was in a fix; she didn't know what to do. She wanted to apologize, but she didn't know how, because she had never said 'sorry' in her life so far, so she tore out a page from her note book and wrote down in big letters, 'I will never smear ink on your notebook'. After writing it down she did a lot of things to attract his attention. Tarapada watched her and then he burst out laughing as he could not hold himself any longer. Charu ran out of the room feeling angry and humiliated. How she wished that she could destroy the piece of paper. At least that would have given her some satisfaction.

Shonamoni was shy by nature. When she wanted to talk to Tarapada she peeped into the room and if she found Tarapada busy with his books she went back. Though Shonamoni and Charu were good friends once again, but she was not sure as to how Charu would react if she spoke to Tarapada. So Shonamoni usually came and met Tarapada when Charu was in the inner quarters of the house. She stood outside Tarapada's room and waited patiently for his attention. When it came to his notice Tarapada would raise his eyes from his book and ask affectionately, "What's it Shona? How are you? And how is *mashi*?" On most of the days Shonamoni would say, "Ma has asked you to come home, she couldn't come as she has a back ache." Sometimes at this juncture Charu would appear suddenly. Shonamoni would appear frantic as though she has been caught red handed while trying to steal something which belonged to Charu. Charu would glare at her and shout, "How dare you come and disturb him, I am going to tell father." As though she was Tarapada's guardian and that she was genuinely concerned about Tarapada's undisturbed pursuance of studies. Everybody knew as to why Charu went to Tarapada's room even Tarapada knew that she had come there with the intention of disturbing him. But it would embarrass Shonamoni no end and she would try to get out of the situation by telling lies. Charu would call her a liar disdainfully and Shonamoi would leave the place crestfallen. Tarapada would feel bad, he would call her back and say, "Shona don't worry I will go to your house this evening." This would make Charu very angry, she would flare up and say, "How can you go there, when you haven't finished your task, I will complain about you to *Mastermoshai* (tutor)."

But this did not daunt Tarapada; he went to Shonamoni's place in the evening in spite of Charu's threat. When Charu realized that her warning was not going to have any effect on Tarapada, one day she came very quietly and bolted the door of his room from outside, then she locked him up with a lock that she had removed from her mother's box of spices. She kept him locked up for the entire evening and opened the lock only at dinner time. Tarapada did not speak a word. He did not touch his food when it was served to him and left the room. Charu repented for what she had done. She requested him to forgive her and eat his dinner, but Tarapada did not relent. Charu started crying, she cried profusely. Tarapada gave in finally— he came back and had his dinner.

After this Charu had sworn many times that she would not misbehave with Tarpada and would never bother him again. But her resolutions were had a short life. Whenever Shonamoni or some other person came to meet Tarapada she would lose her cool and misbehave. When Charu was on her best behavior for three to four days, Tarapada would be extra careful because the attack could come from any side, at any time and on any pretext. Charu's attack could be compared with a storm; lashing wind, followed by torrential rains and then absolute peace.

6

Two years went by. Tarapada had never been a captive for such a long time. It could have been his interest in learning a new language that had kept him bound. Or maybe the fact that he was growing up and a stable, comfortable and orderly life had attracted him. And the third reason could have been that Charu by her mischief and childish pranks had occupied a special place in his heart. Charu had crossed eleven years and Motilal babu had started looking for a match for her. He had short listed a couple of them. With this new development Charu's English education came to an abrupt end and she was firmly told by her father not to go out of the house. This sudden prohibition made Charu rebellious; she started throwing tantrums once again.

Then one day Annapurna took Motilal babu aside and said, "Why are you looking around for a match for Charu, when we have Tarapada right here—with us. He is a nice boy, and I have a feeling that Charu likes him."

Moti babu was surprised by her suggestion, he said, "Come on! How can that be possible? We know nothing about his family. Charu is my only daughter; I want her to get married into a good and well to do family."

After some time, the representatives of Raidanga *babus* came to see Charu. Her mother and her attendants dressed her up for the occasion. But when the time arrived for her to go out and meet them, she refused and she locked herself up. No amount of pleading from Motilal babu made her come out, he even threatened her with dire consequences, but Charu did not open the door. So ultimately, they were told that the girl cannot meet them as she was not feeling well. They concluded from this that the girl must be suffering from some physical disability and that is why she did not come out.

Motilal babu began to mull over his wife's proposal, other than coming from an unknown family Tarapada had all the attributes of an ideal groom, he was young, good looking, well-mannered and talented – a suitable boy for his daughter no doubt. Another positive point about his wife's proposal was the fact that if Charu got married to Tarapada they would not have to send Charu away to her husband's house, the two of them could continue to stay with them. Another point which merited consideration was that all this time they had treated Charu's mischief, whims and fancies and disobedience with indulgence and at times they were even amused by her antics. But her in-laws might not tolerate them. They might frown upon her wayward behavior.

Motilal babu and his wife discussed the matter thread bare and then they sent someone to Tarapada's village to find out about Tarapada's family. He came back and told them that Tarapada hailed from a good family, but they were poor. Moti babu and his wife promptly sent a proposal of marriage to Tarapada's guardians. They were overjoyed when they read the letter and accepted the proposal without any delay.

In Kathaliya Charu's parents started discussing the probable wedding dates and arrangements. Charu's father was very cautious by nature so he didn't let anybody know about it.

Charu on the other hand could not be kept under control, she was back to her former self. She started invading Tarapada's room like she did before. Her mood changed at the drop of a hat angry, affectionate, irritable, happy—her sudden appearance – which was nothing less than a Maratha invasion, broke the quiet and peace of the study room, but Tarapada didn't seem to mind, he was no longer indifferent towards her antics. In fact, he found them amusing. At times he felt a momentary spark in his heart when she was around. Tarapada was a person who loved moving ahead as though he was riding the crest of a wave, but of late he had become absent minded and was given to a lot of daydreaming. On some days he would push his books aside and get into Motilal babu's library where he would immerse himself in the pages of picture books. The pictures tinged by his own imagination would appear more interesting than before. He had stopped making fun of Charu of late. He didn't scold her any more or raise his hand on her when she crossed the limits of his patience. This change in him was something very new – like a dream to him.

Motilal *babu* Fixed the date of their marriage, it was to be held in the month of *Shravan* (fourth month of the Bengali calendar). Then he sent someone to bring Tarapada's family. Tarapada was not told that they were coming. He deposited money in advance and booked a band to play for the wedding. He made a long list of things to be bought and placed an order for the same in Kolkata.

The monsoon arrived and the sky got covered with dark clouds. The river flowing by the village which had no water in it other than a few stagnant pools got filled up. Little boats that were kept in the pools floated up. The ruts left by the wheels of the bullock carts on the dry river bed got filled up with water. Water rushed down the river bed chattering and laughing like a girl who has been set free. Children bathed and played and embraced the gushing water. Women came out of their houses and watched their old friend 'the river 'dancing and frolicking. The dry, dusty and sleepy village woke up and became full of life. Boats from distant places carrying merchandise started plying on the river. The quay became a market place, where merchandise from the boats were sold. Some of the boats stayed back at night. In the evenings the quay rang with songs sung by the boatmen, and the people of the village got to hear songs of faraway places. Throughout   the year the villagers who lived on either side of the river remained confined to their homes, they kept themselves busy with their daily chores. During the rainy season the boats on the river brought tidings from distant places and for some time even the insignificant villagers of the sleepy little hamlet came in touch with rest of the world. They established a relationship with the world beyond their villages and no longer felt small or insignificant.

59

A fair on the occasion of *Rath yatra* (chariot festival) is held in Kudulkatha every year around this time patronized the Nag babus.

It was a moonlit night; Tarapada had gone to the quay where he saw many big boats passing by. They seemed to be in great hurry and their cargo was varied. One was carrying an orchestra party from Kolkata, he heard them practice. Another boat had a *yatra* party on board; some people were singing accompanied with violin. A few boats were laden with merchandise. There were boats which carried *Nagor dolna* (hand operated Ferris Wheel). The boat men from the western part of the country were very noisy. They did not sing but played a special kind of percussion instrument accompanied with *kartaal* (like cymbals) they were full of enthusiasm and energy. All of them were going to Kurulkatha. Very soon dark clouds gathered and the moon got covered by them as though someone had unfurled a black sail over it. Strong westerly wind rose. Dark sail-like clouds ran one after another across the sky and the swollen river roared with laughter. The darkness became denser over the jungles nearby, the frogs croaked and the cicadas joined them. There was movement, as though the whole world was celebrating 'Chariot festival' the wind, the clouds, the river, the boats, the flags and the wheel of time nothing was still. Thunder rumbled; lightning leaped across the sky.   It started raining, the smell of rain as it fell on the earth wafted in the air. Kathaliya village slept peacefully.

Tarapada's   mother and brothers arrived the next day. Three boats from Kolkata carrying goods ordered by Motilal *babu* too arrived on the same day. Shonamoni packed some pickles in a leaf and *aamshotto* (cake made from juice of ripe mango) in a piece of paper and stood quietly near the door of Tarapodo's room. But he was not there. He was nowhere to be seen, no one knew where he had gone.

Tarapada left the village on that dark stormy night, before the shackles of love, affection and friendship could tie him down permanently. He left behind people who would remember him and pine for him. He went back to his unattached indifferent mother, the world.

Glossary

Zamindar — Land lord

Babu — Mister

Gaunj — Market

Dhoti — A piece of cotton material tied around the waist extending up to the ankles

Bramhin — Member of the highest Hindu caste

Tapaswi — Religious ascetic

Janeu — Sacred thread worn by brahmins

Yatra party — Itinerant opera group

Sanyasi — Religious Hindu mendicant

Ashwath — A type of ficus

Adhikari — Owner and director of the yatra party

Panchali — Bengali poems based on mythology and set to tune

Jaishtha — Second month of the Bengali Calander

Ashadh — Third month of the Bengali Calander

Paan — Beetel nut and condiments wrapped in a beetle leaf.

Ramayan — Hidu epic based on life of Lord Ram.

Dada — Elder brother

Khura — Uncle

Didi — Elder sister

Aari — Not on talking terms

Mashi — Aunt

Sal — North Indian tree with broad leaves which yield teak like timber

Mastermoshai — Teacher

Shravan — Fourth month of the Bengali Calander

Rath yatra — Chariot festival

Nagor dolna — hand operated Ferris wheel

Kartaal — Cymbal

7

The Notebook (Khata)

From the time she learnt to write, Uma pestered everybody in the house with her newly acquired writing skill. She wrote '*jol poray pata noray*' on every wall of the house in her crooked childish hand writing with charcoal, which meant leaves move as water falls on them. She found a book called *Hori Dasher Gupto kotha* (secret life of Hori Dash) under her sister-in-law's pillow and wrote with a pencil on every page of the book, *kalo jol lal Phul* (dark waters, red flower).

She wrote in big letters on the new almanac used by the members of the house hold obliterating all the important information regarding the movements of the planets, list of days on which *pujas* (religious rituals) are to be performed, list of auspicious and inauspicious days and so forth.

On her father's note book which he used for writing the daily household expenditure she wrote, '*lekha pora koray jay gari ghora choray shay*' (only those who read and write will get to ride carriages). Uma continued with her literary pursuit for quite some time in this fashion, nothing came in her way till one day something happened.

Uma's elder brother Gobindolal was a quiet person. He wrote in the local newspaper very often. The way he spoke did very little to reveal that he was a thinker at least not to his relatives and friends so no one could blame him for being a thinker, but he wrote all the same. And strangely enough most of his Bengali readers agreed with him.

According to him there were a few misconceptions among the western scientists regarding human physiology. Gobindolal wrote an article criticizing them. Funnily enough he did not take help of any logic or scientific theory to write the article, he relied just on his skill of writing and his sense of humour.

On one quiet afternoon when no one was looking Uma went inside her brother's room and wrote on the pages that contained the article, '*Gopal boro bhalo chele tahakay jaha deva hoy shey tahayee khayeah*.' (Gopal is a good boy he eats whatever is given to him).

The lines that she wrote were from a primer written by *Ishwar Chandra Vidyasagar*, I am sure it was not aimed at the Gobindolal's Bengali readers, but it made Gobindolal very angry all the same. First he beat her up nice and proper to teach her a lesson, then he confiscated the poor child's stub of a pencil, her ink smeared pen which had become blunt with frequent use and other writing implements. The little girl did not understand as to why she was being treated in this fashion. Humiliation brought tears in her eyes and she sat in one corner of the room and wept.

Gobindolal was remorseful for punishing the child so severely. He returned the confiscated property to her after the period of punishment got over. And on top of it, he gifted a beautifully crafted notebook, to make her happy.

This happened when Uma was seven years old. The notebook was her most priced procession. She kept it under her pillow when she went to sleep at night, and during day time she took it with her wherever she went.

Soon she started going to the village school. The maid who looked after her tied her hair into two small braids and took her to school. Uma took her note book to school. The girls of her class were full of awe when they saw it. It gave rise to different feelings among them; some were curious, some were envious while others wanted to possess a similar note book.

The first thing that she wrote on the book was, '*Pakhi shob koray rob. Rati pohaeelo*. (the birds are chirping and the night is ending). Very often she would sit on the floor of her bed room, holding the note book to her chest and recite loudly the poems that she had learnt. Gradually her collection of poems and stories grew and she wrote them down painstakingly in her note book.

In the second year a few of her own writings appeared on the note book, very short, but to the point without any preface or conclusion. I am quoting a few.

In the note book just below the story about a tiger from *Kathamala* (a story book for children written by Ishwarchandra Vidyasagar) that she had copied she wrote 'I love Joshi very much'. The line was self-composed because so far no one had come across these words in any work of Bengali literature. The reader should not presume that I am going to narrate a love story. Joshi is not a twelve-year-old boy of the village befriended by Uma. Joshi is an old maid servant who looked after Uma; and the name Joshi is an abbreviation of 'Jashoda'.

But this line does not indicate the exact feelings of the child towards Joshi. If one wants to know what is the exact relationship between the Uma and Joshi I advise him to flip one two pages ahead and there he would find another line showing an exactly opposite feeling towards Joshi.

But this is not the only example of contradictory statement. She wrote on one page 'I am *aari* with Hari for my entire life' which means that she will never talk to Hari. Incidentally, Hari is not a boy; she is a girl who studied in the same class as her and her full name is Haridasi. A few pages later, she wrote something that left no doubts in one's mind that Hari was her best friend and the dearest person in the whole world.

When she turned nine, one day *shehnai* started playing in her house, early in the morning. Uma was getting married. The groom was Parrymohan, a friend of Gobindolal. Parrymohan too wrote in the local newspapers. Parrymohan was an educated young man, though one can't call him highly educated; unlike other young men of his time his outlook was conservative. The residents of his locality praised him for that. Gobindolal used to emulate him though he was not entirely successful.

After her marriage at a tender age of nine, Uma left her home dressed in a red *Banarasi sari* with her face covered and crying profusely. Before leaving her mother said, "My child obey your mother-in-law and learn how to perform the house hold chores from her. And please stop reading and writing."

Gobindolal blessed her before she left and said, "Uma please do not practice calligraphy on the walls of your new home! They are very different from us. Be careful; do not write on Parrymohan's papers like you did on mine."

The instructions made her jittery. She realized that she was going to a place where no one would excuse her mistakes. And she will have to unlearn many things that she had learnt in her father's house. She will have to find out what is considered 'wrong' in the new house hold and so that she did not get admonished for not knowing customs followed in her new family.

Shehnai played in the morning when she was leaving her house. The place was full of people when she was going away from her father's house, but no one among the crowd knew what was going on in the mind of a nine- year-old covered from head to toe in a red Benarasi sari.

Joshi accompanied her, she was supposed to come back after few days, after settling her in her new home. Joshi was very fond of Uma and after a lot of thought she had packed her notebook along with her other belongings in a small tin box. The notebook was an essential part of her life in her paternal home; it was a loving reminder of her short stay in her father's house. A short history of her childhood days expressed through a few words written in her unformed childish hand writing. The notebook gave her a feeling of freedom in the middle of learning wifely duties.

She hadn't written anything during the first few days of her stay in her new home as she was kept very busy. But she could not hold herself when Joshi went back after settling her, that afternoon Uma shut all the door and windows of her room and took out her notebook from the tin box. She sobbed and wrote in her notebook, 'Joshi has gone home. I even want to go back to my mother.'

After coming to her husband's house, she hadn't copied down any story from her primers as she hardly had any time and also, because she did not feel like doing it, so there was no gap between her first entry and her second. Her second entry was, 'If *dada* (elder brother) takes me home I promise not to spoil his writing ever again.'

People say that Uma's father had wanted to bring Uma back home quite a few times, but Gobindolal inspired by Parrymohan, objected to it. They were of the opinion that this was the time when Uma should develop strong bond with husband, if Uma went to her father's house frequently, it would disrupt the process. Gobindolal had written an article in the newspaper premised on this belief of his. In the article he had taunted the people who thought otherwise. The article was good and the local gentry appreciated it. When Uma came to know about it, she wrote in her notebook, 'Dada I beg of, please come and take me home, I promise not to make you angry ever.'

One day Uma was writing on her notebook secretly, it was nothing much just something trivial which helped her to assuage her feelings, which she did this quite often. Uma's frequent disappearance behind the closed doors of her room made her sister- in- law Tilakmanjari curious; she peeped in through a crack in the door. When she saw Uma writing it surprised her no end. So far Goddess Saraswati (goddess of leaning) had never set her foot in the woman's quarters of the house; not even secretly!

Tilakmanjari's younger sister, Kanakmangeri too tried to see through the crack in the door. After a lot of effort, the even the youngest sister Anangamanjari too stood tiptoe and saw Uma writing. All three of them giggled gleefully after discovering the reason behind Uma's frequent disappearance behind the closed doors of her room. When the sound of their giggles reached Uma's ears, she understood that her secret was no longer a secret. Feeling embarrassed she closed her note book and placed it back in her tin trunk and locked it. Feeling scared about the repercussion she lay down on her bed and hid her face in her pillow.

Parrymohan came to know about the discovery after some time. It got him worried. He felt that this might lead to the arrival of reading material in the women's quarters of the house, which would distract the inmates. They would neglect their chores and spend their time in reading.

He had spent a lot of time in thinking about it and had propounded a theory on the subject. He said the power of a woman and the power of a man combine to give rise to the power behind the bond between a woman and a man. But education gives rise to male power in a woman and that is dangerous. The male power in woman clashes with the male power in a man. This may lead to destruction of the man and the woman may become a widow. Strangely enough no one refuted his theory.

Parrymohan scolded Uma in the evening. Not only that he mocked her and said, "It seems like we will have to order a *shamla* (a kind of turban worn by office-going men) my wife, after all she will be going to office very soon with pen stuck behind her ear."

Poor Uma! She did not understand, as to why he said so. Uma had never read his articles, may be that is why she couldn't understand why he taunted her. But she felt very small all the same. She wished that the mother earth would open up and take her in her arms like she did for her daughter *Sita*.

After this incidence Uma did not write anything on her note book for a very long time; but one autumn morning it so happened that Uma heard a beggar woman sing an *agomoni* song. *Agomoni* songs are sung in Bengal just before Durga puja. These songs describe the home-coming of goddess Durga to her paternal home. Uma stood next to a window and heard her sing resting her chin on a bar of the window. Nearly everyone is reminded of their childhood on such mornings when the earth is awash with soft golden yellow sunshine of autumn. The *agomoni* song brought back the memories of her childhood.

The beggar woman was singing

> "*Purobashi bolay Umar ma*
>
> *Tor hara Tara elo oyee.*
>
> *Koyee Uma bolee koi.*
>
> *Kenday Rani bolay, amar Uma elay,*
>
> *Ekbar aay ma koree kolay*
>
> *Omonee do bahu posharee, maer gola dhoree*
>
> *Obhimanay kandee Raniray bolay*
>
> *Koyee meyea bolay antay giyeachilay.*"

[People tell Uma's (Goddess Durga is also called Uma) mother

look you're your Tara (The Goddess is also called Tara) is coming back

When she hears this the queen (Uma's mother) rushes out to meet her

She asks, "Where is my Uma?"

and when Uma comes to her mother—the queen

She sobs and says, "Come to me my darling let me hold you

in my arms"

When Uma hears this, she throws her arms around her mother's

neck and weeps.

Uma says with a hurt pride to the queen, "Mother why didn't you

Come to take me?"]

The song touched her, her heart filled up with resentment and tears welled up in her eyes. Uma was not a singer so whenever she heard a song that she liked she would write it down, may be to make up for what she lacked in. She had been doing this right from the time she had learnt to write.

Uma called the singer to her room, when no one was looking; and started writing the song secretly.

But the sisters had seen her. They had peeped through the crack in the door and had discovered that Uma was writing on her notebook, something that she had been forbidden to do by her husband.

The sisters were thrilled because they had caught her red handed. They laughed with glee. And shouted, "We have seen what you were doing *boudidi* (sister-in-law)."

Uma rushed out of the room with folded hands and requested them not to tell anybody. She said, "Please do not tell anybody that I have been writing. I promise never to do it again."

As she was talking to them Uma noticed that one of the sisters was eyeing her notebook for quite some time. She ran inside the room and grabbed the notebook and held it close to her chest. The sisters tried to snatch it away from her, but they did not succeed. They ran to their brother and told him everything.

Parrymohan entered the room and sat down on the bed. Then he ordered in a solemn voice, "Give me the notebook."

When she did not obey he brought down his voice and repeated, "Give it."

Uma held the notebook close to her and looked at him beseechingly. When Parrymohan got up to take the book forcibly from her she threw the book down and threw herself on the floor covering her face with her hands.

Parrymohan started reading. He read loudly from the notebook. Uma clung to the ground beneath her in a tight embrace. The other three girls laughed uncontrollably as they heard their brother read.

Uma did not get back her notebook after that. It seems Parrymohan too had a notebook full of cynical essays, but alas there was no well-wisher of mankind around who could snatch it away from him and destroy it.

Glossary

Ishwar Chandra Vidyasagar — He was an educator and a social reformer. He simplified and modernized Begali literature. He championed the cause of female education in Bengal.

Puja — worship

Shehnai — A wind instrument played in northern India while celebrating an occasion.

Banarasi — Silk woven in Benaras hence the name

Shamla —Turban worn by males when they went to office

Sita — In the epic Ramayan Lord Rama asks his wife to prove her purity by walking into fire for the second time. Sita feels humiliated and request her mother the 'Earth' to take her into her arms. The Earth opens up and takes her in her embrace.

8

Postmaster

Just after joining the postal department, the postmaster came to Ulapur village. It was a small and insignificant village. The post office was new; it had come into existence because of the efforts made by the *Sahib* (British officer) of the Indigo factory nearby.

Our postmaster was from Kolkata, his condition in this back of beyond village was somewhat like a fish out of water. The post office was housed in a dark *atchala* (a large hut with eight thatched roofs one on top of another) situated close to a pond clogged with water hyacinth. The pond was surrounded by thick vegetation, comparable with a jungle. The clerks of the indigo factory who came to the post office were very busy people they had no time to talk, moreover, the postmaster did not find them genteel enough to mix with.

People from Kolkata are not affable by nature. When they arrive at a new place, they behave arrogantly or are nonplussed. That is why the postmaster could not mix well with the local people. Time hung heavy on his hands as there was hardly any work. At times the postmaster tried his hand at poetry. He wrote about the pleasures of watching clouds amble across the blue sky and of watching leaves and branches tremble when the wind blew over them. But it was not hidden from the almighty that, no one would be happier than the postmaster if the gene of the 'Arabian Nights' came to him and offered to cut down the trees, make a tarmac dam road and build tall houses of cement and concrete which would hide the sky and clouds from view. May be that could have rejuvenated the gentleman from Kolkata who was wilting away.

The postmaster's salary was meager. So he had to cook his food himself, an orphaned girl from the village assisted him in his domestic chores. The postmaster gave her food in return. Her name was Ratan. She was around twelve to thirteen years of age. Ratan had no prospects of getting married in the near future.

In the evenings when smoke curled out from the cow sheds of the village, (to drive away the mosquitoes), when the cicadas started their chorus from the bushes nearby and the inebriated *baul* (mystical minstrels of Bengal, who live together in groups in villages) singers sang at the top of their voices accompanied with *Khol* and *kartal* (drums and cymbals))--- that was the time, watching the shivering tress in the dark would give an eerie feeling even to poets like the postmaster.

Then the postmaster would light a lamp inside the hut and called out,

"Ratan!"

Ratan sitting close to the doorstep would be waiting for this call. But she never came inside on the first call. She would reply back from outside, "*Dadababu* (elder brother) are you calling me?"

The conversation that followed was like this

Postmaster: What are you doing?

Ratan: I will be going to the kitchen now and light the fire for---

Postmaster: Your work in the kitchen can wait, fill up my *kalkay* (smaller version of hookah) with tobacco and bring it.

Very soon Ratan would enter the room holding a *kalkay* and blowing on it with her cheeks puffed- up. The postmaster would take the *kalkay* from her and start talking.

Ratan, do you remember your mother?

She remembered her mother sketchily. She was more attached to her father. Her father loved her more than her mother. Ratan remembered vividly some of those evenings when her father came back home after the day's work. While speaking Ratan would enter the room and sit on the floor next to the postmaster's feet. She remembered her younger brother and spoke about the times that they had spent together. She told him about how once during rainy season she and her brother sat next to a pond and pretended to catch fish with branches of trees as fishing rods. Ratan gave more importance to this insignificant incidence than many other important things that had happened in her life. They would chat till quite late in the night. Quite often the postmaster did not cook as he felt lazy. Then   Ratan would quickly make some *rotis* (unleavened bread cooked on a skillet) and the two of them would eat *rotis* with the left over *sabji* (cooked vegetables) from lunch.

On certain evenings the postmaster too spoke about his home and family members. He poured his heart out while talking about his younger brother, mother and elder sister. What he could not share with the clerks from the indigo factory who came to the post office, he shared with the illiterate girl without any restraint. Gradually there came a time when Ratan established a relationship with his relatives. While talking to the postmaster, she would often refer to them as '*ma*' (mother), *didi* (elder sister)' and '*dada* (elder brother)', as though she had known them for a long time. The little girl had painted a picture of the postmaster's family members in her mind.

That was a bright and sunny afternoon in the middle of rainy season, a warm and balmy breeze was blowing, a typical fragrance was rising from the sun-drenched grass and leaves, the warm air which was rising from the vegetation made one feel as though the tired earth was breathing. A bird had gone berserk somewhere, his persistent call was sounding like a complaint in the court of nature.

The postmaster had no work that afternoon--- the dance of rain washed shining leaves as the wind blew through them and the dazzling white puffy clouds in the blue sky illuminated by the bright sun was something to behold. The postmaster was enjoying. He was gazing at them idly and was fervently wishing that he had someone who he could call his own, someone close to his heart. He felt that even the bird was trying to tell him the same thing over and over again and the breeze that rustled through the leaves in that quiet afternoon carried the same message. No one would believe neither anyone would want to know that such feelings can arise in the mind of a lonely postmaster of a little-known village in a lazy afternoon.

The postmaster let out a sigh and called Ratan.

At that time Ratan was sitting under a Guava tree with her legs spread out in front, busy chewing an unripe Guava.

Ratan got up and ran as she heard her master call.

"You called me *dadababu*?" she was panting.

The postmaster said, "Yes from now onwards I am going to teach you to read and write."

That afternoon he taught her the vowels. Ratan's lessons continued for some time, soon Ratan started learning conjoined letters.

Month of *Shravan* (July-August) came, and it rained incessantly. The ponds and the canals became brimming full of water. The sound of the falling rain and croaking frogs was all that one could hear. The roads had become rivulets; people could not come out of their houses, and they had to use boats to go the *haat* (market).

It was a cloudy morning; the postmaster's pupil was sitting outside his room waiting for his call. But unlike other days he did not call her. When she didn't hear him, she quietly picked up her notebook and entered the room. She found him lying on his bed. Ratan thought the postmaster must be resting so she left the room without disturbing him. As she turned back to leave, she heard him call, "Ratan."

Ratan went back and said, "*Dadababu* were you sleeping?"

"I am not feeling well Ratan ---feel my forehead," the postmaster sounded tired.

When a person is not well and far away home, especially on a dismal cloudy day he yearns for the tender touch of a female relative. He misses the loving care of a mother or a sister. Our postmaster too felt the same. His prayers did not go unanswered because in no time little Ratan changed her role and became a caring mother. She called the *vaidya* (practitioner of Ayurvedic medicine). He examined him and left some medicine. Ratan strictly followed the instructions left by the *vaidya* she gave him medicines and, cooked special diet, fed him and sat next to his bed throughout the night.

She repeated the same question over and over again, "*Dadababu* are you feeling any better?"

The postmaster got up from his sickbed after many days. The illness had made him very weak. He felt that he could no longer live in a place so unhealthy. So he wrote a letter to the head quarters in Kolkata requesting for a transfer to some other place, citing the unhealthy and unhygienic surroundings.

Being relieved of her nursing duty Ratan took up her position once again outside the postmaster's door. She kept waiting for the Post master's call, but the postmaster did not call her. Whenever she peeped inside, she found him lying on the *chowky* (dewan, often used in make shift offices with a desk placed on one end) in the office room or on his bed staring at the ceiling unmindfully. While the postmaster awaited a reply to his application eagerly Ratan revised her lessons over and over again so that she did not make any mistakes. Finally, after a week or so the postmaster called her one evening. Ratan ran inside expectantly with a trembling heart, "You were calling me *dadababu*?" She asked.

The postmaster said, "Ratan, I am going away tomorrow."

Ratan: Where are you going *dadababu*?

Postmaster: I am going home.

Ratan: When will you come back?

Postmaster: I will not come back.

Ratan kept quiet, she did not ask anymore questions. The postmaster explained, that he had applied for a transfer from Ulapur, which was turned down so he has resigned from the post and was going back home. No one spoke for some time. The lamp twinkled in one corner of the room and water dripped into the room from the old broken-down roof.

Ratan went away to the kitchen to make *rotis*, for dinner. She was not quick like other days. Her mind was preoccupied. After the postmaster finished his dinner Ratan asked him, "*Dadababu* will you take me home along with you?"

The postmaster laughed and said, "How can I?"

The postmaster did not consider it to be necessary to explain to the little girl as to why he couldn't do so.

Ratan did not sleep well that night. She slept in snatches and dreamt. The postmaster's laughter and the words, 'How can I?' reverberated in her ears.

When the postmaster got up in the morning he found, that Ratan had already kept water ready for his bath. The postmaster bathed in water drawn and kept in vessels, a common practice in Kolkata. Ratan did not know about the time of his departure. So she had risen early and had fetched water for his bath from the river, so that he did not get late. The postmaster called Ratan after his bath. Ratan entered the room quietly, looked at her master's face and waited for his orders. The master said "Don't worry I will tell the person who will be coming in my place to employ you, he will look after you like I did, I am sure." He spoke from his heart with a lot of love and affection no doubt, but a woman's heart is difficult to understand. Ratan had never complained or cried on being scolded in the past, but these words of concern drove her to tears she said "Please *dadababu* you don't have to tell anything to anybody, I don't want stay here after you go."

The postmaster was dumb founded because he had never seen her cry.

The new postmaster arrived. And our erstwhile postmaster handed over the charge to him.

Before leaving   he called Ratan and said, "Ratan I have never given you anything. I want to give you some something before I leave. This will look after your needs for some time." He kept aside some money for his journey, and took out the rest of his salary from his pocket to give Ratan.

Ratan fell on the ground and held his feet. She said beseechingly, "*Dadababu* please do not give me anything, and for God sake don't worry about me I will be alright," after that she ran away from the place.

The postmaster let out a long sigh, picked up his carpet bag and placed his umbrella on his shoulder. The porter lifted his blue and white tin trunk on his head and started walking slowly towards the waiting boat. The postmaster followed him.

The boat started off just as soon as he got into it. The turbulent water of the river swollen by rain which lapped around the boat made him feel as though they were steams of tears shed by the long-suffering mother earth. It moved the postmaster and sadness gripped his heart. The face of the destitute village girl appeared in front of his mind's eye representing the sorrow of all lonesome and neglected orphan girls. For a moment the postmaster thought of going back and taking the lonely girl with him, but by then the sail had filled up with wind and the boat had picked up speed, it had already crossed the village boundary and the burning ghat of the village was visible. As the swift flowing river took him further and further away our sad traveler tried to put his aching heart at rest by telling himself that 'in life he would have to confront many partings, death being the most painful one among them, he has to take such partings in his stride, thus there was no point in going back to the village'.

But no Philosophical thought came to Ratan's mind. She was inconsolable. She roamed around the premises of the post office with her eyes brimming full of tears, Ratan still nurtured the hope that her *dadababu* would come back for her. Her attachment with her *dadababu* was strong and that did not let her leave the place.

Alas! The human heart is irrational it doesn't listen to any reason. It takes very long to accept reality. It clings on to false hopes, even the *strongest* proof is brushed aside. And finally one day the tie gets severed leaving behind a barren heart. But that is not the end very soon it gives in willingly to another betrayal.

Glossary

Sahib — British officer

Atchala — A large hut with eight thatched roof one over another

Baul — Mystical minstrels of Bengal

Khol — A percussion instrument

Kartal — Cymbals

Dadababu — Elder brother

Kalkay — Smaller version of hookah

Roti — Unleavened bread cooked on skillet

Sabji — Cooked vegetables

Haat — Market

Vaidya — Doctor of Aurvedic medicine

Choekey — Dewan often used in offices with a small desk on one end

9

Shubha

When she was born, she was named Shubhashini, which means the one who speaks sweetly. No one could imagine at that juncture that she would never speak. She had two elder sisters, whose names were Shukeshini (one who has lustrous hair) and Shuhashini (one who has a beautiful smile). She was named Shubhashini, the one who speaks sweetly, because it rhymed with the names of her elder sisters. People shortened her name to Shubha.

The parents got the two older daughters married after a good deal of searching (for a suitable groom) and expenditure. Shubashini was still a child, but the burden of a dumb girl child weighed heavily on the parents' minds.

Not everybody has the sense to understand that even though a person cannot talk, they are capable of feeling. So often, people discussed her dark future before her without realizing that she understood everything. This led her to believe that her disability was the result of a curse by the gods above. So, she tried her best to hide herself from the rest of the world. She wanted people to forget about her existence. Try as she might, her parents did not forget, especially her mother. Her mother thought that it was because of some fault of hers that Shubhashini was born dumb. Most mothers think of their daughters as an extension of their own self, so if there is something lacking in their daughters it embarrasses them. Banikantha, her father, was very fond of Subha; he loved her more than his other two daughters. On the other hand, Shubha irritated her mother no end because she felt that the girl's disability was because of her own deficiency.

Shubha could not talk, but her eyes were very expressive. They were large, dark and fringed by long eyelashes. When she was moved by something, her lips trembled, like the new russet leaves which tremble at the slightest touch of the breeze.

Expressing our thoughts through our talk is akin to a translation. To do it, we make a conscious effort. But it is not always very successful because not everybody can express their thoughts verbally; people make mistakes. But dark eyes do not have to translate anything. The mind casts its shadow on them. The thoughts that go through one's mind open the eyes wide or shut them, make them sparkle or make them dull. Sometimes the eyes stare unmindfully without focusing on anything, like the setting moon late at night, while an exciting event makes them flash like lightning. The eyes express a wide range of emotions in those who cannot talk; the language of the eyes is limitless, like the sky or like the ocean, every mood and every expression is reflected in them. Subha led a quiet and lonely life, children never included her in their games. Being untouched by the humdrum everyday life imbued her appearance with an aura. Probably this was the reason why children left her alone. She was like the afternoon, desolate and quiet.

2

The name of the village was Chandipur. A small river flowed by it. The nature of the river was like a comely village girl, it flowed quietly between its banks, and the people living on the banks had a close relation with the river. The verdant, high banks on either side were shaded by trees. The river was like a benevolent goddess for the villagers who benefitted from it.

Banikantha's prosperous homestead was close to the river. The main house was an *aatchala*, a big mud-plastered house covered by eight thatched roofs one atop another. The compound was fenced by thin bamboo slats. There was a mango and jackfruit orchard within the compound. In addition, there was a cowshed, a granary a *dheki shala* (a place where rice is husked manually) and huge piles of hay. The homestead attracted the attention of the people who went past in their boats. Shubha's folks were well-to-do, but they did not have time for her, she was left to herself most of the time. So, after finishing her tasks, she would sit on the river bank.

Shubha could not talk, but the surroundings fulfilled what she lacked. The murmur of the river, the distant hubbub of people, the songs of the boatmen as they rowed past, the chirping of birds, the rustling of leaves and the sound of the footsteps of people passing by reached her heart like the waves of the sea that break on the shore. For her this was a language, an extension of the language spoken by her dark eyes – a universal language.

In the afternoon, when the boatmen and the fisher folk went home for lunch, villagers settled down for a siesta, the birds stopped chirping, the ferry boats stopped plying, the sun rose to its peak and it became very quiet, only two people would be out in the scorching sun – the mute mother earth and the mute girl.

It would be wrong to say that Shubha had no intimate friends. She had two very close friends, the cows Sharbashi and Panguli. They had never heard Shubha call them by their names, but they recognized the sound of her footsteps. They understood her silent language. They understood when she admonished them and when she cajoled them for something, they responded when she petted them. In fact, they understood her better than human beings.

As a routine, Shubha went to the cowshed thrice a day. On entering the shed, she would put her arms around Sharbashi's neck and rub her cheek against the cow's head. Panguli would observe them quietly and lick Shubha's arm. There were days when she would visit the cowshed more than thrice. Those were the days when someone had spoken rudely to her. On those days, she would seek the company of her friends for solace. The look on her face would make them understand that Shubha was unhappy about something, they would nuzzle her and rub her arms gently with their horns – it was their way of comforting her.

Other than Panguli and Sharbashi, she had two more friends – a goat and a kitten. Shubha was not as close to them as she was to the cows, but they considered Shubha to be a good friend. The kitten's favourite place was Shubha's lap. He would climb onto her lap without any hesitation and drift into a peaceful slumber. Shubha would stroke his neck and back with her soft hands. This would help him to fall asleep faster. At times he would make it amply clear that he wanted Shubha to caress his back so that he could fall asleep.

3

She had yet another friend who belonged to a higher rung in the developmental ladder. A good-for-nothing fellow called Pratap. It is difficult to say what was the relation between the two of them, because he lived in his own world, and she couldn't speak, so there was no common language between them.

He was from the Gosain family. His parents had lost all hopes that he would do something useful someday. Such people are generally disliked by their relatives, but liked by people who are not related to them. That is because they have a lot of free time and they can be utilized whenever there is a shortage of manpower. Their situation can be compared with that of the gardens in every town; they are looked after by the government, but enjoyed by everybody. Every village has a good-for-nothing man or two who can be utilized for various odd jobs; Pratap fell in that category.

Pratap's main interest in life was fishing; maybe because this was an ideal way of spending time for a person like him. He could be seen sitting on the river bank with a fishing rod in the afternoon. And this is where he met her very often. This suited him because he liked to have someone around while doing any work and a silent companion was ideal for fishing. While others called her Shubha, he called her Shu affectionately.

Shubha sat under a tamarind tree and Pratap sat a little away from her holding his fishing rod and staring at the water. She would bring a *paan* for him every day – rolling it herself. She wanted to help him and make him look upon her as a capable person, but she did not know how she could do that. How she prayed for some special power with which to surprise Pratap and make him say, 'Oh my God, Shu can do all this!'

What if she became a mermaid? She mused. She would emerge from the water quietly with a *mani* (a bright jewel) taken from the head of a water serpent and place it on the steps of the quay, close to Pratap. On seeing the *mani*, Pratap would abandon his useless pursuit, take it in his hand and dive into the water. The *mani* would guide him to *patal loke*, the netherworld. On reaching *patal loke*, he would walk into a palace made of silver and who would he find there? None other than Shu, Banikantha's mute daughter, the one and only princess of patal loke, sitting on a golden bedstead in a room illuminated by the light reflected from jewels. Too far-fetched! Absolutely impossible, can't happen ever, she would tell herself. But what if it happened? She desperately wanted to surprise Pratap, but didn't know how. Alas! Her father Banikantha was an ordinary person and not a king, and she was not a princess, just a mute girl.

4

Shubha was growing up. She had begun to discover a new person within herself and had started feeling different. Her heart was experiencing a new kind of emotion. This new feeling swept through her like the tide rising on a full moon night. Shubha was confused. There were many questions in her mind; she thought about them and looked inward for answers, but didn't find any.

On full moon nights she would open the door of her room and peep out timidly to look at the moon – she would find a lonely moon, as lonely as herself, looking down at the sleeping world below. The full moon would stare down at the baffled young girl who had many questions in her mind.

Shubha's coming of age worried her parents. People in the village were talking about it. It was rumoured that the elders of the village were planning to make the family *ek ghoray* (ostracize), because Shubha was not married even though she had reached the marriageable age. The family was well-off and lived well. This made matters worse because many people were jealous of them.

Subha's parents discussed the problem at great length. And then one day Banikantha went away from the village for a while. When he came back, he told his wife, "Let us go to Kolkata and settle everything."

Preparations started for the journey. Like a fog-shrouded morning, Shubha's heart became heavy with tears and sadness. The prospect of an unknown future troubled her; she followed her parents all over the house like a mute animal and cast her large eyes on their faces every now and then to gauge what was going on in their minds, but she didn't find a clue and no one tried to explain anything to her.

One afternoon Shubha met Pratap; he was fishing as usual. When he saw Shubha he said, "Shu, I am told that they have found a match for you. I hope you don't forget us, once you get married." After saying this he concentrated once again on his fishing. Shubha looked at Pratap the way a doe looks at the hunter after being struck by an arrow, as if to say, "Why did you hurt me? What have I done?" That day she didn't sit down under the tree. She went back home. Banikantha had just woken up from his afternoon siesta and was smoking. Shubha sat next to his feet and sobbed. Banikantha tried to console her, but he couldn't, tears rolled down her cheeks.

The day before their departure, Shubha went to the cowshed to bid farewell to her friends. She fed them and put her arms around their necks. There was so much to tell them; her eyes did the talking as she poured out her heart to them and tears cascaded down from her beautiful eyes.

It was a moonlit night; Shubha came out of her room and walked to her favourite spot on the river bank. She lay down on the grassy bank and spread her arms as though she was trying to embrace the earth like a child embracing its mother. She pleaded, "Oh mother, please stop them. Hold me tight and don't let me go."

Shubha went with her parents to Kolkata the next day, where they rented a house. One day her mother dressed her up with a lot of care because some people were coming to see her. She pulled back her hair and tied it tightly with a golden ribbon and made a bun. After that, she decked her up in heavy gold ornaments. It didn't help much because the dazzle of the gold subdued her natural good looks. On top of that Shubha couldn't stop crying. It worried her mother because Shubha's eyes were swollen with incessant weeping. She scolded her and tried to stop her, but Shubha could not hold back her tears.

The prospective groom came with a friend to see her. Shubha's parents were on tenterhooks. After all, the god himself had come to choose the sacrificial animal! Her mother's admonitions increased the flow of her tears. She was still crying when she was sent to face the examiners.

The main examiner looked at her for a while and said, "Not bad."

Seeing her cry, the groom felt that the thought of separation from her parents after marriage was making her cry. This led him to the conclusion that Shubha must be a sensitive person and that after their marriage she would have similar feelings for him. The value of an oyster increases when a pearl is found in it; similarly, the tears increased Shubha's value. They did not ask her any questions.

She was married on an auspicious day after consulting the almanac.

Her parents went back to the village after giving away their mute daughter to the groom. They were happy because they would not be ostracized by the villagers and they would not have to face the wrath of their ancestors in the next world for leaving behind an unfinished task.

Shubha's husband worked somewhere in the western part of India. He took her there with him after their marriage. Within a week after the marriage people realized that Shubha could not speak. No one understood that this was not her fault, that she had no intention of deceiving them. She had tried to explain with her eyes so many times, but no one understood her because those who could understand the language of her eyes were not there. She wanted to say so many things, her heart was heavy with unspoken words and her eyes were full of tears which no one but the almighty heard or saw.

Her husband married again; this time he made use of his eyes as well his ears to select a bride.

10

Conclusion (Samapti))

1

A purvakrishna was coming back to his village on a boat. He had just completed graduation from Kolkata. The river was not wide. It was a rain-fed river that dried up after rains, but now as it was the end of *Shravan* the river was full of water. It flowed very close to the village. The sky was clear and the sun had come out after many days of rain.

If one could peep into Apurvakrishna's mind he would have seen yet another river flowing, brimming full of youth, undulating and shimmering in the bright sunshine.

The boat stopped at the quay. The terrace of Apuva's *pucca* house was visible from there. He had not informed about his arrival; so no one had come to receive him. He declined the boat man's offer to carry his bag till his place, picked up his bag got down from the boat and started walking towards home in a happy frame of mind.

The river bank was slippery and as soon as he stepped on the bank he fell down. Moments later he heard someone laugh, though it was loud, but it sounded sweet, waves of the laughter reached the birds sitting on an *ashwath* tree nearby it alerted them and they flew away. Apurva felt embarrassed. He picked up his bag arranged his clothes as far as possible and got up. Then he looked around and found the source. It was a girl. She was sitting on a pile of bricks near the quay. The force of laughter was so great that she was shaking.; so much so that Apurva felt she might burst into pieces if she didn't stop.

Apurva recognised her; she was Mrinmayee, his neighbour's daughter. They had settled down in Apurva's village two to three years back. Their house used to be on the bank of a big river a little away from Apurva's village. The river had washed away their property, so they moved into a house next to Apurva's house.

The girl was famous in the village. The male residents called her 'Pagli 'the mad one affectionately, but the females were not too happy with her conduct. They felt that she needed to be disciplined. Her antics were a cause of worry for them. Mrinmayee's friends were mostly boys as she had very little to do with girls her age; in fact, she was indifferent towards them. Mrinmayee and her group were capable of causing chaos in the village within minutes like the *bargis*.

When someone complained about Mrinmayee's behaviour her mother would say, "Mrinmayee's father pampers her a great deal and that is why she has become so unmanageable." Her mother never scolded her or punished her because she felt tears in her daughter's eyes would make her husband miserable. Mrinmayee's father was working in a place far away from home.

She was dark complexioned; her hair was short which reached just beyond her shoulders and was very curly. Though her face was attractive, but there was nothing feminine about it. It was boyish, her eyes were large and dark and there was not a trace of shyness in them, they were bold and frank and so was her behaviour. She was tall and healthy, and it was difficult to make out her age. Had the villagers known her age they would have criticised her parents for delaying her marriage.

When a boat from a faraway place stopped at the quay for a few days, the people of the village would gather around the boat and treat the new comers respectfully. The village women would cover their heads with the end of their saris and made sure that the cover extended beyond their noses. But Mrinmayee would land up there without hesitation, holding an infant in her arms and watching their activity attentively. After satisfying her curiosity she would go back to her friends describe the newcomers in minutest details.

Apurva had met this tom boy a couple times before this, when he had come home during his vacations. She had left an indelible impression on his mind. There have been many times when he had thought about her after going back to Kolkata. In this world there are many faces that one does not forget easily; they remain with you forever. Not because, they are very beautiful. You remember them because of their transparency. Generally, everything about a person is not revealed by their faces, but the faces that do not hide anything are difficult to forget. Her face told that she was an untamable girl, like a fawn who enjoyed her freedom.

It is very important to tell the reader at this juncture, that the laughter might have sounded sweet, but for poor Apurva it was not at all enjoyable. He handed the bag to the boat man without hesitation and started walking towards his house rapidly.

The ambience was just right, river bank, shady trees, chirping birds, soft glow of the morning sun and the age of the two; the hard pile of bricks on which she was sitting was of hardly any significance, because the person who sat on it was capable of making any place appear inviting and attractive by her mere presence. But unfortunately, the ambience came to nothing after what happened following the first foot fall, fate was not fair to the young ones.

2

Apurva continued to hear the laughter cascading down from the pile of bricks as he walked towards his house with his bag and clothes smeared with mud.

His mother was thrilled to see him. She sent the servants to get fish, sweets and curd from the market. The news of his arrival created a stir among his neighbours too.

After lunch Apurva's mother brought up the subject of his marriage, Apurva had anticipated it. She had spoken to him about it long back, but Apurva being quite modern in his outlook had dismissed it and had said that he would get married after completion of his graduation. But now he had no excuse. He said, "Let me see her first and only then I would say yes." His mother said, "You don't have to worry on that account, I have already seen her." Apurva did not want to leave the worry on his mother's shoulders he said, "Till I see the girl I will not marry." His mother found it rather odd, but she agreed.

That night when Apurva blew off the lamp and went to bed, the sound of laughter surpassed all other sounds of a rainy night and reverberated in his ears. How he wished he could erase the part of his fall from the whole episode. He regretted that he could not bring out the fact that he was after all a learned person and had spent many years in Kolkata in pursuit of knowledge and just a fall because of the slipperiness of the ground cannot make him an object of ridicule like any other rustic youth.

It was decided that Apurva would see the girl that his mother had chosen for him next morning. Their house was in the same locality as his. He took special pains to dress up. He abandoned his usual *dhuti* and *chadar* and wore a silken *chapkan and jobba* . He put on a pair of polished shoes and wore a round turban on his head; having dressed up resplendently he set out in morning taking his silk umbrella along with him.

The moment he set his foot in the house of his would be-in-laws the atmosphere of the house-hold changed; it became like a festival. He was welcomed with great honour and was treated like a guest of high esteem. Finally, the girl was brought into the room. Washed and dolled up for the occasion. Her hair was done up in a bun adorned with shiny ribbons and she was covered from head to toe in a red sari. She sat down in one corner of the room, with her head so lowered that it touched her knees. She was chaperoned by an old maid servant who sat behind her to give her confidence. Her younger brother crept into the room, may be to gauge the person who was going to become a part of the family. His eyes got stuck on Apurva's turban, watch chain and soft growth of hair around the chin and upper lip.

Apurva twirled his barely visible moustache for a while thinking of what to say, then he asked, "What do you study?"

No answer came from the heap of clothes in the corner of the room. She responded after being prodded in the back by the maid servant.

"Charu path book two, Vyakaransar book one, Bhugol Vivaran, Patiganith and Bharoter Itihaas," She recited the names of the books that she was studying in one go breathlessly and then she took a long breath at the end. Just then the sound of rapid footsteps was heard and within seconds Mrinmayee ran into the room panting with her hair disheveled. Without paying any attention to Apurva she walked up to Rakhal, the girl's younger brother and started pulling his hand. Rakhal was deeply engrossed in observing Apurva so he did not stir from his position. The old maid servant scolded her in a voice as low as possible keeping the gravity of the occasion in mind. Apurva straightened himself held his turbaned head up and played with the chain of his watch. Finally, when Mrinmayee could not dislodge Rakhal from his position she gave him a resounding slap on his back, pulled down the veil from the girl's head and stormed out of the room. The old maid servant growled in anger. Rakhal giggled seeing the plight of his sister. He didn't feel too bad about the slap, because such give and take was the norm between the two of them.

When Mrinmayee's hair had crossed her shoulders and had reached her back, one day Rakhal had come stealthily from behind and had chopped off a hand full of her hair. Aggrieved by this she had snatched the scissors from him and had chopped off hair mercilessly—her glossy black curls lay like bunches of black grapes on the ground.

The interview did not last long after this; the stationary spherical object in the corner straightened itself, became ambulant and left the room along with the maidservant. Apurva twirled his newly risen crop of moustache for a while and then he too got up to go. He came out the room; found that his shoes were not there where he had left them. A pandemonium ensued after this. They searched for them all over the house, but no one could find them. It embarrassed the family members no end. Everybody cursed the prankster who had taken away the shoes. Apurva left the place minus his new shoes, wearing a pair of old flip-flops of the master of the house.

He heard the same laughter again as he walked on a lonely path near a pond; as though some forest nymph was laughing at Apurva's incongruous footwear. Apurva stopped and started looking around to find the source of laughter. He didn't have to wait long. The unabashed culprit came out from the nearby thicket placed his new shoes in front of him and tried to run away. She was not fast enough; Apurva caught hold of her arm.

Mrinmayee tried her best to wriggle free, but she couldn't. The sun rays fell through the foliage on her mischievous face famed by dark curls. Like a curious traveler who looks at a water fall and tries to gauge its depth, Apurva too looked deeply into those liquid eyes full of mischief and he gradually slackened his grip. He let go his prisoner without punishing her. Mrinmayee would have understood had Apurva punished her by beating her, but this new way of punishing a person and that too in a quiet and lonely place was beyond her power of comprehension.

She started laughing again after he let her go. It rang in his ears as he walked back home in a pensive mood.

3

Apurva did not go to the inner quarters to meet his mother after coming back. He had thought of some excuse for not meeting her, moreover he had an invitation for lunch, so he went out without meeting her.

It was really very difficult to understand as to why a learned person like him was so keen to impress an uneducated village girl like Mrinmayee. How does it matter if she considered him to be an ordinary person! Or for that matter she had laughed at him at a certain point of time or that she preferred Rakhal's company to his? Why was it so important to let people know that he wrote book reviews in a monthly periodical called Bishwadeep; and that there was a note book in his trunk containing his works awaiting release in the form of a book. It was a mystery or may be Apurva Krishna B.A. was not willing to accept rejection.

Apurva entered the inner quarters of the house in the evening and met his mother. The moment she saw him she said, "Apu, did you meet her? Did you like her?"

Apurva looked a bit embarrassed and said, "Yes I have seen them and I liked one of them."

His mother asked, "You were supposed to meet one girl who else was there?"

After a bit of hesitation, he revealed that he had met Mrinmayee too and he liked her.

It was a shock for his mother. What a taste she thought, and that too after being educated in Kolkata! Initially Apurva was a bit hesitant, but his mother's vehement opposition made him stubborn and he declared that he will not marry anyone else other than Mrinmayee. The he more thought about the stationary bundle of clothes he became all the more averse to the idea of getting married to her.

After two to three days of agitation which included hunger-strike, of not talking to each other and insomnia Apurva won the match. His mother came to terms with it by telling herself that Mrinmayee's mother had not groomed her daughter properly and that she would certainly groom her well once she came to the house as a bride. She tried recalling Mrinmayee's face and came to the conclusion that she was pretty. The only problem was that her hair was short and curly; which she thought could be sorted out by oiling regularly and tying tightly.

The villagers had a new name for Mrinmaye, now they started calling her 'Apurva's Choice'. People of the village were fond of her and many called her *Pugli* the mad one affectionately, but none could think of getting their son married to a tom-boy like her.

Mrinmayee's father Eshan Mazumdar worked as a clerk in a steamer company. His office was in a small tin roofed room at the steamer station next to a river, which doubled up as his residence during non-working hours. His job was to sell tickets to the passengers and supervise loading and unloading of the cargo.

Eshan could not hold his tears when he came to know about his daughter's marriage. One can't say if they were tears of happiness or of sorrow because of the impending parting from his daughter. He promptly sent an application to the head office requesting them to grant him some leave for his daughter's marriage, but the boss turned it down. So, he wrote back to his village asking them to postpone Mrinmayee's marriage till Durga Puja as there was a possibility of getting seven days of leave at that time. But Apurva's mother did not agree, as there were quite a few auspicious days in the present month and she wanted to get her son married in one of those days.

Having met with opposition from both the fronts, Eshan had no option, but to agree. He carried on with his work of selling tickets and weighing cargo with a heavy heart like he did before.

Mrinmayee's mother and other ladies of the village started training her for her future role. It continued all through the day. She was asked not to play with her friends, to walk slowly and not run, to smile and not laugh loudly, to control her appetite and to eat only when food was offered; the list of dos and don'ts was long. So many restrictions were imposed on her that she started dreading the idea of getting married. She felt as though she was being sentenced to a life time of imprisonment.

Mrinmayee retaliated to this new kind of treatment. Like an unbroken mare she stepped back turned her head to one side and said, "I will not marry."

4

But she had to get married finally.

Her training resumed after her marriage in her in-law's house and her entire world shrank down to the inner quarters of Apurva's house. Her mother-in-law took over as the main tutor. The first thing that she told her and that too very sternly was that Mrinmayee was no longer a child and her childish pranks and tantrums would not be tolerated.

Mrinmayee did not take the warning seriously; she decided that if her ways were not tolerated in the house then she should go somewhere else. She left the house quietly one afternoon. The house hold was in an uproar when they found her missing. They started looking for her. It was Rakhal—the traitor–who showed them her hiding place. Mrinmayee was sitting inside an abandoned *rath*.

The reader can very well imagine the way she was chastised by her mother, mother-in-law and the well- meaning ladies of the village for this act of hers.

That night the sky became clouded and it rained heavily. Apurvakrishna crept close to his wife in bed and whispered into her ear, "Mrinmayee don't you love me?"

Mrinmayee said, "No, I will never love you." All her anger, frustration and her desire to punish someone for being forced into this marriage came out in that statement. Apurva felt hurt.

But he persisted, "Why what have I done?"

Mrinmayee said, "Why did you marry me?"

It was a difficult question and Apurva was not in a position to answer. Apurva decided to be patient and win over her heart gradually.

Next day her mother-in-law, on noticing certain features of rebellion in her locked her up in a room to teach her a lesson. She shouted cried and banged on the door repeatedly. Her condition was like a bird that has been caged for the first time. When no one opened door, she tore the bed sheet into shreds with her teeth to give vent to her anger and then she threw herself on the floor and wept. She called her father again and again as she cried asking him to take her away.

Apurva came in and sat next to her, and brushed her hair back from her fore head affectionately. Mrinmayee pushed his hand away. He brought his face close to her and whispered into her ear, "I have unlocked the door come let us go to the garden through the rear door. Mrinmayee shook her head vigorously and said, "No." Apurva made an effort to make her get up she pushed him away. He said, "Rakhal has come to play with you. Wouldn't you get up?"

She said, "No," in an angry voice. Rakhal left the place quickly thinking that it would not be safe for him to stay longer. Apurva sat next to her quietly.

Mrinmayee continued to cry. After some time, she fell asleep; Apurva left the room quietly and closed the door softly.

The next day Mrinmayee received a letter from her father. He had written how miserable he felt for not being able to attend his darling daughter's marriage and he had blessed the newly married couple from his heart. After reading the letter   Mrinmayee went her mother-in-law and said, "I want to go to my father." This unusual request made her mother-in-law angry, she said, "How funny! You don't even know where he lives and you are asking me to let you go to him. What a demand!" It was pointless to plead with her mother-in-law so Mrinmayee went to her room and shut the door. Like a person who prays to God as a last resort when all other alternatives are exhausted, Mrinmayee folded her hands and said over and over again, " *Baba* please take me away from this place, there is no one who cares for me in this house. I will die if I stay here."

Mrinmayee left the house late that night when her husband was fast asleep. Though the sky was cloudy, but moon light came through the gaps in the cloud and illuminated her path. She did not know how to reach her father, but she knew that if she walked on the 'mail-runner's path she was bound to reach somewhere. She walked the whole night and was dead tired by the time the birds started chirping. At day break she reached a market place close to the river. No one was there at that time. As she was thinking about where to go, when she heard the familiar sound of bells. It was the mail runner with a bag on his shoulder walking briskly towards the quay. Mrinmayee ran towards him and said, "I want to go to Kushigaunj to my father please take me along with you." He said, "I don't know where Kushigaunj is," having said so he called the boat man of the mail boat got into the boat and set off.

Very busy man indeed! He had absolutely no time to listen to a young girl's plea!

By and by people started coming to the market and the place got crowded. Mrinmayee got down to the quay and called a boatman. She said, "Will you take me to Kushigaunj?" But even before he could answer another boat man in the next boat said, "Oh Minu (Mrinmayee's pet name)what brings you here?" Mrinmayee was thrilled to see him, she said, "Bonomali I want to go to my father in Kushiganj can you take me there?" Bonomali was from her village and he knew this wayward girl very well. He said, "You want to go to your father? Come, I will take you there" Mrinmayee got into the boat.

The boat left the quay. Very soon it started raining. The boat started swaying with the breeze. Mrinmayee was very tired after the long walk the rocking motion and the cool breeze lulled her to sleep.

 When she woke up, she found herself lying in a bed in her in-law's house. A maidservant was sitting next to her bed. As soon as she opened her eyes the maid started scolding her in a loud voice. Her mother-in-law entered the room on hearing the maid's voice and took over from the maid after that. She upbraided Mrinmayee for her improper conduct. Mrinmayee stared at her mother-in-law disbelievingly with widely opened eyes and listened to her as she ranted and raved. She didn't say a word. But when her mother-in-law started blaming her father for the entire incident and said that he had spoilt Mrinmayee by pampering her. Mrinmayee could not tolerate any more she got up and walked into her room, and locked herself in it.

After a little hesitation Apurva made a suggestion to his mother, he said, " Ma why don't you let her go home for a few days, it might help her to adjust."

The suggestion did not go well with his mother she got angry with Apurva and scolded him for his lack of judgement. She said, "Of all the girls in the village you had to choose this devil!"

5

Bad weather continued throughout the day, both inside the house as well as outside.

Next day late at night Apurva woke up Mrinmayee and said, "Do you want to go to your father?"

Mrimmayee held his hand in earnest and said, "Yes."

Apurva said, "Then let's leave the house quietly I have arranged a boat."

Mrinmayee looked at her husband once, and then she got up from her bed to get ready. Her heart was full of gratitude for him. Apurva, in the mean while wrote a hurried letter to his mother to allay her anxiety.

They came out of the house quietly, for the first time Mrinmayee held her husband's hand on her own volition. She trusted him. A wave of happiness flowed inside her, it permeated through her soft hand and reached Apurva he felt the same as she was feeling. The boat set course on the same night. Mrinmayee fell asleep after the initial excitement got over. The next day was a day of happiness and total freedom for her. There were Agricultural fields, forests, villages and markets on either side of the river she missed nothing her eyes took in everything. Many boats crossed their boat from either side. She asked many questions to her husband about what she saw. Even the smallest thing aroused her curiosity and she expected her husband to give an answer. Her questions were, somewhat like this, 'What are the boats carrying? Where are the boats going to? Where are they coming from? What is the name of the village that we are crossing?' And such like, the answers were obviously not there in his college text books and the experience that he had gathered in Kolkata too was not very helpful, but he managed to satisfy the enquirer; though the veracity of the answers was doubtful. The boat reached Kushigaunj next day.

Eshan was sitting in his little tin roofed office writing down the monitory transactions of the day in a leatherbound office register. A small sooty lamp on his desk was the only source of light in the room. The runaway couple entered the room quietly and Mrinmayee called out, "Baba!" Never before had the room heard a sound so beautiful!

Eshan was so happy that couldn't hold back his tears. He was at loss for words as he didn't know how to welcome his newly married daughter and her husband to the ramshackle hut of his. For him they were like the crown prince and princess of some fairyland. He was at his wits end as how to arrange the jute bags in the room and make a place for them to sit.

The next problem was food. He was a poor clerk of meager means and as he was living alone, he had simplified his food to boiled rice, boiled lentils and vegetables. The arrival of his son-in-law and daughter was an occasion for celebration, but he was in a fix as he did not know how to arrange a good meal suitable for the occasion. Mrinmayee solved his problem, she said, "Baba, don't worry we will cook the food." Apurva agreed to it and said, "Yes that is a good idea we will cook together."

The place was small, resources were limited and they were no servants to help them out. But happiness was there in plenty. When the opening is very small in a fountain the water rises very high similarly, happiness gushed out through the tight fist of poverty and reached the zenith.

Three days went by amidst fun and laughter. Steamers came to the quay in the morning as well as in the afternoon at regular intervals. It would get crowded and noisy then. But no steamers came after sundown, and that was the time they liked the best. Then the whole place belonged to them and they had all the freedom to do as they liked. The three of them put in all their culinary skills together to cook the meals, and as none of them knew how to cook the end product was unrecognisable, far removed from the stuff that they wanted to make. But no one complained. The best part was when Mrinmayee's father and husband sat down to eat and Mrinmayee served them affectionately with her hand full of bangles tinkling. They loved the sound. The duo would pull her leg often about the standard of cooking, she too would pretend to get angry and make a face. When three days got over Apurva said that they must get back home, Mrinmayee wanted to stay for a few days more, but Eshan supported his son-in-law, he said, "I think you should go back now."

On the day of their departure Eshan held his daughter close to him and said, "Minu my darling be a good girl make sure no one can find any fault with you, your behaviour should be such that your in-laws feel proud of you."

Mrinmayee left the place weeping. And Eshan went back to his depressing work of selling tickets and weighing cargo.

6

Apurva's mother remained aloof when the culprits reached home. She did not say anything to them, neither did she blame anybody; none of them got a chance to defend. Unspoken words, hurt feelings and complaint against each other made the atmosphere of the house very tense.   When it became unbearable for Apurva he decided to leave. He went up to his mother and said, "Colleges have reopened, I will be going back to Kolkata back to study law."

"But what about your wife?" She asked in a distracted fashion.

Apurva said, "I will leave her with you."

His mother objected she said, "No, don't do that she will not be happy here, why don't you take her with you to Kolkata?" She sounded very restrained, very different from her usual affectionate self.

Apurva felt hurt, he just nodded his head and went away.

Preparation for going to Kolkata started. When Apurva came to his bed room on the night before departure, he found Mrinmayee weeping.

He felt hurt. He said, "Mrinmayee don't you want to go to Kolkata with me?"

Mrinmayee said, "No."

Apurva asked her, "Don't you love me?"

He got no answer. Most of the time the answer is very simple, it is either yes or no, but there are times when other elements of the psyche are associated with it, then it becomes difficult. Thus, it was not fair to expect an answer from her.

"Are you feeling bad about leaving Rakhal?" He asked.

The answer was easy she said, "Yes."

The knowledgeable young man who had successfully graduated from the university with a B.A. degree felt a pinprick of jealousy deep inside him.

He said, "I will not be coming back home for a long time."

There was response from the other side.

"It might be more than two years," he added.

There was a response, but it was incongruous when Mrinmayee said, "When you come back you must bring a three headed Roger's knife for Rakhal." It sounded almost like an order.

Apurva, raised himself from the lying position and asked, "So are you going to stay here while I am away?"

Mrinmayee said, "No I will stay with my mother."

Apurva let out a long sigh and said, "Alright you can stay with your mother, but I will not come back till you write me to come back. Are you happy?"

Mrinmayee did not answer his question, soon she fell asleep. But Apurva could not sleep. He sat up in the bed with his back resting on a pile of pillows.

The moon rose late at night, its light crept into the room and fell on the bed. Apurva looked at her face, he thought she looked like a princess put to sleep by the touch of a *silver magic wand*. He wished he had a *golden wand* with which he could wake her up and tell her so many things.

Apurva woke her up early in the morning. He said, "Mrinmayee it's time for me to go. I will leave you in your mother's house before going to Kolkata."

When Mrinmayee got up from the bed, Apurva held her hands and said, "I have one request. Will you give me something as a reward for helping you out from a few difficult situations in the past?"

Mrinmayee was very surprised, she asked, "What?"

Apurva said, "Please   kiss me once before I go."

Mrinmayee found the request and the solemn expression on his face very funny, she burst into a laughter. After a bit of effort, she managed to control her laughter, she went close to Apurva with the intention of kissing him, but within inches of his face laughter came gushing out from inside and she started laughing again. This happened twice. Ultimately, she gave up and stood with her hand covering her mouth to stop herself from laughing. Apurva gave up and pulled her ears playfully.

Apurva had sworn that he would never force her into doing something that she didn't want. He would stay aloof like a God and accept her gift only if she gave him on her own volition.

 When Mrinmayee stopped laughing, he took her to her mother's house by a less frequented path. He went to his mother after coming back, and said, "I have dropped Mrinmayee in her mother's house as I have decided not to take her to Kolkata, her presence might disturb me and I will not be able to study. Moreover, you don't want her here."

Mother and son parted after that with a heavy heart.

7

Mrimmayee did not feel happy in her mother's place, she could not concentrate on anything. She felt that things were not the same as before. Time hanged heavily, she did not know how to pass her time, where to go and whom to talk to. There were times when Mrinmayee felt that there was no one around her and she was all alone in the house. She would suddenly find darkness enveloping her as though the mid-day sun was eclipsed suddenly. She could not figure out why she had refused to go with her husband to Kolkata earlier and now why she wanted to go to Kolkata so desperately. Even a few days back she used to pine for the life that had she enjoyed before her marriage, but now she had no use for it. It was like a dead leaf fallen from a tree.

People say that there are sword makers, who make swords which are so sharp that the victim doesn't realise when a part of his body is severed, he realises only when someone shakes him and the part falls off. Similarly, when the creator severed Mrimmayee's childhood from her she did not realise. But when the circumstances changed suddenly, she received a jolt and realised that her childhood has slipped away from her. It surprised her and no end and she felt sad about it too.

Her old room in her mother's house seemed unfamiliar, she felt as though the occupant has gone away somewhere and she was a trespasser. Memories of the other house and a particular room in that house came back to her mind over and over again and hummed inside her like a bee.

No one saw Mrinmayee after she came back from her in-law's house. No one heard her laugh. She never went out of the house. Rakhal kept away from her. Her moods frightened him. So, he did not invite her to play with the gang like before.

One day Mrinmayee said to her mother. "Ma I want to go back to my in-law 's house, please take me there."

The hurt expression on her son's face at the time of departure tormented Apurva's mother, and the fact that Apurva left his wife in her mother's house made her feel worse. She was in a bad shape mentally when Mrinmayee walked in quietly and touched her feet. Her mother-in-law took her in her arms and embraced her. Her eyes were full of tears. Apurva's mother looked at her face, she was surprised to see the change in her. It was extraordinary, like a metamorphosis. The tomboy had become a beautiful woman. Only a great force working inside a person could bring about such a change and that too so fast.

After she came back, her mother-in-law decided to correct Mrinmayee's faults one by one, but when she set out to do so she realised that some unseen teacher had already done her job. Mrinmayee was a changed person. She and her mother-in-law started getting along with each other, like two branches which are part of the same tree. They worked together in tandem for the betterment of the house hold.

The change had affected her mind as well as her body, it had calmed her down considerably, but there were times when it bewildered her and tormented her. Like the moisture laden clouds that gather in the sky in early *Ashar*, her complaints against her husband gathered in her mind.

Dark shadows became visible around her eyes under her long and dark eye lashes. When she was alone in her room, she would talk to him in a soliloquy and ask him many questions like 'I did not understand you, but why didn't you make me understand? Why didn't you punish me for being disobedient? Why didn't you force me to go with you to Kolkata? Why did you listen to my request?' and many more questions on similar lines.

Their encounter on a lonely path near a pond under the shade of huge trees came to her mind quite often. Apurva had caught hold of her hand to punish her and she had looked up into his face defiantly. Apurva did not punish her as she had expected, but had looked deeply into her eyes. It was now, that she understood the meaning of that look. On the day of his departure Apurva had asked for a kiss though she did not say no, but she had burst out laughing every time she went close to him. She regretted it and yarned for the moment to come back again. There were many moments that she wanted to relive, very often she would find herself wishing that she hadn't acted the way she did or she hadn't spoken rudely to him.

Apurva on the other hand regretted the fact that Mrimayee never got to know him properly. Mrimayee wondered what impression Apurva might have got about her, she felt bad that Apurva went away thinking that she was an immature girl and he never got know that she too was capable of loving him the way he loved her. She was full of remorse that she didn't kiss him before he left, which she made up by hugging and kissing his pillow over and over again.

Before leaving Apurva had said, "I will not come back home till you write to me and ask me to come home." So, one day she decided to write a letter to him. She went into her room and closed the door and took out some coloured papers with golden borders that Apurva had given to her as a gift. Her greatest problem was how to address him. After a lot of thought she decided to do away with that part of the letter and start straight away. Much to her discomfort she had little control over the size of the letters and the lines. The letters were uneven and the lines were not straight. The pen too let her down resulting in smudges of ink all over the paper. With a lot of effort to write as neatly as possible she wrote, 'Why don't you write to me? How are you? And please come home'. That was all that she wanted to write, but the letter was too short so she decided to add few more things, she wrote 'You must write to me and tell me how you are; Ma is all right and so are Bishu and Punti. Our black cow has given birth to a calf.' She ended the letter as she couldn't think of anything else to write. After that she folded the paper and pushed it into an envelope. She wrote 'Babu Apurva Roy' on the envelope painstakingly and sealed it. In spite of her best efforts the spelling was not correct, the line was not straight and of course the address was incomplete, which she did not know.

Mrinmayee thought it would be embarrassing if everybody got to know about the letter so she asked a maid servant who she trusted the most to drop the letter in the post box.

Needless to say, that the letter did not reach Apurva and he did not come home.

8

Vacations started, but Apurva did not come home. It worried Apurva's mother. She felt that Apurva must be very angry with her and that is why he didn't come home.

Mrinmayee thought that Apurva must be disgusted with her that is why he didn't reply. It embarrassed her no end, when she thought about the contents of the letter. She felt that she had written senselessly about the most insignificant things and had not written to him about her feelings. It troubled her to think of Apurva's reaction on reading her letter surely, he must have thought her to be an immature person, may be because of that he was ignoring her. She asked the maid many time if she had posted the letter. She said, "Don't worry I have posted your letter and the master must have received the letter by now."

One day Apurva's mother told Mrinmayee. "Apurva hasn't come home for a long time; I am thinking of going to Kolkata to meet him. Would you like to come with me?"

Mrinmayee was so happy that she couldn't utter a word, she ran into her room and closed the door. After that she lay down on her bed. Her mind was charged with emotions. She laughed, cried and spoke loudly to the pillow that she held close to her. After some time when her excitement subsided, apprehension took over and she cried for a long time.

Soon the two repentant women set off for Kolkata to seek Apurva's forgiveness. They did not inform anybody. Apurva's mother and Mrinmayee landed up in Apurva's sister's house.

On the same day disappointed by not receiving any letter from Mrinmayee Apurva set aside his resolve and got down to write a letter to her. Like

Mrinmayee even Apurva faced the problem of addressing her; He wanted a word which would express his love for her and at the same time tell her that he was hurt by her indifference. While he was still struggling to find a suitable word in his mother tongue and was gradually losing confidence in the language, he got a message from his brother-in-law informing him about the arrival of his mother. He had asked Apurva to his reach his house as early as possible. He had invited Apurva to dinner. He had ended the letter by saying that he should not worry and that everything was all right. The assurance at the end of the letter did nothing much to allay his anxiety. Apurva reached his brother-in-law's house as early as possible.

The moment he met his mother, he enquired, "I hope everything is all right at home?"

His mother replied, "Yes everybody is all right. Your vacations started quite some time back, but you didn't come home, that is why I came to take you back."

Apurva said, "You shouldn't have troubled yourself. Law is a tough subject, I had planned to stay back and study, that is why...

His sister interrupted, "But *dada* you should have brought your wife along with you."

Apurva replied, "That would have disturbed me, law is a difficult subject."

His brother-in-law pulled his leg he said, "All lame excuses! Actually, he got scared of us."

His sister said, "We must be quite scary no wonder he did not want us to meet the little girl."

The evening passed amidst friendly banter and laughter, but Apurva remained glum. It did not amuse him one bit. He wondered as to why his mother didn't bring Mrinmayee to Kolkata? Then on second thoughts he felt that may be his mother had asked Mrinmayee to come, but Mrinmayee being a whimsical person must have refused. He felt odd about asking his mother about why Mrinmayee didn't come. He was very depressed at that point of time everything appeared futile to him including his own existence.

By the time dinner got over a storm started blowing and the rain pelted down heavily.

Apurva's sister said, "Why don't you stay back *dada*?"

Apurva said, "No, no I have to go back as I have some work at home."

His brother-in-law accosted him he said, "What work can you do at this time of night? You are not answerable to anybody even if you don't go back to-night, so why are you insisting on going back?"

Apurva agreed to stay back reluctantly after a lot of coaxing.

His sister said, "*Dada* you are looking very tired, you must go to bed. Let me take you to the bed room."

Apurva too wanted to go to bed. Actually, he wanted to be left alone; he didn't feel like talking, the idle chat was irritating him. The bed room was dark. The wind had blown off the lamp. His sister said, "The lamp must have got blown off by the wind, I will get another lamp,"

Apurva said, "There is no need, I don't keep the lamp on when I sleep."

His sister went away. Apurva walked towards the bed cautiously in the dark. As he was about to get in to the bed, he heard the tinkle of bangles and without any warning he was imprisoned by soft arms. A pair of soft lips covered his face with kisses and washed his face by a flood of tears. Apurva got taken aback. And then he understood; what got interrupted by a storm of laughter finally concluded in a torrent of tears.

Glossary

Shravan — Fourth month of the Bengali calendar

Pucca — Made of cement and bricks

Bargi — They were light cavalry mercenary group of Maratha Empire who indulged in large scale plundering of the country side

Dhuti — A piece of cloth worn from the waist down wards by male Hindus covering most of the legs.

Chapkan — Long robe

Jobba — Long top

Pugli — mad one

Rath — wooden chariot used to carry idols during Chariot Festival.

Baba — Father

Silver magic wand — From a famous Bengali fairy tale in which a princess is put to sleep by the touch of a silver magic wand.

Gold magic wand — In the same story as above the gold wand wakes her up.

Ashar — The third month of the Bengali Calendar

Dada — Elder brother

11

The Story of a Muslim Woman
(Musholmanir Golpo)

It was the time when lawlessness and anarchy was at its peak in the country. Tyranny and oppression were the order of the day. Each day was like a nightmare for the house-holder. Other than God there was no one from whom he could expect help, so for every little thing that he did, he looked up to God for his blessings. A common man was perpetually under the specter of some imaginary evil spirit who might harm him. People did not trust each other. There was hardly any difference between the consequences of good work and bad work. Stumbling blocks were there at every step, which distressed the common man no end.

The birth of a beautiful girl child was thought to be a curse. The parents and the relatives would wait eagerly for the girl to grow up, get married, and leave the house as early as possible so that she would not come to any harm before marriage. Ill fate befell Banshibadan the *talukdar* of Teen-Mahala when a beautiful girl called Kamala joined his household. She had lost both her parents in infancy, it would have been better had she died too, but unfortunately, she didn't. Banshibadan, her uncle brought her to his house. He showered her with affection and made sure that she was well looked after and safe.

But her aunt was not very happy. While talking to her neighbours, she would often say, "Kamala's father has landed us in great trouble by leaving his daughter with us. In a household where there are already quite a few children, Kamala's responsibility is an added burden on us. People with ill intentions are all around and I am perpetually scared because of her. I am sure that this girl would land us in trouble some day! My worry for her keeps me awake at night."

Days were passing by somehow. One day, a marriage proposal came for Kamala. All this time Kamala was kept within the premises of the house, so that people did not get to see her. Her uncle's worry was that during marriage many people would see her, which may jeopardize her safety, so her uncle wanted her to get married to a rich and powerful groom who would be able to protect her. Luckily the man who sent the proposal was the second son of Paramananda Seth of Mochakhali. They were rich and powerful. People said that he would inherit a lot of wealth from his father. Like a typical idle rich man, the groom had expensive hobbies like falconry, gambling and betting on bulbul fights. In these fights two bulbul birds are made to fight with each other till one dies or is grievously injured, people take sides and lay bets on them. He was very generous so far as spending money on his hobbies was concerned. The man was very proud of the fact that he was from a rich family. His family had employed famous Bhojpuri wrestlers as guards; very often people had heard him boast that no one could touch him because of them. As far as his taste in women went, he had a penchant for beautiful women; though he was already married, he wanted a younger and beautiful second wife so when he came to know about Kamala he sent a proposal to her uncle. The man was hell bent on getting married to her.

When Kamala came to know about it she cried and said, "*Kakamoni* why are you sending me away."

Her uncle said, "Dear child, if I had the means to protect you from the evil forces I would have never let you go. I would have always kept you close to me."

The marriage was finalized. On the day of marriage the groom walked in with great pomp and show. He was accompanied by a band of musicians who announced his arrival loudly. Kamala's uncle approached the groom with folded hands and said, "Please ask them to subdue the music, these are bad times, it is not safe to let people know about the marriage!"

The groom said, "Please don't worry no one would dare to come anywhere close to us."

Kamala's uncle said, "Till the marriage ceremony gets over Kamala is our responsibility. After that she is yours so you will have to ensure her safety till she reaches your house."

He said, "Please don't worry we will look after her."

The Bhojpuri guards twirled their moustaches and stood up holding their staff as a show of strength, when they heard their master.

After the ceremony got over the groom took his bride and set off for home accompanied with his retinue. As they were crossing the infamous Taltori grounds, Madhu Mollah the notorious dacoit and his group attacked them holding *mashals* in their hands. The Bhojpuri guards disappeared within seconds. They were aware of the fact that Madhu Mollah was a ruthless man and he didn't spare anybody. Others followed them.

Kamala got down from her palanquin and she was about to hide herself in the bushes when someone came and stood behind her. It was Habir Khan, the locals revered him like a *paigamber*. He stood erect like a commander and said, "Brothers stand at a distance. I am Habir Khan."

The dacoits moved backwards, their leader said, "Khan *sahib* we can't disobey you, but why are you interfering and spoiling our chances of getting some money?"

Ultimately, they had to leave.

Habir turned towards Kamala and said, "You are like my daughter. Come along with me to my house. This is not a safe place for you."

Seeing Kamala's hesitation he said, "Oh I see, you are hesitating to go with me because I am a Muslim and you are a Hindu's daughter. But please remember a true Muslim will always respect a pious Hindu. You will live like a Hindu girl in my house I promise. I am Habir Khan and my house is very close to this place. You will be safe there."

When Habir noticed her reluctance in spite of his assurance he said, "As long as I am alive no one in this locality will come in between you and your religion. You need not be fearful about that, so please come with me."

Habir khan took Kamala to his house. What she saw surprised her no end. There were eight self-contained sections in his house called *mahal* and one *mahal* was like a typical Hindu household, there was a temple in it too, dedicated to Lord Shiva. She met an old Hindu Brahmin there. He said, "You don't have to worry about anything. You can lead the life of a Hindu here. No one will stop you from doing so."

Kamala wept and said, "Please inform my uncle. He will come and take me home."

Habir smiled and said, "You are making a mistake. They will not accept you anymore. They will throw you out. But you can try. I will take you there."

Habir Khan took her there. She entered the house through the rear gate. Habir Khan told her that he would wait for her, outside the rear gate.

Kamala went to her uncle and said with tears in her eyes "Uncle please let me stay here, Please don't abandon me."

Her uncle was quiet, but his eyes were full of tears.

Her aunt walked into the room and when she saw Kamala, she kicked up a row. "Throw out this ill-starred woman immediately," she told her husband. Then she turned towards Kamala and said, "Don't you have any shame! How dare you come to our house after staying in a Muslim's house?"

Her uncle said, "My dear child this is a Hindu household. No one will accept you here, and if we let you stay here, we will be ostracized by the rest of the village. I have no option, but to ask you to leave."

Kamala stood crest fallen for a while and then she walked out of the house slowly through the rear gate. She left the village with Habir Khan. The doors of her uncle's house shut for her forever.

In his house Habir Khan made arrangements so that Kamala could lead the life of a Hindu girl. He said, "My sons will never come to this portion of the house. The old Brahmin will help you to perform all the Hindu rituals that you are supposed to follow."

The *mahal* in which Kamala was staying had an interesting history. The locals called it 'Rajputni mahal.' The erstwhile Nawab of the place had brought a Rajput's daughter to his kingdom. Rajputs are staunch Hindus. They are inhabitants of Rajputana. Rajputana included mainly the present-day Indian state of Rajasthan, parts of Madhya Pradesh, Gujarat and some adjoining areas of Sindh in modern-day southern Pakistan. The Nawab kept her separately in this portion of the house and allowed her to follow her religion. She was a devotee of Lord Shiva and at times she went on pilgrimages too. The aristocratic Muslims respected the pious Hindus during those days. Many abandoned Hindu women took refuge in the Rajputni mahal. They were allowed to follow their religion. People say that Habir Khan's mother was the Rajput woman brought by the Nawab. Though Habir Khan was a Muslim, he respected and worshipped his mother. Even after the death of his mother Raputni mahal continued to give shelter to Hindu women abandoned by the society.

The love and respect that Kamala got in Habir Khan's house was beyond her expectations. She was not treated well in her uncle's house. Her aunt continuously made her feel small. She accused her of being a harbinger of misfortune, an inauspicious person, a burden on the family and many other things. Her aunt wished that she would die soon, so that the jinx of misfortune in the family would break. Her uncle treated her well, he gave her small gifts at times like clothes and things of everyday use, but he gave them behind her aunt's back. But in Rajputni mahal she was treated like a queen, a retinue of servants looked after her. All of them were once from Hindus families.

Kamala continued to stay in Rajputni mahal, after some time she stepped into the realm of womanhood. She started noticing changes in her; she was swayed by strange emotions that she had never experienced before. At this time one of Habir Khan's sons started visiting Kamala secretly and she fell in love with him.

She went to Habir Khan one day and said, "Father right now I do not belong to any religion. My God is the one who I love. I have nothing to do with the religion which has deprived me of love and treated me like dirt. No God has ever showered his blessings on me. How can I forget that I have been insulted every day by his people? *Bapjan* I got love and affection in your house. For the first time in my life, I came to know that the life of a destitute woman like me is as precious as any other person. The person who has given me shelter is my God. For me he is neither a Hindu nor a Muslim. I have something more to say, and that is I have accepted your second son Karim's proposal for marriage. I will not object if you ask me to convert and become a Muslim, or maybe I could follow both the religions at same time?"

Life went on; connection with her uncle's family got totally severed. Karim Khan's family accepted her. She got a second name—Meherjan.

In the meanwhile, her uncle's second daughter got married. The arrangements were the same as before, fraught with the same risks once again. As they were going to the groom's house the same group of dacoits attacked them. This time, they were hell-bent on taking revenge as they had been deprived of their share of the booty last time.

As they came close to the marriage party, they heard someone shout "*Khabardar,*" from behind. It sounded like a roar.

"Oh hell it is Habir khan again, he will not let us live in peace it seems," said one of the dacoits.

The palanquin bearers left the palanquin on the ground and ran away. The bride's party was about to run away when a dauntless woman stopped them. She was holding a spear. Habir Khan's standard with a crescent moon drawn on it was tied on her spear.

She walked up to the palanquin and said, "Don't be scared Sarala. I have come with an offer of shelter from a person who shelters people irrespective of caste, creed and religion."

Then she turned towards her uncle and said, "My *pronam* to you dear uncle. Don't worry I will not touch your feet and make you unclean. Uncle you daughter is clean no one has touched her take her home if you can. Tell my aunt that I was indebted to her for the food, clothes and shelter that she had given me reluctantly during my stay in your house. I have paid back my debt. I never thought that I would get a chance to do so. I have brought a bridal sari and a small *Kinkhab* carpet. Please take them. And dear sister, if you ever need help, please remember that you have a Muslim sister to help you."

Glossary

Talukdar — Administrative head of a Taluk. Taluk is a subdivision of a district

Kakamoni — Affectionate way of calling one's uncle

Mashal — Lighted torch

Paigambar – Messenger of God

Sahib — Sir

Bapjan — Father

Khabardar – Halt for safety

Pronam — Elders greeted by youngers by touching their feet.

Kinkhab — Silk damask cloth with floral design

12

The Living and the Dead
(Jibito O Mrito)

Sharadashanker *babu* was the *jamindar* (land lord) of Ranihaat. His younger brother was dead and the widow of his younger brother was living with them. There was no one left in her father's house. They had all died one after another. She was child less, thus she had no one to call her own, but she was very close to Sharadashanker's infant son who was the apple of her eye. Sharadashanker's wife had suffered from prolonged illness after the birth of this boy. It was Kadambini the widow of his younger brother who, had taken care of the child since then. When you look after someone else's child the attachment with the child becomes very strong. You have no claim over him; it is only the bond of love that makes the attachment so strong. And that is why you tend to love him inordinately. The widow poured the dammed-up love that was there in her heart on the infant and he grew up nourished by it.

Kadambini died suddenly one night in the month of *Shravan*. No one knew how she died, her heart just stopped beating all of a sudden. Nothing else stopped in the household, everything went on as usual, it was only that a heart so full of love for the infant stopped all of a sudden.

Sharadashanker did not want to get into any hassles with the Police, so he asked four brahmin employees of his estate to take the body to the cremation ground and complete the last rites as quickly as possible.

The cremation ground of Ranihaat was far away from the locality. It was practically bare other than a pond, a hut, and a huge banyan tree that stood next to the pond. A river used to flow across the ground, but it had dried up quite some time back. A pond had been dug in the old river bed. The pond represented the river, which the people considered to be holy.

They placed the body inside the hut and waited for wood for the funeral pyre to come. When the wood did not arrive even after waiting for a long time Nitai and Gurucharan volunteered to find out what was causing the delay. Bidhu and Banamali stayed back to guard the body.

It was a dark night. The sky was overcast. Not a single star was visible. They waited inside the hut quietly. The lantern blew out and the room was plunged into darkness. One of them had brought a matchbox tied to his wrapper. They tried to light the lantern with it, but it had become damp so they could not light it.

One of them wanted to smoke, he said, "Oh brother! How I wish we had the sense to bring a *chilim of tobacco*. Too bad we had to leave in such a hurry."

The other one said, "I can run and get everything."

Bidhu caught on to Banamali's intention of running away, he said, "What the hell! You expect me to sit here all by myself!"

There was a long silence after this. Five minutes felt like an hour. They cursed those people who had gone to collect wood— as time dragged on, they had no doubts that those two must be smoking and chatting somewhere.

It became very quiet; nothing could be heard other than the continuous chant of cicadas and croaking of frogs next to the pond. Suddenly they noticed some movement on the cot where the body was lying. It seemed that the body turned.

Bidhu and Banamali started chanting '*Ram Ram....*' (the lord's name) loudly and trembling at the same time. Suddenly they heard someone sigh. That was the ultimate, they couldn't take it anymore they jumped up and started running towards the village.

After going on for one and a half *krosh* they met the other two. Banamali and Bidhu were right in guessing. The other two had gone for a smoke, they hadn't found out about the wood; though they told Banamali and Bidhu that wood was being chopped and it would be brought very soon.

Bidhu and Banamali described all that had happened in the hut. Nitai and Gurucharan disbelieved them and scolded them for dereliction of duty.

111

Without wasting any time all four hurried back to the hut. They discovered that the body was missing from the cot.

They looked at each other. And they discussed the matter for some time. What if jackals had taken away the body, but in that case the sheet covering the body should have been there. The sheet was missing. They looked around some more and discovered small footprints, most likely of a woman on the wet soil close to the door.

They were sure that Sharadashanker would not believe their cock and bull story; after all, Sharadashanker was a smart person. So, after a lot of discussion, they decided to tell a lie; they would tell him that the last rites had been completed.

All those who came with the wood in the morning were told, as the cremation was getting delayed, they searched around and found a pile of wood inside the hut and they had cremated the body with it. No one suspected anything; after all a dead body can't be all that precious that someone would steal it.

2

We know that when there are no apparent signs of life in a person, they are declared dead, but in rare cases life remains dormant in a body and then starts working once again after a while. Kadambini had not died. Suddenly for some reason her life had gone into a suspended animation.

When she came to her senses, she found herself in a place which was absolutely dark—an unfamiliar place, it was not the place where she slept every day. It scared her. She sat up and called out to her sister-in-law, "*Didi, didi*(elder sister)!" No one answered. She remembered all that had happened. She had a severe chest pain followed by a choking sensation. Kadambini's legs had buckled under her and she had crashed on her bed. She had somehow managed to say, "*Didi* please bring *Khoka* (the infant). I want to see him for the last time. I feel as though I am sinking." After that everything became black as though someone had poured a bottle of ink on a clean sheet of paper. She lost her senses; she didn't remember if she heard *khoka* call her "*Kakima*" for the last time; A sweet voice that she loved so much, the memory of which was her only treasure to carry on her last journey.

The first thing that came to her mind was that she must be in *yamalaya* (it is believed that people go to *yamalaya* after death) that is why it was so dark and silent. A place where there is nothing to see, nothing to hear, nothing to do, just wait and wait.

Then a gust of cool breeze entered the room through the half open door. After that she heard frogs croaking. It brought back memories of many rainy nights of her short life from her childhood days till now. That helped her to connect with the earth. Lightning flashed across the sky, and in that light, she saw the pond, the banyan tree, the huge expanse of barren land and the trees at a distance. She remembered that she had bathed in the pond on auspicious occasions in the past. She remembered how the sight of dead bodies had scared her then.

First, she thought of going back home. Then she decided against it, people at home would not accept her because she was dead. Her presence in the house would be considered inauspicious by them because after all she was a ghost.

She thought had she been alive she wouldn't have been permitted to come to the cremation ground at such a late hour and that too all alone. And if her last rites were not completed then where are those people who had brought her there? She remembered her last moments in the well- lit house of Sharadashanker. Finding herself in a dark and silent place she concluded that her last rites must be over, and she no longer belonged to this world; she was a ghost, inauspicious for the living.

The moment this thought came to her mind she felt that she can break free from all the norms, customs and rules that are there for the living. She felt that she had immense strength and all the freedom to do whatever she felt like doing. Armed with this new feeling she came out of the hut and started walking across the cremation ground like a possessed person. Her mind was uncluttered free from fear, worry and diffidence.

She walked and walked till her feet grew tired and she felt weak. She crossed many meadows and walked along long stretches of paddy fields full of stagnant rain water. The sun rose, villages became visible, and the birds started chirping in the bamboo clumps.

Now she felt apprehensive because she was not sure as to what would be her relationship with the living. As long as she was in the cremation ground or covered by the dark night, she had nothing to worry about. But human habitation in daylight scared her. Human beings are afraid of ghosts, but ghosts too are not very comfortable in the presence of human beings!

113

3

Mud splattered clothes, and a strange expression on her face because of tiredness and sleeplessness made her look like a mad woman. She would have scared people by her looks, children would have thrown stones at her had it not been for a kind gentleman who noticed her.

He came close to her and said, "You appear to be from a good family, where are you going all by yourself so early in the morning?"

She looked at him without answering his question as she did not know what to say. She found it difficult to believe that she looked like someone from a good family. The fact that a gentleman had tried to find out about her seemed unreal to her.

The man said again, "Tell me where you live, I will take you there."

Kadambini did not want to go back to her husband's house because she knew that she would not be accepted there and as there was no one alive in her father's house so there was no point in going there too —she remembered her childhood friend Yogmaya at this juncture.

Kadambini and Yogmaya had separated from each since child hood, but they had kept in touch with each other through letters. Their letters were full of friendly banter, each trying to outdo the other in expressing her love. Kadambini would write that her love for Yogmaya was very strong and Yogmaya would insist that Kadambini didn't reciprocate to her love and affection. They both felt that if they met each other again they would never part.

Kadambini told the gentleman that she wanted to go to Shripaticharan babu's house in Nishchindapur.

The gentleman was going to Kolkata and Nishchindapur was on the way. He made arrangements for her to be taken there.

The two friends met. At first, they could not recognize each other because both had changed. It took them some time to rediscover the little girls hidden inside them.

Yogmaya said, "Oh God I am so lucky. I never thought that I would get to see you again. But tell me something, how did you manage to come here? How come your in-laws let you come here all alone?"

Kadambini kept quiet for a while after that she said, "Please don't ask me about my in-laws. Just let me stay in your house. You can treat me like a servant. I will work for you.

Yogmaya said, "Please don't talk like that, why you will live like a servant in my house. You are my best friend."

It was then that Shripati (Yogmaya's husband) entered the room. Kadambini looked at his face directly and then she went out of the room. She did not cover her head with her sari, as was the custom, in fact she appeared the least bit bashful neither did she show any respect.

Yogmaya was upset by her friend's brazen behavior. She tried to explain to her husband as to why she behaved in that fashion. Shripati accepted Yogmaya's explanation. Yogmaya had expected that there would be some objection from her husband's side. But this easy acceptance on his part made her uncomfortable.

Though Kadambini, landed up in her friend's place, but she could not mix up with her old friend— death was a factor which did not let her get close to her friend. When you are not sure about yourself, you cannot be friends with another person. Kadambini's suspicion about her own status kept her away from her friend. Whenever Kadambini looked at her friend's face, many thoughts crossed her mind. Yogmaya was a part of a household where she lived with her husband and other members of the family; whereas she belonged to a world which was very different. This world was comparable with a shadow. Yogmaya existed in a well-defined world where feelings like love and affection, duty and responsibility bound people to one another, whereas she belonged to a world which was boundless.

Yogmaya was ill at ease; she found it difficult to understand her friend. And like a woman Yogmaya did not like mysteries—mysteries can tempt a researcher to unravel it, one can write stories based on mysteries, but running a household with a mystery nagging at you all the time is difficult. That is why when a female does not understand something she ignores it and over a period of time it becomes non-existent for her; otherwise, she tries to give it a new form –a creation of her own, which she can understand. When she does not succeed in doing either of them it angers her.

As days went by Kadambini's behavior became more and more incomprehensible to Yogmaya, it annoyed her. The added burden of her friend on her shoulders irritated her.

There was another problem which came up; Kadambini started fearing her own self. Try however she may she could not run away from her new identity. People who are scared of ghosts usually avoid looking behind them, whatever they can't see properly scares them. But Kadambini's fear was inside her—nothing scared her from outside.

For this reason, sometimes she would scream loudly in the middle of the afternoon while sitting all alone— she got an eerie sensation when she saw her own shadow in the lamplight in the evenings.

This scared the servants and the other members of the family. Some of them complained of seeing ghosts inside the house. Yogmaya too started seeing ghosts.

One day around midnight Kadambini ran out of her room crying, she stood at the door of her friend's bed room and pleaded, "*Didi* please do not leave me alone I beg of you!"

This annoyed Yogmaya no end. She could have thrown her out of the house at that very moment. But Shripati was a kind person, he pacified kadambini and made a place for her in the next room.

Next day Shripati was called to the *antapur* (women's quarters) by his wife. Yogmaya scolded him and said, "What kind of a man are you? A woman walks out of her in-law's house and lives in your house for more than a month and you are mum about it! There has not been any objection from your side! You will have to explain yourself to me. What is your intention? All males are the same I suppose."

Males are a bit partial towards females in general and females blame them often for this. Kadambini was not only a helpless person; she was beautiful too. Shripati's sympathy for her was a little more than what it should have been. He had sworn to Yogmaya many times that he had no ill intentions, but his conduct said something else.

He believed that Kadambini, a childless widow was ill-treated by her in-laws and that is why she had run away from them and had taken shelter in his house. Her parents had died quite some time back; she had no one to call her own, so how could he turn her away? He did not want to hurt her by asking unpleasant questions, that is why he hadn't tried to find out what compelled her to leave her in-laws house.

But his wife Yogmaya started bothering him and finding faults with his attitude and conduct. In order to bring back peace and harmony in his own house, Shripati decided to find out about Kadambini's in-laws. He felt writing a letter to them will not serve the purpose, so he decided to go Ranihaat and find out personally.

After Shripati's departure Yogmaya went to Kadambini and said, "*Shoyee* (friend) it doesn't look good if you keep staying here, what would people say?"

Kadambini looked at her friend's face and replied back solemnly, "It doesn't make a difference to me as I have nothing to do with them."

Her answer surprised Yogmaya no end she said, "You may not be bothered, but it bothers us, how long can we keep a woman belonging some other household in our house!"

Kadambini said, "But tell me which household do I belong to?"

Yogmaya was shocked by what she heard, good heavens she thought, why is this woman talking like this!

Kadambini continued, "I have nothing to do with anybody, I don't belong to this earth. You people laugh, cry, love each other, everybody is busy in his own world. And I just watch you people. You are human beings, and I am, but a shadow. I can't understand why God has sent me here amidst you people. I know that you people are uncomfortable in my presence. You think that I am inauspicious. God has not given us a place where we can stay, that is why in spite of broken bonds, we remain near you."

Kadambini spoke at a stretch without taking her eyes off from Yogmaya's face. Yogmaya understood somewhat, but not everything. She did not ask her any questions. She got up and left the room looking a little preoccupied.

4

Shripati returned back from Ranihaat around ten 'o' clock at night. It was raining very heavily at that that time. The sound of the falling rain made one feel as though it would never stop; the night too seemed to be endless.

"What happened there?" Yogmaya wanted to know.

"Quite a bit, but I will talk about it later." He went in to change his clothes. After that he had dinner, he smoked and then went to bed looking worried.

Yogmaya had controlled her curiosity all this while, but she couldn't hold it any longer, the moment she got into the bed she said, "Tell me what happened there."

Shripati said, "I am sure that you have made a mistake."

Shripati's remarks annoyed her, she said to herself, 'Women never make mistakes in such matters and even if they do a sensible male does not talk about it, acceptance is the best recourse.' "But tell me what happened there," she sounded angry.

"The woman who has been sheltered by you is not your friend Kadambini."

It is quite normal to feel angry when one hears such a thing, especially from one's husband. Yogmaya said, "What a thing to say, you mean I have not recognized my own friend! You know better than me!"

Shripati had no doubts that Kadambini was dead, but to convince his wife he would have to prove it.

Yogmaya said, "I have no doubts that you have been to a wrong place. And you have been given wrong information. Who told you to go there? All that you had to do was to write to them. Every doubt would have been cleared."

Shripati felt peevish at the lack of his wife's confidence in his capability. He made a fresh attempt at telling his wife in great detail with proof, but that did not help. It became quite late about twelve o'clock, but their argument did not stop.

They agreed that kadambini should be ousted from their house without further delay, but their reasons were different. Shripati believed that Kadambini was an imposter and that she had cheated his wife. Yogmaya felt that kadambini had run away from her home, which made her a loose character. So, the argument went on and gradually the volume of their voices rose. They forgot that Kadambini was in the next room.

The husband said, "What a mess we are in. How can I disbelieve my own ears?"

The wife retorted back, "Why should I agree? How can I disbelieve my own eyes? I see her every day."

When their argument was leading to nowhere Yogmaya said, "Ok tell me the date, they said that she died on."

Shripati thought that by comparing the date of kadamini's death and the date on which kadambini had written to Yogmaya, she would try to prove him wrong.

Shripati told her the date, they calculated and found that the day of Kadmbini's death was one day prior to the day of her arrival at their house. A shiver ran down Yogmaya's spine. She trembled, Shipati too felt uncomfortable.

At this point of time the door of their room was suddenly flung open by a gust of wind. The lamp blew out. And darkness from outside leaped into the room. Kadambini walked into the room. It was past twelve thirty and it was raining continuously.

She said loudly, "*Shoyee* I am not the kadambini that you have known, I am not alive any more, I am dead."

Yogmaya screamed loudly out of fear and Shripati could not utter a word.

She continued, "Is it my fault that I have died? I have no place to go neither here on this earth nor in the next world! Then tell me where should I go?" She screamed out the last few words as though she wanted her voice to reach the almighty. After that she walked out of the room and left behind two unconscious people.

5

It is difficult to say how Kadambini reached Ranihaat. No one saw her when she reached the place. She spent the entire day in a broken- down temple.

In the evening when the sky became heavily clouded and the people went into their houses to avoid getting drenched in rain Kadambini set off for her home. She felt apprehensive when she reached the main door. So, she drew a long *ghomta* covering her head and face and walked into the house. The servants did not notice her and no one stopped her from going inside. It started raining again. It was a very heavy downpour accompanied with strong wind.

At that time Sharadashanker's wife was playing cards with her widowed sister-in-law (Sharadashanker's sister). The maid who looked after the little boy was in the kitchen, and the little boy was resting in his bed as he had a fever. No one spotted Kadambini as she entered the room. Her intention was to see the little boy. She had no plans after that.

She saw him sleeping on his bed, he looked ill and had lost weight his hands were balled into a fist. She had the urge to pick him up and hold him close to her chest. She felt that the boy had been neglected in her absence. His mother loved chatting and playing cards with her friends. She hardly spent any time with him. Right from his birth Kadambini had been looking after the child. She wondered who looked after the child in her absence. These thoughts came to her mind as she gazed at him.

Khoka (the boy's name) turned on the bed and said sleepily, "*Kakima* give me water."

"Oh my darling you haven't forgotten your *Kakima*!" she said. Then she filled a tumbler with water from an earthen pitcher, lifted the boy from the bed and held the tumbler close to his lips. He was half asleep, he drank water from her hand like he always did; he didn't find it unusual. Kadambini kissed him and put him back into his bed. He had woken up by then. He hugged her and asked, "*Kakima* you had died?"

"Yes Khoka," she replied.

"You have come back to me? You will not die again? Will you?"

But before she could answer, the maid entered the room with a bowl of sago soup, the moment she saw Kadambini the bowl fell from her hand, she screamed loudly, and fell on the ground. Her scream attracted the boy's mother's attention and she ran into the room. She got petrified with fear when she saw Kadambini. She could neither move nor utter a word.

All this scared Khoka, he cried and said, "*Kakima* you go now."

Kadambini felt after a long time that she was alive. Nothing had changed in her absence. The household was the same as before. The little boy who she loved so dearly still loved her like he did before. When she was in her friend's house, she had felt that she was not alive, but now while standing close to Khoka in his room she felt that she was fully alive.

"Why are you so scared of me *didi?* Look at me, I am the same person as before," she said desperately.

Her sister-in-law could not stand any longer, she fainted and fell on the ground in a heap.

After hearing everything from his sister, Sharadasanker's came running into the *antapur*. He folded his hands and said to her, "*Choto bou* is it becoming of you? Satish is the only son of our family, why have you cast your spell on him, weren't you a part of our family once? The boy has not been thriving after your departure. He misses you and keeps asking for you. You don't belong to this world anymore so why don't you sever your ties with this world? We will perform your last rites elaborately, so please leave us. (Hindus believe that unless the last rites are performed properly the soul does not come to rest)

Kadambini could not tolerate it any more. She screamed, "Please listen to me, I am not dead. How can I prove that I am still alive? See for yourself that I am living."

She picked up the bell metal bowl from the ground and hit her forehead with it. Blood spurted out from the wound. And she said, "See I am still alive."

Sharadashnker stood there like a statue. The little boy started crying and calling his father. The two women still lay unconscious on the ground.

Kadambini ran out of the room shouting, "I am not dead, I am alive." She repeated the same words over and over, as she descended down the stairs, and jumped into the pond in the women's quarters.

Sharadashanker heard the splash from the room upstairs.

It continued to rain. It rained at night, it rained in the morning and in the afternoon too.

 Kadambini died to prove that she was alive.

121

Glossary

Jamindar — Land lord

Shrawan — Fourth month of the Bengali calendar

Chilim — Quantity of tobacco that can be put in a chillum

Krosh — One and a half mile is equal to a krosh

Kakima —Aunty

Yamalaya — nether world, it is believed that people go there after death

Didi — Elder sister

Antapur — Women's quarters

Shoyee — friend

Ghomta — the free end of a sari that is used as a veil to cover face and head.

Chotobou — Wife of younger brother

13

Story of the Quay
(Ghater Kotha)

If stories could be written on stone, then you would have read many tales of bygone days written on my steps. As that did not happen, please sit on my steps and listen to the gurgling water flowing by it will tell you many stories.

I remember that day very distinctly; it was just like this day. The month of *Ashwin* (mid-September to mid-October) was coming to an end with a couple of days left. A cool breeze was blowing since early morning. There was a nip in the air that rejuvenated all those who had woken up. The breeze made the leaves shiver as though they, too, were feeling cold.

The Ganges was brimming full. Only the last few of my steps were visible. Land and water were in a close embrace. The water had reached the *Kochu* (Taro) plants growing under Mango trees of the orchard nearby. Three stacks of bricks lying on the bank near the bend of the river were nearly submerged, only a few bricks could be seen above water. The fishing boats tied to the trunk of *Babla* (Acacia) tree were floating on the water brought in by the morning tide. The water was splashing around them and rocking them, as though it was pulling their ears in jest.

Early morning sunlight of autumn had lit up the water surface, it looked like molten gold; A rare sight, one does not get to see such splendid colours very often. Sun had lit up the *Kash* forest (Kans grass) on the bank. The flowers of *Kash* had just begun to bloom.

The boat men untied their boats. The wind filled their sails and the boats sailed out on the sun lit river, they looked like swans swimming, with out-stretched wings.

Bhattacharya *moshai* (mister) was already there with his kosha-kushi (two small copper utensils used in holy rites). Women were filling water in their pitchers.

You might think that it happened a long time back, but to me it appears as though it happened just the other day. My days are like the waves on the river that rise and fall on the river surface, and I watch them sitting stationary, at one place. That is why it does not seem very long ago. The day light and the shadow of the nightfall on the river and get erased every day without leaving an imprint behind. That is why though physically I look very old; I am young at heart. I have accumulated years and years of memory somewhat like layers of moss that grow one on top of one another, but sun rays still penetrate the inner depths of my mind and illuminate it. At times a small clump of moss lodges on my steps and then it gets swept away. But it would not be right if I said that, they all get swept off, some stay. Creepers, weeds and moss grow in my cracks where the water does not reach. They are my witnesses because they have seen everything that has happened in the past. They have held together my past lovingly. Their love has helped me to keep my memories fresh. The river Ganges is moving away from me every day exposing my steps as I become older.

I can see the old lady from the Chakrabarty family going back after a bath. A *namabali* (prayer shawl with the name of the lord written all over) is around her shoulders. She has her prayer beads in one hand and she is counting them. When her grandmother was a little girl, her favourite game was to pluck an Aloe vera leaf and float it on water like a boat. There was an eddy pool on my right side. When the leaf reached there, it went round and round, she would keep her pitcher on my steps and watch the leaf with rapt attention. After some time, the same girl grew up and started coming with her daughter. The daughter too grew up and started coming to the quay all by herself. When the younger girls became boisterous and threw water at each other she would scold them and try to discipline them, then I would be reminded of the Aloe vera leaves that went round and round in the pool and feel amused.

I had started to tell you a story, but I started rambling, a lot of other stories came up and I sidetracked. Stories keep coming to me and soon they are replaced by others, there are only a few that go round and round in my mind like those Aloe vera leaves. I will tell you a story which has been going round and round in my mind, like an Aloe vera leaf in the eddy pool, carrying a precious a ware—a story of two flowers.

There used to be an acacia tree, next to the temple where you see the fence of the Gosain's cow shed now. A haat (itinerant market) was held there every week. The Gosains had not settled down there by then. There was a leaf thatched shack where the Gosains have erected a *Chandimandap* (a raised platform where villagers gather to discuss important issues related to the village). The *ashwath* (holy fig) tree that you see today which has extended its roots inside me and has held me together was a sapling then, the shadow of its tender leaves danced on me when the sun rose. Its soft roots would clutch me like the tiny fingers of a child. It would hurt me a lot if someone tore even a leaf of the plant.

I was quite old by then, but I was straight and erect, not like what I am today. My surface was smooth; though today I have many cracks on my surface like wrinkles and my nooks and crannies are used by frogs for their winter sleep. At that time only two bricks were missing on my left side. A *drongo* had made its nest in the cavity. He woke up with the arrival of dawn. When he rustled his feathers, dipped and raised his fork tail, and took off on his first flight after whistling a few notes I knew it was Kusum's time to come to the quay.

The girls who came to the quay used to call her Kusum and that is how I know her name. When her small shadow fell on me, I had this fervent desire to be able to hold her shadow a little longer. She was very charming. If only I could hold on to her shadow forever! Her anklets tinkled when she walked, the moss and the creepers trembled with delight when they heard the tinkling sound of her anklets. Not that Kusum used to play, chat or laugh a great deal, but surprisingly she had a lot of friends. All of them loved her company, especially the boisterous ones. They just couldn't do without her. She had many names, some called her Kushi, some called Khushi (happiness) a few called her Rakkushi (demoness) affectionately, her mother called her Kushmi. Very often I would find her sitting next to the river. She had a special bond with the river.

I stopped seeing her after some time. Her friends Bhuwan and Swarna would weep for her when they came to the quay. I came to learn from their conversation that she has gone to her In-law's place. I gathered that Ganges did not flow in the place where she had gone. New people, new house hold, new city, new surroundings I wondered how she was coping? It felt as though a Lotus had been pulled out from water and taken away to be planted on soil.

I forgot about Kusum. One year went by. The girls who came to the quay stopped talking about her. One evening I was taken aback by the touch of the familiar feet. They must be her feet I thought! But the tinkling sound of her anklets was not there. The music was missing. I had always associated the touch of her feet with the sound of her anklets. The delightful gurgle of the water sounded sad when it did not hear her anklets. The wind blowing through the leaves of the mango grove lamented.

Kusum was widowed. Her husband used to work in some faraway place. She must have met her husband for a couple of days only before he went away. Her in-laws had received the news about his death through a letter. Kusum, who was just eight years old, changed into 'widow's white sari,' after hearing the news. The vermillion mark (sign of a married woman) on the parting of her hair was wiped off and her ornaments were taken away. She returned to her home once again next to the river Ganges. Most of her friends had gone away by then. Bhuwan, Swarna and Amala had gone to their in-law's house. Only Sharat was left, I heard that she too was getting married in the month of *Aghrayan* (mid-November to mid-December). Kusum had no friends now. Sometimes when she sat on my steps with her head resting on knees, I felt that the river was waving at her and calling her "Kusi, Khusi, O Rakkhushi... like her friends called her.

Like the Ganges that fills up during the rainy season Kusum, too started filling up with youthful beauty by and by. Her faded old clothes and her quiet demeanor left a shadow on her beauty, so people did not notice the change in her. Even I did not. To me she was still a little girl though her anklets did not tinkle any more, but I could hear them when she walked.

Ten years passed, and the month of Bhadra (mid-August to mid-September) was nearing its end. Your great grandmothers must have woken up that morning to see a softly glowing sun. They must have covered their heads with their sari ends, picked up their pitchers, walked on the uneven path of the village to reach the quay, chatting with each other on the way. Their presence had brightened up the quay. I am sure they wouldn't have thought about you at that juncture, just like you cannot imagine they were little girls once upon a time. And just like you, even they played, laughed and chatted with each other, those days were as delightful as they are today, full of joy. Even their tender hearts were like yours, swaying between happiness and sorrow.

The northerlies had just started blowing since morning that day. It had blown down a few *Babla* blossoms on me. The first dew of the season had moistened my surface. That morning, a tall, fair, young ascetic with a radiant face took shelter in the Shiva temple close by. The news of his arrival spread in the village like wildfire. Women started calling him 'Baba thakur'. They would put down their pitchers on my steps and enter the temple to touch his feet. The crowd of visitors increased day by day. He was handsome and very attentive towards those who came to see him. He made small children sit on his lap, when their mothers came to visit him and ask the mothers about their household affairs. He struck a chord with the women and became very popular. The men too started coming to him. He recited from the Bhagwat Geeta to them and explained the inner meaning of the verses. He discussed various religious texts with them at length. Some people came for advice. Some came to him for medicines for their ailments. A few requested him to teach sacred Mantras, which would guide them through their lives. The women spoke about his beauty when they got together at the quay. They said, "Oh! He is so handsome! It seems as though lord Shiva himself has come to live in his temple."

Every day at dawn he stood in waist deep water and chanted mantras dedicated to the morning star in his deep sonorous voice, I did not hear the gurgling water when he chanted the mantras, I just heard him. Gradually the eastern sky would turn red. The borders of the clouds would turn crimson. The darkness would peel off like the sepals of a blooming bud. And in the lake like blue sky a red flower would bloom gradually. As his chanting continued the night would make way for the morning, the moon and the stars would descend, the sun would ascend in the eastern sky and the ambience would change. Who was this enchanter? I wondered. After bathing when he rose from water the rays of the early morning sun touched his fair, tall and wet body and made it glimmer, like the flame of a sacrificial fire.

A few months went by. Many people came to the village to bathe in the Ganges on the occasion of a solar eclipse in the month of Chaitra (mid-March to mid-April). A big *haat* came up in the acacia grove. Many people came to see the ascetic. A few women from Kusum's in-laws' place came to take a dip in the holy Ganges.

He was sitting on my steps in deep meditation. On seeing him one of them nudged her companion and said, "Good lord! He looks very much like our Kusum's husband!"

Another one parted her *ghomta* (end of the sari which covers the face and head) slightly and said, "Oh yes! I have no doubts, he is the youngest son of the Chattujay family".

There was one among them who was quite bold and did not bother about purdah, she peered at him and said, "Yes, it has to be him! same nose, eyes, forehead!"

Another one hardly looked at him. She went into the water and pushed her pitcher in the water and said, "But how can it be? He is not alive. How can he come back? Our Kusum is not all that lucky!"

Then one of them commented, "He did not have a beard."

Another one said, "He was not so slim."

Someone said, "He was not so tall!"

The doubt was settled this way and no one spoke about it after that.

Everyone in the village had seen the ascetic except Kusum. She had stopped coming to the quay as many people had started coming there.

It was a full moon night; she was probably reminded of our association when the moon rose and she came to the quay.

No one was there at the quay. The cicadas were humming in unison. The temple bells had stopped ringing, sometime back. The full moon was at its brightest, the tide was making the water lap at the banks. Kusum was sitting on my steps, her small shadow had fallen on me. There was no breeze, the trees were not moving, it was very quiet. Wide stretch of Ganges flooded by the moon light was in front of her, behind her darkness had enveloped everything, the bushes, the trees, the broken temple, the palm grove, the foundation of a dilapidated house, everything. The bats were hanging upside down on the *Chatim* (devil's tree) tree. An owl perched on the temple spire screeched. A jackal howled loudly once and then stopped.

The ascetic came out of the temple slowly. He came to the quay and walked down the steps. He was about to go back on seeing a woman sitting on the steps all by herself, when Kusum turned back to see. Her sari slipped off her head. Moon light fell on her face like it falls on a new bloom. They saw each other. In that one glance they got to know each other as though they had known each other from their last birth. An owl flew over them. Kusum was startled she covered her head quickly. She got up and prostrated herself at his feet.

The ascetic blessed her "What is your name?" He asked

She said, "Kusum."

No one spoke after that. Kusum's house was near-by she went back home slowly. That night the ascetic sat on my steps for a long time. When the moon started going towards the west, his shadow fell in front of him, he got up and entered the temple.

From that day onwards Kusum would come and touch his feet every morning. When he explained the inner meaning of religious texts to the assembled gentry Kusum would stand in one corner and listen to him. After completing his morning prayers and rituals, he would call her and talk to her about religion and advise her, she would sit quietly and listen to him attentively. Kusum followed his advice to the last word and letter. She worked very diligently for the temple. She washed the temple daily with the water that she carried from the river and picked flowers for the offering. She never neglected her task.

After listening to him, Kusum sat on my steps and thought about what she had heard. Her vision broadened gradually. She started hearing what she hadn't heard before. She started seeing what she hadn't seen before. The dark shadow of sorrow which was there on her face disappeared. She reminded me of a dew washed fresh flower offered to God when she prostrated herself at his feet every morning. The purity of her intent brightened up her entire being. She looked radiant.

A cool breeze blows mostly at this time of the year when the winter is about to end, but there are days when southerlies blow in the evening and the chill in the breeze is gone. On such days one can hear sound of flute and songs coming from the village, the boat men stop rowing and let their boats drift as they sing songs dedicated to *Shyam* (the dark lord) and the birds fly from branch to branch answering the call of their mates. The time was such.

Spring was in the air. My stoney heart was touched by the advent of spring and I was feeling young. The creepers growing in my crevices were laden with flowers. I hadn't seen Kusum for quite some time. She had stopped coming to the temple for a while.   She no longer attended the discourses; she didn't even come to the quay. I wondered why!

I really do not know what happened in the meantime. One evening she met him on the steps. Kusum bowed her head and said, "Master, did you ask me to meet you?"

"Why don't I get to see you these days? Why are you so neglectful towards your duties?"

Kusum kept quiet.

"Please tell me what is bothering you."

Kusum turned away her face slightly and said, "Master I am a sinner. That is why I do not come to the temple anymore."

"Kusum I can make out that you are very disturbed." He spoke in an affectionate manner.

She was startled by what she heard. Maybe she was worried as to how much he knew already.

Her eyes filled up with tears. She covered her face with her hands and sat down next to his feet and wept.

He moved away slightly and said, "Please tell me everything. I will show you the way to peace."

Kusum started speaking, she spoke in a reverential tone. There were times when she halted as she found it difficult express herself. She said, "I will try my best to tell you since you have asked me to tell you, though I may not be able to narrate everything properly. I am sure that you will understand. Master, I used to revere someone like God. I used to worship him. This filled my heart with happiness, but one night I dreamt that I was sitting next to him in a *Bukul* (a large evergreen flowering tree) grove. He was holding my right hand with his left and was speaking of love. Strangely enough it did not strike me as improbable. When I woke up, I felt as though I was in a trance. When I saw him in the morning, I remembered the dream. I ran away from there, but what I saw in my dream remained with me I could not brush it off from my mind. Since then, I have been agitated. I see nothing, but darkness in front of me."

 As Kusum spoke and wiped her tears I could feel, him gripping my surface with is right foot.

When Kusum finished talking he said, "Can you tell me the name of the person who you saw in your dream."

Kuaum folded her hands and said, "I can't."

He said, "I am asking you to tell me his name because it will be good for you if you do so."

Kusum wrung her petal soft hand together and said, "Do I have to tell his name!"

"Yes, you have to."

"Master, it was you," Kusum spoke immediately.

As soon as her own voice reached her ears she fainted on my hard lap. He stood there like a statue.

When she came to, he spoke to her gently, but firmly, "You have obeyed me all these days. I am going to ask you to do something, which you will have to obey. I will be leaving this place just now, so that we don't meet again. You will have to forget me. Promise me that you will try your best."

Kusum got up, she looked at him and said slowly, "Master that will be done."

He said, "Then I am going."

Kusum said nothing, she touched his feet. He left.

After he left Kusum murmured to herself, "He has asked me to forget him." After this, she walked to the river and descended into it. Kusum had grown-up next to the river. The river was her friend since her childhood. Who else could shelter her, other than a friend? The moon went down. The night darkened. I heard a splash, but could not make out what caused it. A strong wind started blowing. Maybe it did not want anything to be seen so it blew off the stars.

She grew up on my lap. She played here. We were friends, but she didn't tell me where she went!

Glossary

Ashwin — Mid September to mid-November

Kochu — Taro

Babla — Acacia

Kash — Kans grass

131

Moshai — Mister

Kosha-kushi — Two small copper vessels used in holy rites

Namabali — Prayer shawl

Haat — Itinerant market

Chandi mandap — A raised platform in the village where people gather and discuss important matters pertaining to the village

Ashwath — Holy fig

Rakkhushi — Demoness

Aghrayan — Mid- November to mid-December

Bhadra — Mid-August to mid-September

Chaitra — Mid-March to mid-April

Ghomta — Free end of the sari which covers the face and head

Chatim — Devil's tree

Shyam — The dark Lord Krishna

14

Mahamaya

Mahamaya and Rajivlochan met in a dilapidated temple next to the river. She did not utter a word, just looked at him solemnly like the way she always did, but this time she was angry. Though she did not say anything, but it appeared as though she wanted to say, "How dare you call me here to meet you and that too at this hour? Till now I have listened to whatever you have told me to do, is that the reason why you have taken the liberty of calling me here?"

Rajiv was a little scared of Mahamaya and on top of it the look on her face unnerved him. So, he decided to tell her why he had called her and get over with it. He said, "Let's run away from here and get married." Though Rajiv told her what he had in his mind, but he had planned to say this after a preface which he had practiced at home. What he said sounded insensitive to his own ears too. He felt embarrassed, he was so nervous that he couldn't add a few words afterwards to soften the impact. So, it boiled down to the fact that this foolish man had called her to the broken-down temple in the middle of an afternoon just to say, 'let's run away and get married.'

Mahamaya was unmarried, she was from a *kulin (high class Brahmin)* Brahmin family and was twenty four years of age . Getting a match for a girl from a *kulin* family was difficult, that was the reason behind Mahamaya's unmarried status.

 She was very beautiful and fair, her complexion was like the autumn sun shine—mellow and golden. Though she did not talk much, but her personality was radiant like the Sun. She had an open mind and was fearless by nature.

She didn't have a father. Her elder brother Bhawanicharan Chattopadhyay was her guardian. The brother and sister were of the same nature. He too

133

was a man of few words, but he had a fire within him capable of reducing a person to nothing. People were scared of him.

Rajiv was an outsider. He had come with his boss who was the *burra sahib* of the local *resham kuthi*. Rajiv's father had worked under the *burra sahib*. After the death of his father the *burra sahib* supported him financially and took over the responsibility of bringing him up. When the *sahib* got transferred to Bamanhati *kuthi* he brought Rajiv with him. Rajiv was a child then. The only blood relation that Rajiv had was his *pishi*, (aunt, father's sister) who was a very affectionate person. She too came along with Rajiv and they started living in Bamanhati in a house next to Bhawanicharan's. They became neighbours. Rajiv and Mahamaya were childhood friends and Mahamaya was very close to Rajiv's *pishi*.

Rajiv grew up, he crossed sixteen, seventeen, eighteen and even when he reached the age of nineteen, he refused to get married in spite of *pishi's* repeated requests. The *sahib* was very happy by Rajiv's decision of not getting married— very uncommon among Bengalis. The *sahib* was a confirmed bachelor, he was glad that Rajiv was following his foot-steps.

Rajiv's Pishi died after sometime.

On the other side it was getting more and more difficult to find a match for Mahamaya—the demand for money from the prospective grooms was astronomical, which her brother could not afford. Mahamaya was aging, and very soon she fell into the category of an unmarried girl from a *kulin* family.

It is needless to tell the reader that the god responsible for tying the wedding knot between young men and women somehow overlooked these two, but the god of love was alert. When old *Prajapati* (the God who fixes marriages) was asleep, young *Kandarp* the cupid was wide awake.

Lord *Kandarp* has a different effect on different people. Rajiv, under his influence kept trying to find an opportunity to talk to her and tell her about the love he had for her in his heart, whereas Mahamaya kept avoiding him. Her quiet and calm looks intimidated him.

It was after a lot of effort that he mustered some courage and told her to meet him in the temple. He had thought of telling her everything that he had kept locked up in his mind; which would either lead him to lifelong happiness, or maybe to a life full of sorrow. But unfortunately, all that he could say on an occasion as momentous as that was, "let's get married."

After that he was mum, like a confused student who had forgotten his lesson mid-way in spite of learning. Mahamaya had not expected that Rajiv would propose to her so she too kept quiet for a long time.

Certain sounds that are heard during afternoons have an element of pathos in them, and they become more audible when the surroundings are quiet. The broken door of the temple moaned as it moved slowly with the breeze. The pigeons sitting on the ventilator cooed, a woodpecker drummed on the branch of the silk cotton tree outside, a lizard ran over dry leaves making a crackling sound, a gust of warm wind rose suddenly and agitated the river; waves rose and fell on the broken steps of the quay making a splashing sound. Amongst all these sounds the plaintive tune of a shepherd's flute came wafting in the air. Rajiv avoided looking at Mahamaya as he felt scared. He stood with his back against a wall and gazed at the river dreamily.

After a while Rajiv made another effort and looked at Mahamaya, like a beggar begging alms. Mahamaya shook her head and said, "No that is not possible."

Rajiv's hopes came crashing down. Rajiv knew full well that Mahamaya was a self-willed person; no one could make her do anything against her wishes. She was fiercely proud of her *kulin* status. Though Rajiv was a Brahmin by birth his ancestors were not *kulin*. Mahamaya could not dream of getting married to a Bramhin who did not belong to a *kulin* family – loving someone and getting married was not the same thing. It came to her mind that she should have discouraged him from getting friendly with her from the start. After a while she started walking towards the exit.

Rajiv made one last effort; he said, "I am going away from this place tomorrow."

Mahamaya initially thought that she would behave as though the news did not affect her and say, 'So, why are you telling me?' But she stopped herself and said, "Why?"

Rajiv said, "Sahib has got transferred to the Sonapur *kuthi* and he is taking me along with him."

Mahamaya kept quiet and thought for some time then she came to the conclusion that as their paths were going to run in opposite directions it would not be fair to give him false hopes so she said, "Ok" through her pursed lips which sounded like a sigh. She was about to leave after saying this when Rajiv said in a startled voice "Your brother!"

Mahamaya saw Bhawanicharan was coming towards the temple. She realized that her brother has come to know about their meeting. Rajiv made an attempt to jump out from the broken wall of the temple to save Mahamaya from embarrassment. Mahamaya caught hold of his hand tightly and prevented him from doing so. Bhawanicharan entered the temple—he looked at them only once and turned away.

"Rajiv I will come to you. Please wait for me," Mahamaya said in an unperturbed voice.

Then she followed Bhawanicharan silently as he went out of the temple.

And Rajiv stood there dumb founded like an accused who has been sentenced to death by hanging.

2

That night Bhawanicharan gave Mahamaya a *cheli* (red bridal sari) and said, "Wear it and come."

When she wore it and came back. He said, "Now come with me."

So far no one had dared to disobey Bhawanicharan's orders. Even Mahamaya didn't.

He started walking towards the cremation ground. Mahamaya followed him. The cremation ground was not far from their home.

Hindus believe that if a person breathes his last on the bank of the holy river Ganga he is released from the cycle of rebirth, so in many cremation grounds next to the river Ganga there are rooms where people on the verge of death are kept till, they die. These rooms are called *gangayatrir ghar*.

A very old Brahmin was awaiting his death in one of the rooms. Bhawanicharan stood next to his bed. A priest was sitting there, Bhawanicharan looked at him and nodded. The man got up and started making arrangements. Mahamaya understood that she was about to get married to the dying old man who was lying on the bed. She did not oppose. The light coming from two pyres burning outside the room lit up the room. Mahamaya got married amidst groans of the old man and inaudible mantras chanted by the priest.

Rajiv was very upset when he came to know about her marriage, but the news of her becoming a widow did not upset him in fact he felt happy. But the happiness did not last long. A news hit him like a bolt from the blue. Someone told him that there was going to be a great celebration in the cremation grounds as Mahamaya has decided to immolate herself on the funeral pyre along with her husband.

His first reaction was to inform the *sahib* so that it could be stopped. Then he remembered that the *sahib* had left for his new place of work on that very day. He had wanted to take Rajiv with him, but Rajiv didn't go, he took a month of leave and had stayed back instead.

Before going with her brother Mahamaya had said, "Wait for me." That is why Rajiv had stayed back. He had taken a month's leave and had thought of extending his leave to two months or may be three and wait. And if nothing happened even after that he had decided to quit his job and wait forever.

The news made him go berserk with worry he didn't know what to do—he seriously contemplated on taking his own life. As a storm raged inside his mind; another storm rose outside, a deluge of rain hit the village, like no one had seen before. It was raining so hard that he felt the roof would cave in at any time. The storm outside augured well, it made him feel as though nature had come to his assistance, out of sympathy. Rajiv knew that he wouldn't have been able to stop the immolation of Mahgamaya by using force single handedly, but now he felt relieved, that the nature had joined in to help him.

There was a loud knock on the door. Rajiv got up and opened the door quickly. A woman entered the house. Her clothes were wet. Her face was covered with a *ghomta*. Rajiv recognized her, she was Mahamaya.

He was thrilled to see her, he said, "Oh my God! It's you, Mahamaya! You managed to escape from the funeral pyre!"

She said, "Yes, I had promised to come to you, so here I am. But Rajiv I am not the same Mahamaya that you have known. There has been a lot of change in me physically. But mentally I am the same person. If you promise that you will never remove my *ghomta* (the end of the sari which is draped over the head covering the face like a veil) and insist on seeing my face, I will stay with you. Tell me what should I do? I can go back because still there is time."

Getting Mahamaya back from the jaws of death was enough for him; Rajiv did not want anything more. He said, "Please stay the way you want to, but please don't leave me. I will not live if you do so."

Mahamaya said, "Then let's leave this place at this very instance and go to the place where your sahib has been transferred."

They left everything that was there in the house and set off. The storm had not abated. The force was so much that it was difficult to stand. The wind lifted little pebbles from the ground and hit them like pellets. They avoided walking on the roads lest they came under a falling tree. The wind pushed them onwards.

3

The reader might find the story unrealistic. But such incidents did occur sometimes when *Satidah* was practiced. *Satidah* was a custom practiced long ago, in this a widow immolated herself on her husband's funeral pyre. The women who did it were considered to be virtuous and were revered for this act.

Mahamaya's hands and feet were tied and she was placed on the pyre next to her husband's body. The pyre was lit and the flames rose high, but the storm and rain came to her assistance. The people who had gathered there ran away to seek shelter from the rain. It did not take very long for the rain to quench the fire. Mahamaya managed to free her hands as the rope had got burnt. The pain of the burns on her body was excruciating, but she did not cry. She got up and undid the rope tying her feet. Her clothes were burnt at places. She managed to cover herself somehow and reach home. Luckily no one was at home, as everyone had gone to the cremation ground. She lit a lamp and changed her clothes. Then she saw herself in the mirror. What she saw shocked her; she flung the mirror on the ground and thought for a while. After that she drew a long *ghomta* over her head and face and went to Rajiv's house which was near-by. The reader knows what happened after this.

Mahamaya started living with Rajiv, but he was not happy, because of the barrier of *ghomta* between the two. The barrier was permanent like death, but was more painful than death. After the death of a loved one a person's feelings become numb for some time because of despondence. But this barrier created by the *ghomta* kept hope alive and that was very painful for Rajiv.

As it is Mahamaya was a quiet person, but the barrier created by the *ghomta* made her quieter. Rajiv found this unbearable. He felt that she was perpetually living under the shadow of death; and this was permeating into his life too. Rajiv too was dying by bits every day. The Mahamaya that he had known since his childhood was lost. Even the beautiful memory of his childhood friend was fading in the presence of this hooded figure. The distance between him and Mahamaya was increasing every day. Rajiv lived outside the boundary that she had created around herself and from there he tried to gauge her; like the stars at night that look down and try to fathom the dark night.

Days went by. Two of them continued to live together like two islands.

One night on the tenth day of a lunar fortnight when the moon came out through the tattered clouds and flooded the earth with its light. Rajiv was awake. He was sitting next to a window, a chorus of cicadas and fragrance of wild flowers from the jungle accosted him. The pond nearby fringed by trees, shone like a mirror in the moonlight. Usually, people's minds do not remain confined to a particular thought on such nights, but Rajiv's thoughts flowed in a particular direction. His thoughts were fragrant like the wild flowers and they hummed in his mind like the chorus of the cicadas. God knows what came over him he felt that a night like this was meant for breaking rules. The night was beautiful, the sky had thrown away its cloud cover and the moon was shining. It reminded him of Mahamaya of the bygone days, beautiful, quiet and solemn. His entire being wanted to be with Mahamaya.

Rajiv walked into Mahamaya's room like a sleepwalker. She was sleeping. He went close to her and lowered his face. Moonlight had fallen on her face. But alas! Where was the face that he loved so much? The hungry fire of the funeral pyre had satiated its hunger by eating a portion of the face which was once so beautiful. Rajiv was shocked. He sucked in his breath an indistinct sound came out from his throat. Mahamaya woke up. The first thing that she saw was his face lowered over hers. She got up from her bed and covered her face. Rajiv knew what he had done was unpardonable, but still he held her feet and begged forgiveness.

Mahamaya did not utter a word; she left without so much of a backward glance. No one saw her after that. She left Rajiv to burn in her quiet and unforgiving rage all his life.

Glossary

Kulin — The ancestors of these Brahmins came from Kannauj to Bengal on invitation of the king. They were very orthodox and married within their group. They considered themselves superior to the local Brahmins

Burra Sahib — Senior most British official

Resham Kuthi — Silk factory

Pishi — Father's sister

Prajapati — The god who fixes marriages

Kandarp — Cupid

Cheli — Red bridal sari

Ghomta — The end of the sari which is draped over the head covering the face like a veil.

Satidah — The practice of widows burning themselves on the funeral pyre of their husbands.

15

Punishment
(Shasti)

When Dukhiram Rui and his brother Chidam Rui left home in the morning for work carrying their *das* (a heavy chopper with a wooden handle), their wives were shouting and squabbling with each other at the top of their voices. Their neighbours had got used to the noise; they considered it to be normal like any other sound that they heard every day in the surroundings. It was a daily routine. When they heard them start fighting, they would say, 'There they go', as though they were expecting it to happen. No one wanted to know the reason behind their fights like, one doesn't ask 'why has the sun risen' or 'why is it setting down'.

Though their fights did not affect the neighbours much, they affected the husbands; unfortunately, the wives couldn't care the less. The discomfort suffered by the husbands because of their fights could be compared with the irritating sound made by a spring-less wheel of an *ekka gari* (a carriage drawn by a single horse). When one travels by such a transport the irritating sound made by the wheels becomes an essential part of one's journey similarly, they had accepted the daily fight between their wives as a part of their daily existence. The brothers felt apprehensive if it was all quiet in the house. The fear of some unexpected catastrophe made them chary.

That evening, when the two brothers came home after toiling for the entire day, they found the house quiet and eerie. It had rained heavily around twelve, that day. The sky was still covered with clouds. The growth of wild vegetation around the house because of rains, the smell of submerged jute plants in the fields nearby and the moisture rising from the wet vegetation had given rise to a congealed mass of darkness around the house. The atmosphere was suffocating.

The swollen Padma River, flowing under a canopy of dense and dark clouds looked ominous. The river had washed away the agricultural fields and had eroded the banks. Mango and jackfruit trees on the bank were somehow holding on to the soil. Their visible roots reminded one of fingers desperately trying to cling to something.

Dukhiram and Chidam, had gone to the *jamindar's* (land lord) *Kachari bari* (office) to work. Most of the people in the neighbourhood had gone to their fields on temporary islands which had risen out of the river to harvest paddy before they got washed away by the rising water level. A few others had gone to their jute fields. Only Dukhiram and Chidam had gone to the *Jamindar's* house. The *jamindar* had sent his *Peyada* (armed footman) to fetch them, who took them forcibly. The thatched roof of the *kachari bari* (office) was leaking at places and they were asked to repair it. It took them the entire day to fix it. They worked in spite of rain because they had to finish the work that day. They did not go back home for lunch; some light refreshments from the *kachari bari* was given to them in lieu of lunch, but the money that was given to them for their labour was far less than their expectations. When they objected, they were rudely turned away with a shower of expletives, which was more than what they deserved.

When they reached home in the evening after wading through slush and water, they found Chandara, the wife of the younger brother lying on the verandah. Chandara had shed a lot of tears that day. She was quiet and sulky like the hot and sultry day. The elder brother's wife Radha was sitting in one corner of the verandah with a sullen and threatening look on her face. Her one-and-a-half-year-old son had cried himself to sleep.

Dukhiram, the elder brother, was very hungry. The first thing that he told his wife was, "Give me food."

Her husband's demand for food was like a spark in a pile of gunpowder. She exploded in her loud and high-pitched voice, "Did you leave any rice for me to cook? Do you expect me to go out and earn money to buy rice!"

He was very hungry, tired and was smarting from the humiliation that they had suffered in the *jamindar's* place. On top of that his wife's dirty insinuation made him flare-up. He roared like a lion and said, "What did you say!" And then without blinking he hit his wife on the head with his *da*. Radha fell down near her sister-in-law and died on the spot.

"Oh, what have you done!" Chandara screamed as blood gushed out and soaked her clothes.

Chidam rushed to his wife and clapped his hand over her mouth. The *da* slid down from Dukhiram's hand and fell on the ground. Nonplussed by the situation, Dukhiram fell down on the ground in a heap. The little boy got up and started crying out of fear.

It was very peaceful outside. The shepherds had come back with their herd. The peasants who had gone to the opposite bank to harvest paddy had rowed across the river with their share of the crop.

Old Ramlochan Chakrabarty had come back home after posting a letter in the post office, he was pulling at his hookah and relaxing, when he remembered that his tenant Dukhiram's rent was overdue. Dukhiram had promised to pay a part of his rent to Ramlochan on that very day. Presuming that Dukhiram has come back home he placed a folded Chador on his shoulder and set off for Dukhiram's house holding an umbrella.

He got an eerie feeling when he entered the courtyard of the house. The house was dark, no lamp had been lit. He could make out a few shadowy figures on the dark verandah. Someone was crying. A child was repeatedly asking for his mother and Chidam was trying to stop him.

"Is Dukhi there?" Ramlochan asked hesitantly.

Dukhiram, who was sitting still like a statue all this while, broke into loud sobs like a child when he heard his name.

Chidam got up and came down to the courtyard and stood next to Ramlochan.

"What is it? The women have fought again?" Enquired Ramlochan, "We have heard them shout at each other all day long."

Chidam was in a confused state. He did not know what to say. All kinds of explanations and stories were going round and round in his head. He had planned to dispose of the body of his sister-in-law quietly late at night. Ramlochan's arrival had unnerved him as he had not catered for someone's arrival at that juncture. As a result of which, he could not think of a suitable answer. He said simply, "Yes the two of them have had a big fight today."

Chakrabarty made a move towards the verandah and asked, "But why is Dukhi crying?" He found it quite unnatural.

Chidam realized that in spite of his best efforts he would not be able to save the situation, so he blurted out inadvertently, "The younger one has hit the elder one on her head with a *da*."

Other than the present predicament, simple minded Chidam could not think of the problems that could arise in future because of what he said. His main concern was how to face the truth, that is why he resorted to telling a lie without realizing that the effect of the lie would be far more serious than the truth—his response to Ramlochan's question was instantaneous.

Ramlochan was startled, he said, "Oh my god what are you saying? Is she dead?

"She is dead!" Replied Chidam and then he fell on Ramlochan's feet.

Ramlochan cursed himself for getting caught in such an awkward situation. He would be one of the prime witnesses of the case and would be summoned by the court many times—the thought was already making him weary. Chidam did not let go of his feet. He pleaded, "*Dadathakur* (way of addressing elderly people of some social standing), please tell me how I can save my wife."

The villagers sought Ramlochan's advice in legal matters because of his knowledge, so when Chidam asked him for a way out, he thought for a while and said, "See there is a way out, you go to the police station immediately and tell them that your elder brother Dukhi had asked for food after coming home from work, the food was not ready so out of anger he hit her on her head with his *da*. I am absolutely sure you will be able to save your wife if you say this."

Chidam's throat ran dry, he made some effort and said, "*Dadathakur*, I can get another wife, but I won't get another brother if he is hanged for this." Strangely enough when he had put the blame on his wife, he hadn't thought of this— at that time he had spoken without thinking—in a hurry. But now his mind helped him to rationalize his statement and that gave him some relief.

Even Ramlochan felt that it was the right thing to do so he said, "In that case run along and tell them everything. It is not possible to save both."

Ramlochan left the place. The news that Chandara had killed her sister-in-law Radha in a fit of rage spread all over the village in no time.

Police rushed into the village like water flowing out of a broken dam; causing a lot of anguish and anxiety to the innocent as well as to the offender

2

Chidam decided to continue to walk on the same path. He thought it would not be correct to reveal the truth as he himself had told Ramlochan Chakrabarty about it and from him the entire village had come to know. He feared that if he changed his statement then the matter might become worse. So, he made up his mind to repeat the same lie during interrogation and added some cock and bull story to it to save Chandara.

Chandara was dumbstruck when Chidam told her to take the blame on herself. Chidam said, "Do what I am telling you. You don't have to fear for anything, we will save you." Though he reassured her his throat ran dry and his face looked pale.

Chndara was about 17 to18 years old. She was of short and her face was round and chubby. She was healthy, her body was firm and her limbs were shapely. Her movements were unhindered. Somewhat like a new boat, small, swift and shapely. She had a curious mind and she laughed freely. She enjoyed chatting with the women folk of the village. While coming back home after filling water she would lift her *ghomta* (the free end of the sari used to cover head and face so that strangers don't get to see their faces) a bit and take note of whatever her dark eyes saw.

The elder one was just opposite. She was slovenly and disorganized, found it difficult to look after her only child and perform her house hold chores together. She couldn't relax even when there was hardly any work as she was perpetually flustered. The younger one hardly raised her voice even when they were fighting. She would retaliate in a low voice, but her remarks would be caustic which would work like a spark, the elder one would explode and shout at the top of her voice. Her voice would reach the rest of the village and disturb the villagers.

There was a great resemblance between the husband and the wife. Dukhiram was broadly built. His nose was short and his eyes had a perpetual bewildered look; as though he found it difficult to understand the world, which he accepted unquestioningly. He was a rare combination of being harmless yet terrifying, strong yet helpless.

On the other hand, Chidam was like a painstakingly sculptured statue of polished black stone. There was not an ounce of extra fat on his body. Every limb of his spoke of strength and dexterity. Be it jumping into river from a steep bank, propelling a boat with a pole in the shallow parts of the river, climbing a bamboo tree to cut down the thin bamboo shoots, no work was difficult for him, he performed every work with a lot of skill and adroitness. His dark and long hair reached his shoulders, which he combed away from his forehead and oiled regularly. He took special care of his attire.

Chidam was not indifferent towards the beauties of the village in fact he took special care to dress up to attract their attention, but he loved his wife dearly. Though they fought with each other frequently, but that did not come in the way of their affection for each other, their fights mostly ended in a draw as one could not out do without the other, and it did not take them very long to make up. There was another reason which brought the two close, they had similar concerns about each other. Chandara's flirtatious nature was a cause of worry for Chidam, and Chidams roving eyes were a cause of concern for Chandara. She felt that if she didn't increase her hold over him, she might lose him to another woman someday.

The relationship between the husband and wife was going through a bad phase before this mishap took place. Chandara had noticed that her husband had been going away from home for long periods on the pretext of doing some work and had been coming back home empty handed. Sometimes his sudden absence would be for a day or two. Chandara retaliated to this in her own way. She started leaving home and visiting the quay side very often, a place where the village folks bathe, fill water and chit chat. On her way back home, she would tour the entire village and come home late. And then she would talk in great detail about the second son of Kashi Mazundar.

This caused a lot of anguish to Chidam. He lost his sleep over it. He could not concentrate on his work. One day he scolded his sister-in-law for not keeping an eye on his wife. Chidam's sister-in-law retorted back, "Your wife moves faster than a storm, how do you expect me to control her, I am warning you, that this girl is going to land us into great trouble someday!"

Chandara came out of the next room and said slowly in a deliberately controlled voice, "What is troubling you?" And that started a fight again.

Chidam glared at his wife and said, "I will break your bones if I get to hear that you have gone to the quay side again."

146

Chandara retorted back, "It will be a big relief." Having said that she walked out of the house, Chidam sprang on her, held her by her hair and dragged her inside. Then he pushed her inside a room and closed the room from outside.

When he came back in the evening, he found the room open and his wife missing. Chandara had gone to her maternal uncle's house, which was three villages away. Chidam literally had to beg her to come back home. He had to accept his defeat in this battle. He understood that his wife was like quicksilver, something that can be kept on an open palm, but is bound to spill out in between the fingers of a closed fist.

After this incident Chidam never forced her to do anything, but he was perpetually in a state of anxiety. He loved this flippant woman dearly, but this love for her caused him a lot of pain; so much so that there were times when he wished that she was dead, he felt that he would live peacefully after that.

It was at this point in time that this incident took place.

Chandara was shocked when her husband told her that she should take the blame on herself; she listened to every word that he said, as her dark eyes lit up like fire with anger. Chidam smoldered in that heat. As she heard him her mind and body started drawing itself inwards to the point of being nonexistent; she wanted to free herself from the clutches of this monster of a man, who was her husband and after a while she grew apathetic towards the whole situation.

"You have nothing to fear," Chidam reassured her. He tried to coach her regarding what she must tell the magistrate. There was no response from her; she sat like a wooden statue. Not a single word entered her ears.

Dukhiram was dependent on Chidam for everything. But when Chidam asked Dukhiram to blame Chandara for the murder he said, "But what will happen to *bouma* (wife of younger brother)?

Chidam said, "Don't worry I will save her." Dhukiram felt relieved when he heard Chidam.

3

Chidam told his wife to say that her sister-in –law had attacked her with a *bonti*.(sharp knife mounted on wood used to cut vegetables).And she had used a *da* in self-defense, which led to a scuffle; her sister-in-law had got hurt inadvertently in the scuffle. The story was fabricated by Ramlochan. Ramlochan had gone to great lengths in telling Chidam how to make the story sound convincing and what all proofs must be brought forth to authenticate the story.

The police came to investigate. The people of the village were unanimous in their opinion that Chandara had killed her sister-in-law. The statements given by the witnesses pointed towards the same. When the police asked Chandara she said, "Yes I have killed her."

The next question was, "Why did you kill her?"

She answered, "Because I disliked her."

--Was she the first one to attack you?

--No.

--Did she ill-treat you?

--No.

Her answers surprised everybody. Chidam was very perturbed, he could not hold himself and blurted out, "She is not saying the right thing; actually, my brother's wife was the first one…."

The police officer asked him to shut up.

The officer continued his interrogation, to find out how it happened, but Chandara stuck to the same answer, she did not say that her sister-in-law was the first one to attack her.

It is very rare to come across a person as stubborn as Chandara. She was hell bent on ending her life. She was hurt by her husband's attitude. From her behavior it seemed as though she was trying to convey to her husband silently, 'I have chosen the gallows in your place. I have broken my bond with you, my final bond will be with the noose'.

The police arrested Chandara. A young, innocent and fun-loving girl walked through the village; a village that was so familiar to her surrounded by her captors. They crossed the school building, Mazumdar's house, the post office, the quay side and houses of many people who knew her very well. Her friends were so ashamed of her, that they did not come to meet her for the last time. They hid their faces behind their *ghomta* as she walked past. A few hid behind trees and watched her go. Thus, Chandara left the village forever in disgrace.

On being questioned, Chandara told the *hakim*(magistrate) that she had killed her sister-in-law. She did not mention about being provoked or attacked by her sister-in-law.

Chidam started crying when he was called to the witness box. He pleaded with folded hands to the magistrate and said, "Sir, my wife is innocent." The magistrate scolded him for creating a scene. The magistrate's admonition brought an end to his emotional outburst. Chidam revealed the truth to the *hakim* during interrogation.

But the *hakim* did not believe him, because of the statement given by Ramlochan. Ramlochan was the only witness who had some social standing. Ramlochan had said, "I arrived on the spot immediately after the murder, Chidam told me everything in great detail. He wanted to save his wife so he held my feet and requested me for advice. I did not say anything. It was Chidam who said, 'what if I say that my brother had asked for food after coming home and his wife refused, which made him very angry and he hit his wife on her head with his *da*'. I said, 'I warn you, it would be a sin if you tell a lie in court.... '

Ramlochan had thought of telling some stories in the court that he had conjured up, with the intention of saving Chandara. But when he saw that Chandara herself had no intention of saving herself he decided not to bring them out in court lest he got into trouble for lying. He said what he was told by Chidam, not only that he added a few things to make it sound convincing. The deputy magistrate transferred the case to the session's court.

In the meantime, life went on as usual. People in the village went about their daily chores like, looking after their paddy fields, buying things of their daily requirement, fighting with each other, celebrating festivals.... It rained like it always did. The paddy in the fields grew and nothing stopped.

Police arrived at the court along with the accused and the witnesses. Chidam sat next to a window and looked out. The *munsiff* court (lower court) nearby, was full of people, they were waiting for their turn to be called in. A lawyer along with forty-nine people had come from Kolkata. They were witnesses in a case involving the ownership of a part of a small pond situated behind the kitchen of the litigant. Many others had come to claim what they felt was rightfully theirs. They all looked as though nothing could be as important as their claim. Chidam stared at those busy people. He was in a trance—nothing was registering. A cuckoo started calling loudly from a huge banyan tree in the compound, do birds have courts too? He wondered.

Chandara was tired of answering the same questions over and over again, so when the judge asked her about the incident she said, "Oh *sahib* (sir)! How many times do I have to answer the same questions?"

The judge tried to explain the gravity of the case, he said, "Do you know the punishment for the crime that you have admitted to have committed?"

Chandara said, "No."

He said, "Death by hanging."

Chandara said, "Please *sahib*, why don't you tell them to do it, I just can't bear the delay anymore."

When Chidam was brought to the court, Chandara turned away her face. The judge said, "Look at the witness and tell me how he is related to you?"

She covered her face with her hands and said, "He is my husband."

--Does he love you?

--He loves me a lot.

--Don't you love him?

--I love him too.

When Chidam was questioned he said, "I have killed her."

--Why?

--I asked her to serve food. She didn't.

The elder brother fainted when he was called. When he came to his senses he said, "*Sahib* I have murdered her."

--why?

--Because she refused to serve food to me.

After listening to the brothers and the other witnesses the judge came to the conclusion that both the brothers were trying to save her. Chandara stuck to her statement; there was no change. Two lawyers had volunteered to help her. Even they gave up at the end.

A dark chubby little girl left her dolls at home and went to her husband's house. The night when the wedding was solemnized could anyone imagine that the poor girl's life would end so pathetically? Her father had died a satisfied person thinking   that he had sent this daughter to a good household where she would lead a happy life!

On the day prior to hanging the doctor asked her if she would like to meet someone.

She said, "I want to see my mother."

The doctor said, "your husband wants to meet you, should I send for him?"

Chandara said, "*Moron* (a mild rebuke)!"

Glossary

Da - A heavy chopper with a wooden handle.

Ekka gari — A carriage drawn by a single horse.

Jamindar — Landlord.

Kachari bari — Office of the land lord.

Peyada — Armed footman.

Dada thakur — A way of addressing elderly of some social standing.

Ghomta — The free end of the sari used to cover head and face, so that strangers do not get to see their faces.

Bouma — Wife of younger brother.

Bonti — Knife mounted on wood, used by women for cutting vegetables.

Hakim — Deputy magistrate.

Munsiff court – Lower court.

Sahib — Sir.

Moron — An expression of mild rebuke.

16

Wife's Letter
(Strir Potro)

Srichrankamaleshu (to thy lotus feet, a reverential way of addressing someone)

We have been married for the last fifteen years, but I have never written to you before this. We have been speaking to each other for so many years, but there has never been an occasion for me to write to you, because we have never lived apart.

Right now, I am in Puri on a pilgrimage, and you are in your office busy with your work. Your relationship with your office is somewhat like a snail with its shell. Your office has become a part of you, both physically and mentally and that is why you did not apply for leave. I think the almighty too wanted it to be that way. Incidentally, he has approved my leave.

Everyone knows me as the *mejo-bou* of your family, the wife of the second son. After fifteen years of our marriage, today as I stand next to the sea, I have come to realize that I have yet another relationship with the rest of the world and its creator. And that realization has given me the courage to write to you. This letter, by the way, is not from your *mejo-bou*.

When, other than the one who had written my fate, no one else knew about my marriage, my brother and I got afflicted by typhoid. He died, but I survived. The women living in our neighbourhood said, 'Mrinal is a girl that is why she survived. She wouldn't have survived had she been a boy'. *Yama*, the god of death is an expert at stealing and he has a penchant for precious things. I have written this to make you understand that, I am not precious hence I will not die easily, I will live long.

The day your distantly related *mama* (maternal uncle) and your friend Nirod came to our village to select a bride for you I was just twelve years old. Our village is located in the interior part of East Bengal, where jackals howl even in broad daylight. After getting off from the train, they had to travel a little more than twelve miles in a hackney and cover yet another three miles of unpaved road on a palanquin. They were very tired by the time they reached our village. On top of it they had to eat lunch cooked in *Bangal* style (the way food is cooked in East Bengal). Your *mama* still talks about it.

The *boro bou,* the wife of the eldest son, is not good looking so your mother wanted a good-looking wife for her second son. Otherwise, why would your relatives come to a village like ours? Anyway, East Bengal abounds in diseases of the stomach, spleen, liver and beautiful girls of marriageable age. You don't have to look for them, their relatives come to you in hoards with proposals. And once they come, you are spoilt for choice.

My parents were very nervous when your relatives came to our house. Their main concern was how to make the city Gods happy. They had nothing to offer other than showcase their daughter's beauty. Their daughter on the other hand had no airs about her good looks. It was a big opportunity for my parents; and they were ready to accept any price.

Not only my parents, even my neighbours were on tenterhooks regarding my selection. Their collective anxiety sat like a stone on my chest. That day I felt as though the light from the skies above and the strength of the entire world were working like pillars to make a twelve-year-old rustic girl stand in front of two pairs of scrutinizing eyes. There was no place for me to hide.

I was selected. Flutes played and the skies above cried. I finally reached your house and faced a second round of scrutiny. This time it was by the ladies of the house. Their mission was to find faults in me, which they did meticulously, but even they agreed unanimously that I was beautiful. My *boro-ja*, wife of my husband's elder brother, looked grave when she heard it. I wonder why it was necessary to make me beautiful because beauty was of no value in your family. I believe when the almighty creates something beautiful, he does it in his leisure for his own pleasure.

It didn't take you very long to forget that I am beautiful. But my intelligence was something that you were reminded of at every step. Intelligence is an inherent quality so in spite of living in your house for the last fifteen years it hasn't left me. My mother was not happy about it; she was of the opinion that it is not good for a woman to be intelligent. According to her a woman has to accept a lot of dos and don'ts in her life and if she uses her intelligence and raises questions about them, she would surely get into trouble. But what to do when the almighty was distributing intelligence, he must have given me an extra helping, much more than what is necessary for an ordinary housewife. I can't return it back, can I? You people have cursed me for it and have called me *meye jyatha* (impertinent woman) quite often. Calling names is a way of giving vent to one's anger, so I forgive you people for that.

There is something that I did in secret and none of you got to know about it. I wrote poems; nothing much, very ordinary stuff. But in the world of my poetry, I was a free person. There were no barriers around me. I could be myself there. Fortunately, no one knew about it.

The First thing that comes to my mind about your house is the cow shed. It was a very cramped place. The cows were given food in huge wooden basins which were kept in one corner of the yard.

The servant detailed to give them food was kept busy with other jobs in the morning. The starving animals had to wait till he finished his chores. The hungry cows licked the basins till he arrived. So much so that they bit off the sides of the basins and chewed them. My heart wept when I saw their plight. I am from rural background, so I could bond with them very easily. To me they were like an extended family. When I was a new bride very often, I would starve myself and feed them my food on the quiet. When I became older, I started feeding them openly, seeing my affinity with the bovines, you people would pull my leg and joke about my gotra (lineage).

My daughter died very soon after her birth. She called me before leaving, but I stayed back. Had she been alive then she would have made my life different. Then I would have been a mother and not just a *mejo bou*. A mother has a universal appeal, because all mothers are driven by the same emotion. I suffered a lot while giving birth to my child, but unfortunately, I could not enjoy the ultimate happiness of becoming a mother.

I still remember the expression on the English doctor's face who came to see me. The condition of the women's quarters surprised him and the unhygienic condition of the *antur ghor* (room earmarked for deliveries) angered him. He scolded the attendant. The *sadar* (men's quarter) in your house is well furnished and it has a small well-kept garden too. But the women's quarter is like the inner side of a knitted sweater untidy and unkempt. Fresh air does not enter here because of poor ventilation. Natural light does not have an access here so it is perpetually dark. The place is lit by dim lights. The floors need scrubbing. The walls are dirty. And the household refuse lie piled up for days. The doctor had made a mistake; he had thought that this neglect must be making us, the women folk unhappy. But it was not so. When self-respect is at the lowest level neglect does not seem to be unjust. It doesn't hurt any more. Women generally feel embarrassed to let people know that they are unhappy. That is why I feel that if you are born a woman, being unhappy is an inseparable part of your existence. And for you men I would say 'if neglecting women is your ultimate aim, then please do not give them too much attention at any time, because it hurts when all of a sudden you start neglecting them'.

In whichever way you have kept me, unhappiness has never bothered me. So, when *Yama* (the God of death), stood next to my bed I did not feel scared. Why should I feel scared after all what I have got from life? Those who have been cared for, and nurtured lovingly their tie with life is strong. They find it difficult to leave this earth. Had *Yama* made a little effort that day I would have come out like a tuft of grass growing on loose soil, with roots, soil and everything.

I wonder why Bengali women talk about dying at the drop of a hat. What is so glorious about it? I find it embarrassing. Is dying that simple?

My daughter was like the evening star, she came up for a very short time and then she disappeared. After she went away, I got busy with my daily chores which included looking after my bovine friends. Life would have continued like this till the end and the need to write this letter wouldn't have arisen, but something happened that changed the course of my life. Sometimes a small seed of *ashwatha* (a type of Ficus) blown by the wind lands up in your yard, it germinates inside some unseen crack in the yard, a sapling raises its head the roots make their way through the gaps in between the bricks and cracks become visible on the yard.

After the death of her widowed mother the younger sister of my *boro ja* came to stay in our house, because she was being ill-treated by her cousin brothers in her own house. She was an unwanted person in our family too, you people were not pleased by her arrival. But what to do my nature compelled me to take her side. My contention was, a person has to swallow her pride when she takes shelter in a place where she is not welcome. How can anybody ill-treat such a person and ask her to leave?

It was then that I noticed my *boro ja's* plight. She had got her sister to live in our house because of her concern for her, but when she realized that her husband was against it, she started behaving as though she would be relieved the day her sister went away. She did not have the courage to be affectionate towards her sister openly. Maybe this was a way of showing her devotion to her husband. I felt sad.

After some time my *boro ja* started treating her younger sister like a servant. She was given the same food that the servants ate and she wore the same kind of saris that the maid servants wore. It not only saddened me, but embarrassed me too. I think the aim behind this was to show the family members that she has got Bindu (her sister) at a very cheap rate to work as a servant for the family.

My *boro ja's* family was not wealthy, and the daughters were not good looking. But the family was reputed for their *kul* (lineage). You must be remembering how her father fell on your father's feet and begged for his daughter's marriage to your elder brother. My *boro ja* has always considered her marriage to your brother as a mistake, and held herself solely responsible for depriving your brother of getting a good match. And that is why she made herself as self-effacing as possible. She had kept herself confined to a very small space in your household where she would not be heard nor seen by the rest of the people.

But her self-effacing nature set a wrong precedence for me. I couldn't behave like her though, I was expected to. If I feel that something is good, I can't change my opinion and call it bad because someone wants me to say so. There have been many instances in the past which must have made you realize this.

Anyway, I gave Bindu (sister of my *boro ja*) a place in my room. My boro ja was not happy about it. She said, "Why are you spoiling my sister's habit by pampering her? After all she comes from a poor family." She went around complaining about it to everybody as though I had done something terribly wrong. But I know that she must have been happy to see her sister being looked after, which she could not do herself.

My *boro ja* decreased Bindu's age by a few years whenever she spoke about Bindu. But I know that she would not be a day less than fourteen. She was of marriageable age, but there was no one who was willing to take the responsibility of getting her married. Moreover, Bindu was not good looking thus no large- hearted groom came forth and asked for her hand. This was the reason why she lied about Bindu's age.

Bindu was very hesitant and wary when she came to my room for the first time, her reluctance made me feel as though I was a delicate doll and she was worried that her contact would harm me. She avoided company as much as possible. There were times when I felt that Bindu did not believe that she had a rightful place on this earth. She considered herself to be a trespasser. In her father's house after the death of her parents her uncle's sons (cousin brothers) were not ready to leave even a small corner for her in her own house. Unwanted objects which are of no use to the family members are often left here and there, and people forget about them— but it becomes difficult to forget an unwanted person especially if she is a female. Poor insignificant, Bindu she didn't get a place in her own house, not even a small corner. Her cousins at present are leading a comfortable life in the same house which was rightfully her house too.

Bindu looked scared when she came to my room. I felt bad when I saw her in that state. I spoke to her affectionately and made her understand that there was a place for her in my room.

But my room had another inhabitant other than me so it was not easy. Within a day or two after shifting she developed a rash all over her body. The rash was most probably prickly heat, but you people firmly believed that it was pox. It had to be so because she was 'Bindu'. A good for nothing doctor practicing in your *para*, (locality) was called to examine her; he saw her and said that he would not be able to say anything before two to three days. You people were in a great hurry, you were not willing to wait that long. Bindu felt very embarrassed because her ailment was creating such a lot of problems for the residents of the house. I had to intervene, I said, "Please don't worry I will stay with her in the *antur ghor* and we will remain there till she recovers fully." The proposal was not appreciated by the family members. They were angry with me. Bindu's sister wanted to send her to the government hospital for treatment and admission. Fortunately, her rashes disappeared within a few days. But this time there was a new worry, you people said, "Though the rashes have subsided outside, they might be growing inside and will recur." It had to be, because after all she was 'Bindu'.

When people are neglected right from their childhood, they develop an inner strength. As a result, they don't fall sick easily and even if they do, they recover fast. So Bindu recovered fast, the ailment just touched her and went away. But one thing that I learnt from this episode was that it is very difficult to give shelter to an insignificant person and it becomes all the more difficult to provide shelter to a person whose need for a shelter is the utmost.

By the time BIndu's hesitation about coming to my room got over, another problem arose. She became too fond of me, so much that it became a cause for worry for me at times. I have never seen anyone loving another person so much. I. have read great love stories, but they were between a man and a woman!

All these years no one had spoken about my beauty to me it was Bindu who spoke about it again. She would stare at my face and say, "*Didi* (elder sister) it is only me in this house who has discovered so much of beauty in you. They don't have eyes." She loved combing my hair. It would upset her if I combed my hair. She combed my hair gently, and tied it in different styles every day. Earlier I dressed up only when there was an invitation for me to attend some function. But after she came, I had to dress up every evening on her insistence. She helped me to dress up. She had gone crazy about me.

There is not an inch of land in the woman's quarter where trees can grow. But there is a Gaab tree next to the Northern part of the compound wall; it had somehow grown between a drain and the wall. When I saw red leaves on the tree, I knew that spring has arrived. When I noticed a glow on Bindu's face one day like the Gaab tree, I knew that metamorphosis has started in Bindu too. Spring has invaded Bindu's heart.

Bindu was suffocating me with her love and affection so much that, I was finding it difficult to bear. It used to annoy me at times. But through her love I discovered a self- image, which I had never seen before. This image was absolutely free; free from all bindings.

You people found it difficult to digest the fact that I was giving special attention to a girl like Bindu. It annoyed you. You said that I was crossing my limits. The day a gold armlet of mine went missing from my room, you shamelessly blamed Bindu for it. The day the local police came looking for a freedom fighter in our colony and searched our house too, you people had no doubts that Bindu was a police informer. You people had no proof; your suspicion zeroed down on her because she was 'Bindu'.

The maid servants of the house refused to do any work for her. Moreover, Bindu felt very embarrassed if I told them to do something for her. So, I had to employ a maid servant for her. This increased my monthly expenses. You did not like the idea. When I gave my saris to Bindu you got even more annoyed and you stopped giving me money for my personal expenses. From that day onwards I started wearing the cheapest saris made in cotton mills; one rupee and *four annas* (one fourth of a rupee) for a pair of them. When the maid servant came to pick up my plate after lunch, I stopped her. I fed the leftovers to the cows and washed my utensils in the yard. This continued for quite some time. You noticed it one day and it made you very unhappy. Isn't it very funny that it matters very little if we are unhappy, but you people have to be kept happy.

Your anger and disgust for Bindu kept increasing day by day and so did Bindu's age. Both were very natural, but these natural phenomena started becoming a cause of great concern for you.

What surprises me most is that why you didn't throw Bindu out of the house during all these years? Now I know the reason. Actually, you were scared of me. Though you never admitted, you respected me for my intelligence inwardly.

Ultimately you decided to take the help of *Lord Prajapati* (the god who fixes marriage) to throw her out of the house. A groom for Bindu was found. Bindu's elder sister was relieved. She said, "God has been kind. He has saved our family honour (in those days if a girl did not get married in time the family of the girl was treated as an outcast by the society)."

I did not know anything about the groom. But you people said that he was a very good match for Bindu, good in every aspect. When she came to know Bindu held my feet and cried she said, "Didi why do I have to get married?"

I tried to pacify her and said, "Bindu you don't have to worry, I have heard that your 'would be husband' is a very nice man."

She said, "He might be a nice person, but what do I have in me that he will like me?"

One thing that I found very odd was, that the groom's family never came to see Bindu, though her sister was happy about it.

Bindu did not stop crying. I did not have the courage to stop the marriage. How can I stop her marriage? What if I die who will look after her, I thought.

Bindu's complexion was dark. I wondered what kind of fate awaited her! What if they don't accept her? The thought made me shudder.

When only five days were left for her marriage, she came to me and said, "Can't I die in these five days *didi?*"

I scolded her for what she said, but the almighty knows that I would have been happy had she died a painless death during those five days.

One day before her marriage she went to her sister and said, "*Didi* I will stay in your cowshed and do anything that you ask me to do. But please don't throw me out like this."

Her sister had been shedding tears quietly for quite some time. She wept that day once again, but the teachings of the scriptures overruled the heart so she wiped tears and said, "Bindi the ultimate salvation for a woman is marriage. You are getting married, not everyone is lucky like you; it all depends on what the gods have decided for you! Try however you may, you will not be able to change their decision."

Poor Bindu had no options, she had to get married somehow, whatever happened to her after that was no one's concern.

I wanted the marriage to take place in our house. But you people said according to the groom's family custom the marriage should take place in their house.

I understood that it was a lame excuse. Actually, you people wanted to avoid the expense that would have been incurred had the marriage taken place in our house. I kept quiet. I dressed her up like a bride before she left and gave her a few of my gold ornaments. I didn't tell anybody about it, but her sister may have noticed it.

Before leaving, Bindu hugged me and said, "So *didi* you too have forsaken me."

I said, "Bindu, whatever happens to you I will be with you always."

Three days went by after her marriage. I had gone to the coal shed where I had kept a lamb. This lamb was sent to you by a tenant farmer of your estate as a gift. I had somehow managed to save it from your cook who was all set to make a stew out of it. I used to feed the poor animal as I did not trust the servants. That day when I went down, I found Bindu huddled up in one corner of the room. The moment she saw me she held my feet and started crying.

She said, "*Didi* my husband, is a lunatic."

I was shocked, "Are you telling me the truth Bindu?" I enquired.

"How can I lie to you *didi*? My husband is insane. My father-in-law was against this marriage, but he could not convince my mother-in-law, he is scared of her. He left for Varanasi before our marriage. My mother-in-law's stubbornness has led to this marriage."

I sat down on a heap of coal. How can a woman be so unkind to another woman I thought?

Bindu told me that apparently her husband appeared normal most of the time, but sometimes he becomes so violent that he has to be kept locked up. He was normal on the night of marriage, but the strain of the function and lack of sleep made him violent from the second day onwards. In the afternoon when Bindu was having lunch he arrived there and threw away her plate. He claimed that Bindu was a queen and her servants had stolen her gold utensils and had served food to her on brass utensils. On the third night when Bindu's mother-in-law asked her to sleep in her husband's room she died of fear. But she had to obey. Her mother-in-law it seems is a very short- tempered person. One could call her partially mad and such people are more difficult to handle. Fortunately, her husband was quiet that night. When her husband went off to sleep, she left the room quietly and managed to run away from the house somehow.

Anger and hatred made my body burn from head to toe. I said, "They have cheated you. One can't call this a marriage. Bindu from now onwards you will stay with me like you did before. Let me see who dares to take you away from me."

When I told you people about what had happened to Bindu you said, "Bindu is lying."

"Bindu is not lying," I protested.

Your response was, "How do you know?"

"I know for sure," I said.

You tried to scare me and said, "What if they complain to the police."

I said, "When this matter goes to court, we can say that they cheated us and got her married to a mad person."

One of you said, "You mean to say that we will have to fight out the matter in court? But tell me how does it affects us?"

"If you people do not make an effort then I will sell my ornaments and try and do whatever I can," I retorted back.

"You will go to the lawyers' quarters to hire a lawyer!" All of you spoke together.

After this I had nothing to say.

After the meeting got over, I came to know that people from Bindu's in-laws' house had come and were creating a ruckus. The elder brother of Bindu's husband, it seems, was threatening to inform the police.

I don't know what gave me the courage, but I said, "Let them go to the police, I don't care."

I decided to take Bindu into my room and lock ourselves in. But when I went to my room, I found her missing. Someone told me that Bindu had gone to her brother-in-law on her own accord, when she came to know about the ruckus that he was creating.

Probably she did not want to create any further trouble for me.

But by going back to her husband's house Bindu made her life more miserable than before. Her mother-in-law argued that after all her son had not harmed her in any way. There were many husbands who torture their wives regularly compared to them her son was a gem!

Bindu's sister said, "It is her fate, one can't do anything about it. But all said and done she is lucky to have got a husband after all."

I was told the story of a devoted wife who took her leprosy afflicted husband to a brothel so that his needs got satisfied. A story often told by men to glorify the devotion of a wife towards her husband. Wonder why you men never thought this story to be an example of extreme cowardice. You men never think twice before citing this example of a devoted wife to all those who would listen! No wonder you people got angry with Bindu when she ran away from her husband's house. But my heart bled for her and I felt extremely ashamed of you. I grew up in a village, but after marriage I came to a household which is urban and forward in many ways, I wonder how I got to think differently. Honestly, I can't tolerate the moral the lectures that you people give and I don't understand the religion that you follow.

I knew for sure that Bindu would never come back to our house. But I hadn't forgotten that I had promised to help her if she needed my help; I had told her that I will never forsake her. My younger brother Sharat was studying in a college in Kolkata. He was a very helpful person. Sharat spent more time volunteering for social causes than studying; be it killing rats in a plague afflicted area, or helping people affected by flood in Damodar River Sharat would be there working from the forefront. Because of this he had failed twice in his FA exam. But that did not decrease his enthusiasm one bit. I asked him to come and meet me. When he came, I requested him to keep an eye on Bindu and let me know should anything untoward happen. I knew that Bindu would not be in a position to write to me and even if she wrote, the letter would never reach me. That is why I had requested him

Sharat was a little disappointed when he came to know about the task that I had given him. He would have been happier had I told him to kidnap Bindu and bring her to me or maybe if I had asked him to bash-up Bindu's husband.

You came into the room while I was talking to Sharat. You looked at Sharat suspiciously and said, "Now what is the latest trouble that you have got into."

I said, "The trouble started right at the beginning. I came to your house after that, though I had nothing to do with it, the mistake was made by you people." You did not react to what I said.

"Where have you hidden Bindu this time?" You wanted to know.

"Had Bindu come here I would have certainly hidden her, but she will never come here, you need not worry about that,"I retorted back.

Actually, the presence of Sharat had made you suspicious. You people never liked Sharat coming to our house. So much so that I had stopped calling him for 'bhai phonta' (a ceremony in which a sister asks God to grant her brother a long life and marks his forehead with sandalwood paste). You people were scared that Sharat was being watched by the Police because of his social activities. And maybe he might be arrested by the Police because of his political leanings and drag you into trouble. That is why I hardly called him home.

163

You told me that Bindu had run away again. Her husband's elder brother had come to enquire if she had come to our house. I felt terrible when you told me. Poor girl, she was so unhappy in her husband's house! And there was no way by which I could rescue her.

I sent Sharat to find out about Bindu. He came back in the evening and told me that Bindu had gone to her cousins' house. But they were very angry with her, they took her back to her husband's house immediately. It seemed that they were very upset about the expense incurred in hiring a transport to take her back.

Around this time your aunt came to our house before leaving for a pilgrimage to Puri. I said that I wanted to travel with her. My sudden interest in religion delighted you people so no one objected. You people wanted me to be away from Kolkata for some time so that I do not create further trouble as far as Bindu was concerned.

The day of our trip was Wednesday, and by Sunday everything was arranged. I called Sharat and told him to put Bindu on the train leaving for Puri on Wednesday.

Sharat was happy with the new assignment. His face shone with excitement. He said, "*Didi* trust me, I will put her in the train and travel along with her to Puri. It will give me a chance to visit Puri."

Sharat came home on the same evening. His face told me that something had gone wrong. I said, "What happened Sharat? You couldn't meet her?"

He said, "No."

"You couldn't make her agree?" I asked.

He said, "No, that would not be necessary any more. Yesterday night she committed suicide by setting fire to her sari. I had made friends with a nephew of her husband; I came to know from him. It seems she had written a letter to you, but they have destroyed the letter."

Bindu's chapter came to a close. She managed to run away finally.

When you people came to know about it, one of you said, "Such a lot of drama." Another person said, "Oh this is a fashion these days, setting fire on one's sari and dying." I said to myself why does it have to be a sari always? Why not, a *dhoti* (garment worn by males) sometimes!

Poor Bindu when she was alive neither her looks nor her qualities were considered good enough to be worthy of praise, sadly enough her death too was thought to be a drama by the males. Some of them even called it a new fashion among women. Poor Bindu couldn't think of a different way of dying to please the male population and make them clap in appreciation! In her death too she annoyed people.

Her sister cried for a few days quietly, when no one was around. But there was a sense of relief in her crying. She was dead after all. Had she been alive god knows what all she may have had to undergo!

At present I am in Puri. There was no need for Bindu to come, but I have come because it was necessary for me.

While I lived in your house, I experienced no discomfort. In your house there was no shortage of food, it was good and in plenty. The clothes that I wore were expensive and fine. There is nothing in your character that I can complain about. Had you been like your elder brother then maybe like his wife I would have blamed my luck rather than blaming you. I repeat I have no complaints against you. This letter is not meant for that.

I will never return to your house in No 27 Makhan Baral lane. I have seen Bindu. I have seen how a woman is treated by the society and what is the value of a woman in the eyes of a male. I have no taste for it any more.

But I have seen something else too, though Bindu was a woman, God did not abandon her. You had the power to force her into this marriage, but there was a limit to your power. You tried very hard, but you could not keep her under your feet. Your feet were not large enough. Bindu has become sublime through her death. There she is not just an ordinary girl from a Bengali family, she is not a sister to a couple of cruel cousins, she is not a wife of an insane husband. She is limitless there.

When the tune that death played on his flute reached me after touching the broken heart of the poor girl, I felt a deep pain inside me for the first time as though someone had struck me with an arrow. I asked the almighty, "Why is it so difficult to conquer the most useless and insignificant thing on this earth? Why is this bubble of unhappiness created by walls in this lane where I am living so difficult to burst? When the world offered me, wine made by the six seasons, why couldn't I cross the door step of the women's quarters and drink deeply? Why did I have to die by bits within the walls made of wood and bricks? When there is a beautiful world created

165

by you waiting outside the walls? My daily routine, the rules that I followed within the women's' quarters, the repetitive conversations that I have there are so insignificant in comparison with the world outside. Tell me, will I be able to break this barrier ultimately or will I be deprived of the wonderful world created by you?"

There was a tune which kept ringing in my ears. It said, "Where are the walls? Where are the barriers created by rules? How can these flimsy walls and barriers imprison a human being? Can't you see the standard held by 'Death' proclaiming victory. *Mejo bou* you don't have to be scared of anything. It doesn't take long to break the shell called '*Mejo bou*'. Come out of it."

I am no longer scared of your lane where I was a prisoner. Today there is the blue sea in front of me and the dense dark clouds of *Ashar* (third month of the Bengali Calendar) above me. The darkness created by you, had kept me covered. Bindu had seen the real me through a chink in the cover. It was Bindu who tore the cover apart by dying. What I saw and felt when I came out made me very proud of myself. When my lord raised a toast to my unsung beauty and I saw myself against the backdrop of his blue sky above, I knew *mejo bou* was dead.

You must be thinking that I am going to die. Don't worry I will not give you the opportunity to make fun of me. Mirabai was a woman, her shackles too were heavy, but she didn't have to 'die' to 'live'. In her song she had said, "My father may abandon me, my mother may abandon me and so can everybody, but my lord will be with me forever, I don't care what happens…." This is living.

Even I will live.

Mrinal.

[The one who left the shelter of your revered feet.]

Glossary

Mejo bou — Wife of the second son

Yama —The God of death

Mama — Maternal uncle

Bangal style — Style of cooking followed in East Bengal (Now Bangladesh)

Boro ja — Wife of husband's elder brother

Meye jyatha — Impertinent woman.

Gotra — Lineage

Antur ghar — room ear marked for conducting deliveries

Sadar — Men's quarters

Ashwatha — Sacred Fig

Kul — Lineage

Didi — Elder sister

Para — locality/colony

Prajapati — the god who fixes marriages

Gaab — Diospyros embyopteris. An evergreen tree fruit bearing tree.

Bhai phonta — A ceremony in which a sister prays to the gods to grant her brother a long life and marks her brother's fore head with sandal wood paste.

Aashar — Third month of Bengali calendar.

17

Laboratory

Nandakishore was a brilliant engineer; he had studied engineering in London University. Right from his school days till he passed out from university, he was always among the top few in his class.

His intellect was sharp, his monitory requirements were massive but his financial means were limited.

He worked in a railway company and had managed to become a part of two bridge building projects. In this job the expenditure incurred was huge. Though in reality there was a mismatch between what was spent and what was projected. The dealings were not always above board. He had accumulated a lot of wealth in this fashion. His conscience did not bother him even once when both his hands, left and right were busy in accumulating the ill-gotten wealth. He believed that when assets and liabilities were associated with an abstract object called a company, it should not bother an individual.

His bosses called him a genius. He had a head for accounts and numbers, for which he got neither recognition nor remuneration. Being a Bengali could be a reason behind this. He disliked tremendously when low-ranking British officials standing with legs apart with their hands stuffed into their deep pockets, patted his back and said, 'Hello Mr. Mullick' patronizingly. He hated it even more when even after working hard to make a project successful; his British bosses took all the credit and got rewarded for the same. This injustice led him to keep a neat account in his head of what was due to him and he knew very well how to make up for what he did not get.

Though he had earned a lot of money through fair as well as unfair means, he led a simple life. He lived in a one and a half-storied house in Shikdar *para* (locality). He kept himself so busy that he didn't even have the time to change his clothes after coming back from work, thus people mostly found him wearing grease and soot-stained factory clothes, when people made fun of him about his clothes, he would laugh it off and say, "I am a worker and I take pride of my uniform."

He had built a mansion, to house his collection of scientific instruments and a laboratory. He was so busy with this hobby of collecting scientific instruments that he did not realize when people started talking behind his back and casted aspersions on him. Some even said, "Wonder where he got the Aladdin's lamp from?"

Some people get so involved with their hobby that it becomes like an obsession. His hobby was science and he was obsessed with it. He didn't realize when people started getting suspicious about the source of his income. Very often while turning the pages of a catalogue of scientific instruments, the pictures of instruments would excite him so much that he had to clutch the arm-rest of his chair to control his excitement. He bought expensive instruments from Germany and America which were not available even in the leading Indian universities of our country. The lack of facilities in the Indian universities irked him very much. He felt very sorry for the Indian students who were offered the leftovers from the feast of knowledge held in the western universities. The dry and drab textbooks were the only source of knowledge for the students of India. The lack of sophisticated instruments did not permit them to gain practical experience. Very often people heard him say in his booming voice, "We have plenty of talent, but what we don't have is money." He was determined to open the gates of the world of science for the Indian students. So, he started collecting rare and expensive instruments to fulfill his dream. His colleagues got jealous, their righteousness got the better of them and they complained against him. But his boss saved him from embarrassment. He respected Nandakishore for his talent. Moreover, his boss was of the opinion that siphoning off money for personal gains was a common practice in the railways especially in the higher echelons. But Nandakishore had to resign from his job after this.

He bought discarded wood and iron from the railways at a throw away price with the help of his boss and started his own factory. This was the time when Europe was in the middle of the First World War. The markets were doing very well. Nandakishore made full use of the situation and channeled money into his coffers from every possible avenue.

It was at this juncture that he was struck by a new obsession— a woman.

He had gone to Punjab in connection with his business. It was here that he met her.

One morning he was having tea sitting in the verandah when a twenty something attractive woman walked in without any hesitation swaying her long skirt. Her eyes were bright and the smile that played on her lips had the sharpness of a knife. Funnily enough she sat next to his feet and said, "*Babuji* (Sir) I have been watching you for the last few days and I have found you very fascinating."

Nanadakishore smiled and asked her, "how come? Don't you have a zoo here?"

She replied back, "There is no need for a zoo because those who should have been in are roaming around freely. I am looking for a human being."

"Did you find one?"

She pointed towards Nandakishore and said, "Yes I have found one."

Nandakishore smiled and said, "What did you find in me?"

She said, "The big business men of this place resplendent in their thick gold chains and diamond rings wanted to trap you. They had thought after all you are a Bengali, naïve in business dealings, but I noticed how adroitly you evaded all the traps laid by them, and trapped them instead; which they haven't realized as yet."

Nandakishore was surprised to hear this—what a woman he thought, an enigma no doubt! Difficult to fathom!

The girl said, "Let me tell you about myself. There is an astrologer in our neighbourhood and a famous one at that. He had gone through my horoscope and had said that I would be famous someday, but my ruling planet is Satan."

Nandakisore was surprised, he exclaimed, "Satan! Don't tell me!"

She said, "You know something Babuji? Actually, Satan has a big say in everything in this world. People might curse him, but he is true to his word. Look at our *Bom Bhlonath* (oblivious of everything, Lord shiva is often called by this name affectionately) Lord Shiva he is so doped most of the time that he cannot look into the day to day running of this world.

Look at our rulers, they have conquered nearly the whole world by their Satan-like power which, I am sure, has nothing to do with Christianity. But one thing that is there about them, and that is they are true to their word and that is why they have been able to keep their empire intact. The day they go back on their word Satan will deal with them and set them right."

Nandakishore was surprised.

The girl continued, "Babuji please do not get annoyed, I have seen a shade of Satan in you. You are going to win. I have fooled many males in the past. But this is the first time that I have come across a male who has the capability to defeat me. Babuji please don't let me go, please accept me, it will be a great loss for you otherwise."

Nandakishore smiled and said, "What do you want me to do?"

She said, "My grandmother is in debt, she will have to sell her house to clear her debts. You will have to clear her debt."

"How much?"

"Seven thousand rupees"

Nandakishore was surprised by her audacity, He said, "Suppose I give the money, but what happens after that?"

"After that I will never leave you."

"But what role will you play in my life?"

"I will make sure no one cheats you, other than me of course!"

Nandakishore smiled and said, "I give you, my word." He took off his ring and said, "Here's my ring, wear it."

Nandakishore was a great judge of people. Like a touch stone he could evaluate the worth of a person. The girl left an impression on the touch stone in his mind. He could make out that the girl was not a fake. Not only that the girl knew her true worth. Nandakishore   gave seven thousand rupees to her grandmother.

Her name was Sohini, and like a typical good looking North Indian woman she was tall, slim and fair. Her facial features were chiseled. Her looks did not impress Nandakishore though. He was not the kind of a man who would get swayed by good looks; he was too busy for that.

The place from where Nandakishore had brought her was not clean and healthy. But Nandakishore was a stubborn person. He did not care about dos and don'ts prevalent in the society and wagging tongues. When his friends asked him if he had got married to Sohini his reply was, "Sort of, only to an extent that we felt was necessary." It amused people when they found him educating Sohini and molding her so that she could become a true companion. When some of them asked him if he was going to make a professor out of her his reply to such people was, "I intend making a replica of myself. In a marriage both the parties should be on equal footing. I don't believe in unmatched marriages."

To some who could not understand, asked him to clarify, he would say, "It is unacceptable to me if the husband is an engineer and the wife just a homemaker who spends her time in cooking and looking after the house. I have been noticing mismatches between husbands and wives in many households. If you want a wife who is faithful to you then make sure that the two of you follow the same faith."

2

Nandakishor died in an accident while performing a dangerous experiment which went haywire. Sohini stopped all business activities after that. A lot of people came and gathered around her with the intention of cheating on her. Distant relations of Nandakishor started lawsuits against her. Sohini learnt the finer points of law pertaining to her problem and after that she used her feminine charm in the lawyers' quarters; she was a charmer par excellence. Soon she won all the cases against her put up by her husband's relatives. One of them even landed in jail because of submitting forged documents to the court.

They had a daughter, whom they had named Nilima which meant bluish glow, but her name did not match her complexion. She was very fair. Her mother used to say that her ancestors had come from Kashmir, and that is why her skin glowed like the white lotus of Kashmir. Her eyes were blue like the blue lotus. Her glossy hair was golden brown in colour. Nilima had shortened her name to Nila.

When the time came for her to get her daughter married Sohini realized that there was no question of getting her married in the conventional way because of uncertain caste and pedigree. The only way was to let cupid play his part. A young Marwari boy with a lot of inherited wealth and modern education fell into the trap laid by Cupid. One day Nila was waiting near her school gate for her car when the boy saw her. After that day he started strolling up and down in front of her school gate at school closure time. Nila caught on and she started waiting at the school gate much before the expected time of arrival of her car. After a while it was not only the Marwari fellow there were a few more young fortune seekers belonging to many other communities who started walking up and down in front of the gate. Among the lot it was only the Marwari boy who took the plunge and never returned again. It was a court marriage, which was not approved by his society. The marriage did not last long. Fate drew an end to their married life. Typhoid fever set him free.

Her mother noticed her restlessness and was reminded of her own state when she was her age. It worried her. Sohini tried to build a protective wall around her daughter by way of getting her interested in academics. She arranged for a highly educated lady tutor for her daughter. Nila's youthfulness affected her tutor too, and stirred up her mind. Nila's admirers kept coming only to be rebuffed by the barricade created by her mother. Women desirous of her company sent her invitations for tea, tennis, cinema…. but none of the invitations reached the addressee. Many aspirants buzzed around in the fragrant air to taste the nectar, but her mother was careful; she did not permit them to hover close to her daughter. But it was difficult to keep Nila under check as she was perpetually on the lookout for a chance.

Nila read books on the quiet which were not approved by her mother. On the pretext of collecting art material, she collected paintings bordering on obscenity. So much so that even her tutor got distracted by the paintings. One day while coming home from Diocesan school a love struck handsome young man threw a note into her car. The letter made her blood race. She hid the letter in her clothes, but unfortunately it was discovered by her mother. As a punishment she was locked up without food for the next twenty-four hours.

Sohini started looking around for a suitable groom for her daughter among the post graduate students who had been given scholarships by her husband. She was pained to notice that most of them had their eyes riveted on her money bag. One of them even dedicated his thesis to her. She mocked him and said, "You embarrass me young man. I hear that your post-graduation is coming to an end. And still, you are making your offerings to an unsuitable person who will not be of any use to you in future. Please make sure that you make your offerings at the right place and at the right time if you want to progress in life." A young man called Rebati Bhattacharya had come to Sohini's notice for some time. She found him suitable for her daughter. He was already a doctor of science and two of his papers had been adjudged well in some foreign universities.

3

Sohini was good at the art of socializing. Manmatha Chowdhury was one of Rebati's professors during his student days. Sohini got him under her thumb by frequent invitations to tea with tasty snacks of omelets, toast and fried Hilsa roe. One day she brought up the subject while serving fried Hilsa roe to him. She said, "You must be wondering as to why I call you to tea so often."

"I assure you, that is the least of my concerns, Mrs. Mullick."

Sohini said, "People say that I become friendly only when I have an axe to grind."

"Mrs. Mullick let me tell you whatever might be your intention behind getting friendly with me, to me friendship matters a great deal, it is of great value to me. And where is the harm if someone can gain something through friendship with me. Our category of people, the academicians, never get a chance to utilize their brains beyond the pale of academics; I believe fresh air is good for the brain. Well, I can see that you are amused, because you are smiling. Well, I can be droll at times. I think you should know this before you offer me another cup of tea."

"I am glad to know, and relieved at the same time. I have come across many professors, and it is really very difficult to extract a smile from them."

"Oh good, that means, the two of us think alike. Now tell me how can I help you?"

"You must be knowing that my husband's only joy was his laboratory. I don't have a son and I am looking for a suitable young man who can take over the laboratory and use it fruitfully. I have Rebati Bhattacharya on my mind."

The professor said, "You have chosen the right person, but the subject on which he is working would need a lot of money for its fruitful culmination."

Sohini said, "Well it doesn't matter at all. I have a lot of money in the bank waiting to be utilized. Widows of my age spend a lot of money on the brokers of various gods and goddesses to appease the divinity so that when the time comes, they get an easy entry to heaven. I do not believe in all that."

Manmatha opened his eyes wide and asked, "What do you believe in then!"

"If I can get a worthy individual, and hand over the laboratory to him, I will be in a position to pay off my husband's debts as much as I can. This is what I believe in and this is my religion."

"Hurray, this is an extraordinary case of stone floating on water. It is rare that one finds a spark of intelligence among beautiful women. So, you want to establish him in your laboratory, which happens to be a part of your house? Can't he work somewhere else a little away."

"Mr. Chowdhury please do not be mistaken, I am a woman and this laboratory is my husband's temple, his place of worship, if I can find a suitable person capable of keeping the lamp burning, it will make him happy wherever he happens to be at present."

"By Jove! I am hearing a woman speak at last. And I like it. But please remember one thing: if you want to support Rebati till the end, then your expenses will exceed a lakh."

"Don't worry I will still have something with me, to give me two square meals a day."

"And what about the person who you want to make happy. Hope it will not upset him! I have heard they have a lot of power."

"You read the newspaper every day, don't you? When a person dies don't, they write paragraph after paragraph overflowing with virtues of the person in the papers. There is no harm in believing in the dead man's greatness. But remember one thing: when a man accumulates a lot of wealth, he accumulates a lot of sin along with it. What is a wife there for if she cannot upturn the bags of money to lighten her husband's sins? I don't need the money; I have no use for it."

The professor got excited he said, "I really don't know what to say. Gold that is extracted from the mines is called pure gold though it is mixed with a lot of other things, you are purer than the purest gold. Wonder why you did not reveal your true worth so far. Now I know what you are! Tell me what I have to do."

175

"Please make the boy agree."

"I don't think that will be that simple. Anybody else would have jumped at your offer, but not him."

"Where is the problem?"

"Right from his childhood his life has been under the influence of a female. Who by her ignorance and stubbornness has been a hurdle in his path of progress."

"What do you mean?"

"See Mrs. Mullick, you must have heard about matriarchal societies of South, in which women have an upper hand. Once upon a time the waves of this Dravidian custom swayed the Bengali society too."

She said, "Alas that Golden era is long gone; though the custom of female supremacy might still be there in certain quarters of our society, strong enough to confuse a weak minded male, but by enlarge the rudder is in the hands of males. They are the ones who whisper into our ears what is right and what is wrong. We get our ears boxed when we stray from the path laid out by them. At times the pull on our ears is strong enough to tear them away."

"Really you have a way with words Mrs. Mullick, but honestly if times change and people like you start a matriarchal society I will gladly look after the ladies' laundry and send our college principal to pound paddy. Learned people say that matriarchy in Bengal runs in the blood of the Bengali males. Otherwise have you heard of males of any other race utter 'Ma ma' so frequently like a mooing calf! It is only prevalent in Bengal. Let me inform you Rebati's life is controlled by a woman"

"Is he in love with someone?"

"That would have been very good had it been so. This is the right age for him to fall head over heels in love with a young woman, but instead of that he has become a bead in the rosary of a pious old woman. There is no hope for him, his youth, his intellect, his knowledge …..... nothing can save him."

"Can I call him for tea? Will he have tea with us? After all, he may not consider us to be clean enough to have tea with. He is a Brahmin after all."

"Unclean! If he refuses to come, I will clean him nice and proper like a washerman, so that every ounce of Brahmanism gets washed off from him. Let me ask you something, you have a beautiful daughter, don't you?"

"Yes, I do have a daughter and she is a widow, the unfortunate thing happens to be very beautiful. There is nothing much that I can do about it."

"No, no please do not misunderstand me. Frankly speaking I like good looking women; you could call it affliction. But his relatives might get unnerved."

"But don't worry, I am planning to get her married in our own community."

(Which was a barefaced lie!)

"But you have got married outside your community."

"I had suffered a great deal because of that. I had to fight with the relatives of my late husband in court, and only I know what all I had to do to defeat them."

"I know a bit about it. There was a rumour floating about the articled clerk of the other party. You won the case and left the scene after that, but the poor chap was on the verge of committing suicide!"

Sohini was quiet.

The professor continued, "I think you have misunderstood me. I am a scientist and not a judge. I was an onlooker when that happened, so I did not take any sides. The game took its own course. When you won the game, I gave full credit to you and thanked my lucky stars at the same time that I am a professor and not an articled clerk. The distance of Mercury from the Sun has helped the planet to survive. There is nothing good or bad about it, just plain mathematics. I am sure you've understood by now."

"Yes, I know, planetary movements are governed by the laws of attraction and repulsion, and that is something worth learning."

"I want to confess something to you. While talking to you I have realized had I been younger by ten years or so I would have certainly got into big trouble today. The collision was avoided by a few inches. But I can still feel the surge of steam rising inside me! The entire creation is controlled by mathematics."

Professor Chowdhury slapped his knee and burst into a hearty laughter at his own joke. But one thing, that he did not know is that Sohini had spent about two hours before his arrival in making herself appear younger. Maybe, she could have cheated the creator too.

4

The next day the professor found her drying a skinny mangy dog with a towel after bathing it.

"What is the reason behind your honouring this mangy dog?" Asked Chowdhury

"That is because I saved him. He had broken his leg after coming under a motor car, I had picked him up and had nursed him, so I have a strong claim on him."

"But tell me something, won't it upset you to see this horrible ill-fated canine every day?"

"Not at all, I haven't kept him in my house to admire his looks. The fact that he has come out from the jaws of death makes me feel good. I provide him with things that ensure that he continues to live, and he spares me of the ordeal of dragging a poor lamb to *Kali* temple and sacrificing him to absolve myself of my sins. I have decided to open a hospital to treat the maimed dogs, rabbits and other animals which come out of your laboratories after you people finish off with them."

"You surprise me Mrs. Mullick. I discover something new in you every time I meet you!"

"You will get used to it when you see me more often. But have you got in touch with Rebati? Did you get to know anything about him?"

"Well, I am distantly related to him; I know a bit about his family. His mother died soon after his birth. Rebati was brought up by his aunt (father's sister). She is a very strict person, and a great one at following rules. Hell breaks loose in the house if there is any digression from the rules laid down by her. There is not a single person in the household who is not terrorized by her. Poor Rebati was reduced to a pulp in her hands, in his childhood if he was five minutes late in coming back from school, he used to get bombarded by a volley of questions from her, a little short of court martial."

Shohini said, "I thought males discipline and females pamper their wards and that keeps the balance right."

The professor said, "Have you seen a swan walk? It sways from side to keep its balance similarly females too sway from side it is only very few who walk erect with their heads on their shoulders. For instance...."

"You need not say anymore. You can make out that I am very much a typical woman till my roots and my latest need is to catch a certain young man. Otherwise, I wouldn't have bothered you."

"Please don't keep saying the same thing over and over again. I have come today without preparing for my class and I am enjoying this dereliction of duty."

"I must say you are partial to the fairer sex."

"Quite possible, but a shade more partial towards certain members of the sex. We will talk about it on some other occasion."

"You need not tell me, but let us finish what we had started discussing. Tell me how Rebati did so well in academics."

"He could have achieved much more. Once he had to do some research work at high altitude. He had chosen Badrinath as a place for his work. Pandemonium broke out when his aunt came to know about it. It seems Rebati's aunt had an aunt who had died on the way to Badrinath. So Rebati's aunt gave a standing order to him, 'As long as I am alive you will not go to any hills or mountains,' since that day I have hoped and wished for something. I better not talk about it, and forget about it for the time being."

"But why are you blaming the aunt? When will this darling nephew develop a strong back bone?"

"I've told you before, matriarchy makes them weak and confused so much that they start mooing like motherless calves. That was the first incident, the second one was when Rebati got a scholarship from the government to study in Cambridge university. Hell broke loose when she came to know about it, she approached Rebati howling and crying. She had presumed that Rebati was going abroad to marry a *memsahab* (fair skinned European woman). I had said, 'so what even if he does?' That was a grave mistake, what was a presumption became a conviction as though Rebati was already engaged to some lady abroad. The aunt said, 'if Rebati goes abroad I will hang myself'. I am an atheist, so I did not know which God to pray to so that a suitable rope could be spun for the purpose. Ultimately there was no need to procure the rope as Rebati did not go abroad. I called him all kinds of names for his foolishness like, 'Stupid, dunce, imbecile' and so on. Right now, he is trying his level best to go ahead with his research work which can be compared to extracting oil drop by drop from a *ghani* (manual oil extractor)."

This angered Sohini she said, "I feel like dashing my head against the wall. Well, one woman all but drowned Rebati, now just watch another woman rescue him and land him on the shore. I take a pledge to do so."

The professor said, "Well madam you have been adept in holding the poor animals by their horns and drowning them, but you are not so experienced in pulling up the poor creatures by their tails. You might as well start practicing from now onwards. May I ask you something? How did you develop such an abiding interest in science?"

"All branches of science interested my husband, he was completely devoted to them, Other than science he was addicted to Burma cheroot. He had introduced me to them and had almost converted me to a Burmese woman. I gave it up later when I realized that men are not used to seeing a woman smoke. Men mesmerize women by making fools out of them, but my husband had mesmerized me by his knowledge. Mr. Chowdhury, a husband's weakness can never be hidden from a wife, but I found no weakness in him. When I saw him from close proximity, I felt that he was a great man. Today when I see him from a distance, I feel that he was greater."

"What was it that attracted you the most?" asked the professor.

"What attracted me the most was his unattached devotion to knowledge. He was totally submerged in it. We women need a well-defined object like an idol to worship. His laboratory is my place of worship. Sometimes even, I feel like lighting incense sticks and make offerings of flower and ring bells like one does in a temple. But I know that he would hate it. His way of worshiping was different. In this, students flocked around him, and he taught them for hours together and guided them to work with the instruments in his laboratory. I joined those sessions."

"Don't tell me! Could they concentrate?"

"All those who could concentrate, they progressed. I have seen students who were calm and dispassionate like ascetics, while others would try to snuggle close in the ruse of sharing notes. Some even wrote long letters and discussed literature."

"How did it feel?"

"Frankly speaking 'not bad', after my husband left for work and a few romantic ones used to buzz around me."

"Please don't mind, I am interested in psychology, that is why I am asking you; did they succeed in their venture?"

"I don't call myself tainted. But there were a couple of them among those people, who left a deep impact on me, my heart still aches when I think about them."

"A couple of them!"

"The mind is greedy. It keeps the fire of greed hidden inside the body, which flares up on slight prodding. I am not afraid of revealing that I had earned a bad name when I was young. We women do not live like sages all our lives. And we find it difficult to pretend to be what we are not. There are times when *Droupadis* and *Kuntis* had to behave like *Sitas* and *Savitris* (Droupadi and Kunti are characters from the epic Mahabhrata. Droupadi had five husbands and Kunti had four sons; her eldest son was born when she was still a maiden and three younger ones were fathered by people other than her husband. Yet they were considered to be great women. Whereas Sita and Savitri were known for their virtue and dedication to their husbands). Mr. Chowdhury what is right and what is not, were not made clear to me in my childhood. I had no Guru. Thus, plunging into what is considered bad was normal for me. Fortunately, I managed to swim across. It blemished my body, but not my mind. Nothing could cling on to me. His funeral fire cleansed me of all my sins, I have no greed left in me."

"Bravo you did not flinch even once while speaking the truth! What guts!"

"It becomes easy when there is a person who can make you speak the truth. You are so straight forward and so truthful."

Do those boys who wrote letters to you and received favours from you, still come to you?"

"That is how they have cleansed my heart. I noticed that they had gathered around me with their eyes trained on my cheque book. They thought, just because I am a woman, I will not get over my weakness towards them and they will take advantage of the situation and reach the money. What they did not realize is that I am a realist and not a romantic. My Punjabi origin has made me a realist. I can get carried away by the requirements of the flesh and do away with the norms of the society, but I can't be a traitor to my faith. They didn't get a single penny that was meant for the laboratory. My heart has become like a stone that guards the doors of my lord's temple. No one can reach there as long as I am guarding it. The one who chose me did not make a mistake."

"I bow to him. I will certainly box the ears of those seekers of money when I meet them next."

Before leaving, Sohini took the professor around the laboratory.

He said, "Your feminine intelligence has sieved out the unwanted elements and has given the true spirit a chance."

Sohini said, "Whatever you say I still feel apprehensive. Feminine intelligence is a creation of the almighty. When one is young the mind is strong, but when we grow old and our blood cools down the traditional aunt hiding inside us comes out. I want to die before that."

The professor said "You don't have to worry about that, you will die in your full senses."

5

Wearing a white sari with her salt and pepper hair, powdered white Sohini had an aura of pristine purity about her. She took her daughter with her and they came to the Botanical- garden of Calcutta in a motor launch. She had dressed her daughter in a bluish green *Benarasi* sari and a yellow blouse which shone through her sari. There was a small dot of red *kumkum* on her forehead and a faint line of *kajal* outlining her eyes. Her feet were shod in black leather sandals with red velvet work. Her hair was tied in a loose bun which hung at the nape of her neck.

Sohini had found out that Rebati spent his Sundays in a *akashneem* (millingtonia) grove in the botanical garden. Sohini landed up there and touched his feet with extreme reverence. This embarrassed Rebati, he got up in a haste.

Sohini said, "Please don't mind son, you are a Brahmin and I am a *Khatriya's* daughter (*Brahmin* is the highest caste in the Hindu caste hierarchy and *khtriya* is lower than *Brahmin*). You must have heard about me from professor Chowdhury."

"Yes, he told me about you. But where can I make you sit?"

"Why this lovely green grass! No place can be better than this. You must be wondering as to why I have come here. I have come here to fulfill something that I had promised myself. I will never find a *Brahmin* like you who can help me."

Rebati was surprised, he said, "A *Brahmin* like me?"

"Yes, you are. My Guru had told me that the best *Brahmin* today is the one who has the best knowledge of the most important subject of our times –science."

Rebati looked embarrassed, he said, "My father was a *Brahmin* priest, but I had very little to do with it. I have no knowledge of mantras and rituals."

"Oh my God what are you saying? The mantras that you know are the ones that have helped man to conquer the universe. You must be wondering how a woman can talk like the way I am talking, believe me I learnt to talk like this from a great man, my husband. Please promise me to come to the seat of his meditation someday."

"I will come tomorrow in the morning. I am free at that time."

"It delights me to see that plants and trees interest you. Once my husband had gone to Burma in search of plants and I had tagged along with him."

Actually, she had accompanied him not because of her interest in botany. The dregs that were there in her mind used to surface at times and that made her suspicious of her husband's motives and that was the reason behind accompanying her husband. Once when Nandakishore was very ill, he had said, "One good thing about dying is that I will be going to a place where you will not be able to find me and bring me back."

She had said, "At least I can accompany you."

Nandakishore had smiled and said, "Dear me!"

"I had brought a flowering plant from there. The Burmese call it Kkozaitaniyeng, the flowers of the plant are beautiful, but unfortunately, I could not save the plant."

183

Sohini had searched her husband's library that morning and had found out about the plant, she had not seen the plant ever in her life. She knew that the only way to trap an erudite person is to spread a network of knowledge around him.

Rebati was surprised he said, "Do you know the Latin name?"

She said, "It is called *Millettia*", without blinking an eyelid, and went on to say, "My husband had very little to do with traditional beliefs, but one thing that he believed blindly and that is if a woman during the period of her special condition fills up her mind with all good things in nature her children will be beautiful. Do you share the same belief?"

It suffices to say that all this was Sohini's own creation Nandakishore, did not believe in such things.

Rebati scratched his head and said, "Sufficient proof has not been gathered to support this hypothesis so far."

Sohini said, "I've got one proof in my own family. Otherwise, how could my own daughter be so beautiful? She is like a beautiful garland made of spring flowers…. I will not say anymore you will have to see her to believe me."

Rebati looked eager to see her. The stage was made ready by her for the next scene. She called her *Brahmin* cook dressed up like a priest and said, "*Thakur* (the way of addressing brahmins) please bring Nilu."

Sohini had left Nilu in the steam launch and it was decided to present Nilu at the right time. She would climb up the steps holding a basket in her hand. And Rebati would get ample time to see her in the dappled morning light.

In the meanwhile, as Rebati awaited the arrival of Nila, Sohini got a chance to scrutinize Rebati's looks. He was dark, but his complexion was smooth with a tinge of pale yellow in it. His hair was brushed backwards and he had a broad forehead. His eyes were not large, but very bright and they attracted a person at the first glance. His face was round which gave him a soft look. One thing that she had learnt from the information that she had gathered about Rebati was that his childhood friends had a sentimental affection for him. The charm that he had about his face spoke of weakness and that could be the reason behind the affection of his boyhood friends.

That jolted Sohini a bit. She believed that a man need not be handsome to reach a woman's heart, she did not consider it to be important for a man to be intelligent and erudite to win a woman's heart what mattered most is the male magnetism. The invisible waves that emanate from within a man and speak of arrogant desire.

She was reminded of the time when she was growing up. The person who had attracted her was not from a reputed family, he was not good looking, not even highly educated, but an invisible warmth that emanated from within him touched her which led her to feel the intense masculine appeal of the person. Sohini was disturbed by the thought that there will be a time when her daughter too would experience such a turmoil in her life the thought of this worried her.

The last part of youth is the most dangerous time of life for anybody. Sohini's tireless quest for knowledge had kept busy at that time. Fortunately, Sohini's intellect was just right for such abstract studies. Nila did not have the same bent of mind. Her mind was not enlightened enough.

By and by Nila walked up the steps and appeared on the quay. The morning sunlight touched her forehead and her hair and the gold work on her *Benarasi* sari shone in the mellow morning light. Rebati looked up and in one glance took in everything. After that he lowered his eyes. He had been taught right from his childhood that 'beautiful women are temptresses they steal your heart', his aunt's admonitions and warnings had deprived him the pleasure of watching them and getting to know them. That is why whenever he got a chance, he had to satisfy himself with one quick look."

Sohini was disappointed by him, she said, "Oh look! Isn't she looking beautiful!"

Rebati was startled by what he heard, he raised head and saw her once again.

She said, "See doctor how beautifully the colour of her sari is matching with the colour of the leaves!"

"Wonderful!" Said Rebati after a bit of hesitation.

"Really he is incorrigible," Sohini said this to herself and then she said loudly, "Tell me which flower does she remind you of, a hint of yellow underneath and bluish green on top."

Rebati was encouraged by this, he took a good look at her and said, "I am reminded of one flower but the outer petals are brown and not blue."

"Which flower? Asked Sohini."

Rebati said, "Gmelina."

"Oh, I have got it. A flower with five petals, one of them is bright yellow while others are dark in colour."

Rebati said, "It surprises me! How do you know so much about flowers?"

Sohini smiled and said, "Why son aren't we women supposed to know about flowers other than the flowers that are used for worshipping different deities?"

Nila walked up to them slowly and hesitatingly holding a basket and stood at a distance from them. Her mother said, "Please join us, why are you standing there so shyly, but before that you must touch his feet."

Rebati got perturbed and said, "No no please don't." He was sitting cross legged on the ground, she took some time to find his feet to touch them. Her touch made him shiver.

Her basket contained rare orchids and sweets of different kinds arranged on silver platters.

Sohini said, "All this has been made by Nila."

There was no element of truth in it. Nila neither had the aptitude nor the desire to do such things. The sweets had been procured from a well- known sweet shop in *burra* bazaar (a market in Calcutta).

Sohini said, "Please son have some, they have been prepared for you."

Rebati folded his hands and said, "Please do not ask me to eat. I don't eat at this time of the day. If you permit me, I can take them home."

Sohini said, "That's a good idea, even my husband was against forcing people to eat when they didn't want to. He used to say human beings can't eat like pythons."

Sohini arranged the sweets in a tiffin carrier. She asked her daughter to arrange the flowers so that Rebati could carry them home. She said, "Segregate the flowers properly so that one variety does not get mixed up with another. And please cover the flowers with the silk scarf with which you have tied your hair."

The scientist became an art enthusiast. He watched Nila's shapely fingers playing amidst the flowers of different colours and was transported to a world far removed from reality. He looked at Nila's face intermittently. On one side the face was bordered by a gold chain strung with pearls, rubies and emeralds clipped to her hair on the other side it was framed by the red piping of her yellow blouse which could be seen through her sari. Sohini was arranging the sweets, but she was aware of   what was going on. Her inner eye had caught on to the magical spell that her daughter had cast on Rebati.

6

The next day Sohini sent a message to the professor to meet her. When he came, she said, "I have been calling you very often for selfish reasons, which must have hampered your work."

He said, "Please call me more often. It makes me feel good if I can do anything for you. But it would be even better if you call me when there is nothing for me to do."

"You must be knowing that my husband was crazy about buying the latest scientific equipment for his laboratory so much so that he cheated his company to procure these machines, purely for unselfish reasons. He was working towards making this laboratory the best in Asia. I was inspired by him and got drawn into this. This helped me to maintain my equilibrium all these years otherwise the blood that runs through me would have led me astray. Mr. Chowdhury you are a friend with whom I can discuss without any hesitation about the evil that is still clinging on to me. The fact that I can discuss with you freely about my wrong doings and that gives me a lot of relief."

Chowdury said, "We the scientists are used to seeing things in totality. Half-truth is confusing, so you need not hide anything from me, I will understand.

My husband used to say, "People hold their lives precious and want to protect it forever which is not possible. So, they look around for something which is more precious than their lives. This laboratory was more precious to him than his own life. If I don't protect this laboratory then I will be the killer of my own husband. That is why I was looking for someone who will protect the laboratory. Rebati is the ideal candidate."

"Did you try convincing him?"

"Yes, I did try and I am hopeful. But I may not succeed ultimately."

"Why."

"The moment Rebati's aunt hears about it, she will come running and snatch him away. She will think that I have laid a trap to get Rebati married to my daughter."

"No harm done; it will be good if they get married, but if I remember correctly, you had once said that you will get your daughter married in your own community."

"Yes, I had said so because at that juncture I did not know what you thought about the matter. I had lied. In fact, I was very keen to have Rebati as my son-in-law. But now I have given up the idea. I have realized that she will ruin everything. She is capable of utter destruction."

"But she is your daughter."

"Yes, she is my daughter and that is why I know her inside out."

The professor said, "But you must not forget the fact that women are capable of inspiring men."

"Men are fine as long as they don't get addicted to alcohol, but my daughter happens to be a goblet brimming full of wine."

"What would you like to do?"

"I want to give away this laboratory to the public."

"You will be depriving your only daughter!"

"My daughter! If she inherits the laboratory then I do not know which abyss she would push it into. I would like to make Rebati, the president of the trust that I am planning to form. I am sure his aunt will not object to that."

"Many a times I cannot understand the rationale behind a woman's objection, maybe that is why I have been born as a man. But what escapes me is that you don't want him as your son-in-law, but at the same time you want to make him the president of the trust! Why is it so?"

"The instruments are lying lifeless; I want to instill life in them. I need a suitable man to do that. After my husband's death, not a single new instrument has been bought. There is no dearth of money, but there should be an aim behind procurement of new instruments. I have heard that he is working on magnetism. New instruments can be brought to facilitate his research. Money will not be a constraint."

"I really don't know what to say! Had you been a man I would have danced around, with you on my shoulders. Your husband stole money from the rail company, but you stole his brains, I have not seen such an ideal graft of two brains. I am surprised that you've consulted with me."

"That is because you are unalloyed, and you always say the right thing."

"You make me laugh! I am not a fool to say the wrong things to you and get caught. Let's get down to brass tacks. Firstly, the list of the assets has to be made and evaluated and after that, you will have to contact a good lawyer who will settle your rights and frame the rules and a lot of other things."

"Please Mr. Chowdhury, you will have to look after all that from now onwards."

"That will be for name's sake only. You know very well, I will do what you want me to do and say what you will want me to say. As a fringe benefit, I will get to see you every day. I wonder if you know about the feelings that I have for you."

Sohini got up from her chair, walked up quickly to Chowdhury put her arms around his neck, kissed his cheek and went back to her seat as though nothing had happened.

"Goodness gracious! That marks the beginning of my ruination."

"I wouldn't have gone that close if there was any possibility of what you fear. You will be treated in the same fashion off and on."

"Are you sure!"

"Yes, I am sure. I don't lose much. And the expression on your face tells me that you don't gain much either."

"You mean to say like, a woodpecker pecking on dead wood …. Well, I am leaving to see a lawyer."

"Will you come to here tomorrow?"

"Why? For what?"

"To wind-up Rebati a bit."

"And lose my heart in the process."

"Do you think you are the only one who has a heart?"

"Do you have any?"

"Yes, plenty of it is left."

"Yes, enough to make a lot of monkeys dance around you!"

7

Rebati came to the laboratory at least twenty minutes before time. Sohini was not ready. She came out in haste dressed in her everyday clothes. Rebati realized that he had made a mistake. He said, "My watch is not showing the right time."

"So, it seems," said Sohini. She sounded cut and dry.

A sound attracted Rebati's attention and he looked up eagerly. It was Sukhan the servant who had come to give her the keys of the glass cases.

Sohini said, "Should I ask him to bring a cup of tea for you?"

Rebati wanted to say no, but he said, "No harm done," instead.

Poor Rebati, he was not used to drinking tea, only when he suffered from cold, he took hot water with wood apple leaves boiled in it. He had expected Nila to come with a cup of tea for him.

Sohini asked, "Do you like strong tea?"

He said, "Yes." Without thinking.

He thought that saying yes was the custom. When the tea arrived, it was strong, dark like ink and bitter like Neem leaves. The tea was brought by the Muslim *Khansama* (butler). Actually, this was done to test Rebati. Though he was not comfortable about being served by a Muslim, he did not say anything. Sohini did not like his hesitation, she said, "The tea is getting cold please pour it out Mobarak."

Poor Rebati, he hadn't come twenty minutes before time to be served tea by a Muslim butler. Only God knew and so did Sohini how he felt when he raised the cup of bitter tea to his lips. She noticed his plight and took pity on him. She said, "Leave the cup of tea. I will pour some milk for you. And ask them to bring some fruits for you. You have come so early; most likely you haven't eaten anything." It was true that he hadn't eaten anything before coming. Rebati had thought that it would be a repetition of the botanical garden, but it was far from it. The bitter taste of tea lingered in his mouth and the bitter experience of broken hopes troubled his heart.

It was at this juncture that the professor entered the room. He said, "What's the matter with you man! All gone cold! Here I find you drinking milk like a little girl. You think you are sitting in a toy shop surrounded by toys! Let me tell you it is a sacred place where great things have happened in the past! People who have the right bent of mind have even seen *Shiva's* followers doing *Tandava* (Shiva's dance of fury) here."

"Professor why are you scolding him? He has come without eating anything. He looked as though he needed some refreshment which is why I offered him milk."

"Oh my God! Here comes aunt number two. One aunt slaps him on one cheek, the other one plants a kiss on the other cheek. Poor chap! At this rate, sandwiched between the two of you he will become like a handful of soft clay.   Remember when Lakshmi, the goddess of good fortune comes unasked and if one does not take notice of her she goes to those people who go all over the world in search of good fortune. Now tell me Mrs..... Oh, let us do away with Mrs.   I am going to call you Sohini, and I don't care if it makes you angry."

"Oh my God! Why should I get angry, but why call me Sohini, I would I love it if you call me Suhi."

"Well let me share a secret with you. There is another name which rhymes with your name and it is very meaningful (the other name is Mohini, which means enchanting). When I wake up in the morning both the names ring in my ears like a duet."

"This must be a side effect of you research in chemistry, in which you make new compounds by binding different elements."

"Some of them are highly combustible I know of people who have lost their lives while dealing with it." He laughed loudly after saying this. And then he continued, "No, no one should not discuss all this in front of a young person. He hasn't done apprenticeship in a gunpowder factory as yet. He has been under his aunt's protection so far."

Rebati's feminine face had turned red with embarrassment.

The professor said, "Sohini I was about to ask you if you have served opium to him this morning otherwise why was he looking so dopey?"

"I must have given him some inadvertently."

"Hey Rebi (short form of Rebati) please wake up and say something. You should not be so quiet in the company of woman. It encourages them if you remain quiet. They are like disease; they look for your weakness and once they find a chink in your amour they enter and make your temperature rise. I am here to caution young people like you. One must learn from a person like me who has been bitten, but is still alive. Rebi my son, people who do not talk and remain quiet are very dangerous, please don't mind my saying this. Now let me take you around the laboratory.

Those two galvanometers over there they are of the latest variety. That is a high vacuum pump and this one you see is a micro photometer. Please, don't be mistaken, they are not light rafts that help you pass your exams. These instruments are of great importance. I can imagine how peeved you professor would be when you settle down to work in this place. I mean the one with a bald pate I don't want to take his name. I had felt when you started as my student, that a great future awaits you, but I hadn't told you. Please don't let this opportunity slip. And when they write your biography if my name appears in the foot note of the first chapter of the book I will consider it to be a *Gurudakshna* (fees paid to a teacher after completion of studies)."

The Scientist woke up from his somnolent state. His eyes brightened up. There was a change in his visage. Sohini looked at him with admiration. She said, "Those who know you they all wish you great success in your life. This does not happen very often. This certainly increases the magnitude of your impediments both inside as well as outside."

The professor slapped Rebati on his back as an encouragement, but the impact was so great that it shook him. The professor's voice reverberated when he said, "Rebi you are the harbinger of a great future, you should come riding on *Airawat* (elephant of Indra, the king of Gods), but this miserly present moment has given you a bullock cart to ride on, which gets stuck in slushy roads. Sohini…. Suhi? …. Oh no don't worry I won't slap you on your back, but tell me have I said the right thing."

"Yes absolutely."

"Please note it down in your diary, not word should be missed."

"I will."

"I hope I have made it amply clear Rebi."

"I think I have understood."

"Please remember greater the talent bigger is the responsibility. Talent is not your personal property it is a gift given to you by God thus you are answerable to eternity. Are you listening Suhi? Have I managed to express myself properly!"

"You have spoken very well in olden times the king would have honoured you by taking off his necklace and putting it round your neck."

"But that was in the past."

Rebati said, "You don't have to worry, nothing will make me weak."

He bent down to touch Sohini's feet. Sohini stopped him half way.

Chowdhury said, "Oh no you shouldn't have stopped him. It was a good act. Preventing someone from doing a god act is incorrect."

Sohini said, "If you at all have to pay obeisance it should be there." She pointed towards a bust of Nanadakishore on an altar, with a tray heaped with flowers and incense sticks burning in front."

She said I have read in the *Puranas* (scriptures) that sinners were saved by great men. Well, I was saved by this great person. He had to go down pretty low to pick me up from where I was wallowing. And in end he made me worthy to sit…. I would be wrong if I said beside him… to sit at his feet. He led me on the path of knowledge and that was my salvation. He also warned me not to give away the precious gems that he had collected all his life to the daughter or the son-in-law who may not be worthy. He had said, "This is where I am leaving my spiritual salvation—my country's salvation."

The professor said, "Heard what she said Rebu? This is going to become a trust and you will be given the responsibility of running it."

Rebati objected, he said, "I don't think I am worthy of it. I won't able to do it. I have been busy with academics I have no experience in administration."

The professor said, "No duck ever swam before hatching out of egg. Your shell will break today."

Sohini said, "Don't worry I will be there with you."

This reassured Rebati and he left the place looking relieved.

Sohini fixed her eyes on the professor. He said, "There are many kinds of fools on this earth the male fool tops the list. But you must remember one thing a person can prove his worth only when he is given a responsibility. A man is born with a pair of hands and that qualifies him to be a man, if he was given a pair of hooves instead, he would have grown a tail automatically to match it. Have you seen a pair of hooves on Rebati?"

"I am not feeling comfortable with the present situation. Men who have been brought up by women never shed their milk tooth. It's just my misfortune why did I think of someone else, when you are there."

"Makes me happy to hear that, but tell me which good quality did you find in me?"

"You are not greedy."

"I consider it to be a disqualification. You mean to say I don't covet things that are worthy of being coveted! I do...."

But even before he could complete the sentence, she kissed both his cheeks.

He said, "On which account should I bring it on charge?"

She said, "I am indebted to you so much that I don't think I will be able to repay it. This is just the interest."

"On the first day I got one, today I got two, will it keep increasing this way?"

"Yes, it will be compounded!"

8

Chowdhury said, "Sohini ultimately you have made me the priest to conduct your husband's *shraddha* (a ceremony which is conducted after death of a person to pay respect to the departed soul). What a responsibility! To please someone who is beyond your reach is really a stupendous task. Very unusual…"

"But you not an ordinary priest. Whatever you decide to do, will be considered as a ritual. I hope everything is ready! I mean the *dansamagri* (offerings)?"

"Yes, that is exactly what I have been doing all these days. I have got everything arranged in the big room downstairs. The people who would receive them will be very happy no doubt."

Sohini went down stairs along with Chowdhury and found books instruments and microscopes arranged neatly with tags bearing the names of the recipients and their address. Cheques had been kept ready which would be given to two hundred and fifty students as their stipend for one year. Everything had been looked into, till the minutest detail. The expense amounted much more than what is spent on a rich man's *Shraddha*, but it did not appear ostentatious."

"But what will be the fee of the head priest? You haven't told me that." She asked.

"Your happiness Sohini."

"You have made me very happy no doubt, but I want to give you something to express my happiness.   It is a chronometer; my husband had got it from Germany, he used it for his research work."

"I am overwhelmed. I really don't how to express my gratitude. I have got my fees"

"There is a person who I cannot forget till date--- Manik."

"Now, who is this Manik?"

"He was the best mechanic of my husband's laboratory. He was very good at his work. His accuracy was such that he did not deviate even by a hair's breadth. He had a head for machines and could understand the working of machines in no time. My husband treated him like a friend. He took him in his car when he visited factories so that Manik could learn something. But unfortunately, he was an alcoholic and my husband's assistants used to look down upon him for that. My husband used to say that Manik's talent was in- born. Something that one cannot acquire through training. He respected Manik. This might help you understand as to why he honoured me. He understood my true worth. I have a lot of flaws but he must have discovered, that the good part in me far surpassed the bad part. He trusted a foundling like me and I have never betrayed his trust and I am still doing it with my heart and soul. He over looked my weakness and honoured my strength. Had he not discovered my true worth can you imagine in which abyss I would be at present? You might find many faults in me, but I must be having some very strong and good points in me otherwise he wouldn't have tolerated me."

"Sohini, right from the first day that I met you, I felt that you are a genuinely good person. Had you been good in the ordinary sort of way the taint wouldn't have gone off so easily."

"Anyway, whatever people may think about me, I am proud of the fact that I have been honoured by him, and that will remain with me till my last day."

"Sohini the more I am getting to know you I am realizing that you are not the kind of a woman who would become emotional at the mere mention of husband's name."

"No, I am not of that kind, I had felt the power that he had in him, he was a real man, thus I didn't have to follow the examples of the revered women in scriptures to prove my devotion to him. Only he deserved me no one else."

Nila entered the room at this point. She said, "Professor if you don't mind, I want to talk to my mother alone."

"Not at all dear! I was about to go the laboratory and find out how Rebati is getting on with his work."

"Don't worry. His work is going on well, said Nila, "I watch him once in a while quietly through a window and find him deep in his work oblivious of everything around him, writing, taking down notes and at times biting his pen and thinking.... that place is out of bounds for me because nothing should disturb 'Sir Isaac's center of gravity' I mean concentration. I heard ma telling someone that he is working on magnetism. May be for that reason she doesn't allow anyone specially women to enter his work- place lest the needle gets deflected."

Chowdhury laughed loudly and said, "My dear there is a laboratory right inside us where research on magnetism is going on forever. One has to be careful about people who can deflect the needle. After all, one should not lose the sense of direction! Okay I am off to the laboratory."

After Chowdhury's departure Nila faced her mother and said, "Ma how long are you going to tie me to your *aanchal*. You know that you will not be successful and end up being unhappy."

"Tell me what do you want?" asked Sohini.

Nila said, "A new higher study movement has been launched. You have contributed a lot of money for the venture. How about letting me work there?"

"I have feeling that you will be a hindrance to their work."

"Do you feel that stopping all my activities is the best option?"

"No definitely not, and this worries me."

"Ma for God's sake let me do my own worrying. Some day or the other you will have to leave me alone; I am no longer a child. You must be thinking that I will be interacting with all kinds of people which is not safe for me. Ma, people don't move as per your wishes. And no law can stop me from getting to know people."

"I know that. My fears cannot stop things from happening. You want to join 'Higher study circle' do you?

"Yes, I do."

"Okay go ahead, I know that you will drive the male teachers of the institution astray. But you will have to give me your word that you will stay clear of Rebati. And you will not enter the laboratory under any pretext."

"Ma what do you think I am? You think I will go anywhere close to that miniature Sir Isaac Newton of yours? He is definitely not of my kind."

After that she mimicked Rebati , the way he squirmed when he felt embarrassed, Nila continued, "I am not interested in men of that kind. You can keep him for women who love molly coddling grown up little boys."

"I think you are over doing it, and I feel, that you are not speaking your mind. I don't care about whatever you have in your mind, but I will not forgive you if you come in between him and his work!"

"Ma it is really difficult to understand you. Some time back you were so keen to get me married to him that you dolled me up and paraded me in front of him, do you think that I did not understand. And now you are telling me not to go anywhere close to him. Wonder why!"

"Let me tell you this Nila, I will never let you get married to Rebati."

"Then in that case, what if I get married to the Prince of Motigarh?"

"You can get married to any one you feel like."

"Advantageous for me. He has three wives already. My responsibilities will be less. He usually gets drunk and disorderly in night clubs; I will get a lot of time to do whatever I feel like doing."

"Good, that will be the best solution. In any case I am not going to let you marry Rebati."

"But why ma, you think I will make his brains go all hay wire?"

"I don't want to argue any more, but please remember what I said."

"But what if he comes after me?"

"Should that happen, he will have to leave, this place…. You people will have to fend for your selves. He will not get a penny from your father's money."

"Oh my god! Bye-bye then Sir Isaac Newton!"

The curtains came down after that for the day.

9

"Mr. Choudhury everything is going on well my only problem is my daughter. I am worried about her I just can't make out what is she aiming at."

Choudhury replied back, "You should be worried about who all are aiming for her. People are talking about the huge amount of money left by your husband for the up-keep of the laboratory. The amount is increasing by leaps and bounds as the news is travelling from one person to another. People are laying bets on who will win the hand of the princess and get the kingdom finally."

"I know one thing; the princess would be won over very easily. But the kingdom will not change hands till I am alive."

"But people have already started flocking around. The other day I saw Professor Mazumdar coming out of a cinema hall holding your daughter's hand. He turned away his face the moment he saw me. This man delivers very interesting lectures. He talks mostly about the future of our country and he speaks very convincingly. But seeing him turn his face when he saw me made me dubious about his intent."

"Mr. Choudhury the barricade has been removed. She has been set free."

"Yes of course."

"Let the Mazumdars go to hell; my main concern is for Rebati."

Chowdhury said, "At present there is nothing to fear, he is totally immersed in his work. And he is doing extremely well."

"Mr. Chowdhury, his problem is that he might be having a very clear head so far as science goes, but he knows very little about women."

"You are right. He hasn't been immunized so far. A slight contact may prove to be fatal."

"Please come every day and check on him."

"Hope he doesn't bring the germ from somewhere and I get infected at this old age. Please don't worry I am joking. I am sure you understood that it was a joke! I have crossed the epidemic zone. I don't get infected even on coming in close contact. But there is a problem, I will have to leave for Gujranwala the day after tomorrow."

"I hope this is a joke! Please have pity on this poor woman!"

"No, this is not a joke. An old friend of mine Doctor Amulya Addi was practicing there for the last twenty-five years. He died suddenly of heart failure, leaving behind his widowed wife and children. I will have to go there and settle his accounts sell off his property and bring back his wife and children. I can't say how long I will have to be there."

"Well, I don't know what to say."

"In this world whatever has to happen will happen. So please be brave. People who believe in fate are not wrong. Even scientists believe in fate, whatever is inevitable will happen. It will not go even a hair's breadth awry. Try your best, but when it goes beyond your control just raise your hand."

"Okay."

"This fellow Mazumdar that I spoke to you about just now, is not all that dangerous, he has been included in the group to give the group a respectable front. The other members of this group to quote the famous scholar Chanakya, are very dangerous even if they are kept at a distance of a hundred hands. There is an attorney in the group called Banku Bihari he is like an octopus, he has a habit of entangling people, and he has a particular fondness for rich widows. So please be careful. And last, but not the least remember my philosophy."

"Mr. Chowdhury I don't care about your philosophy. I am not going to leave everything to fate, I am going to go against your philosophy of letting the inevitable to happen. If someone tries to takes away the laboratory, I will not let it happen. Please remember I am from Punjab. I will not hesitate to kill should the need arise. It can be anybody, my daughter, aspiring sons-in-law anybody!"

She took out a knife hidden under the waist band of her sari in a flash and showed it, the blade shined. She said, "He chose me....... I am not a Bengali woman who do nothing else, but cry for their love. I can give my life for my love and take some one's life too for love. This laboratory is my life I can go to any extent to save it."

Chowdhury said, "There was a time when I wrote poems. Today I feel I can write once again."

"Write poems if you feel like, but please take back your philosophy. I will never be able to accept that. I will fight till the end, single handed. And I will win."

"Bravo! I take back my philosophy. I will be the drummer of your victory march. I am going away for some time, and I will be back soon."

Strangely enough Sohini's eyes filled up with tears. She said, "Please don't mind."   Then she put her arms around his neck and said, "Nothing lasts forever in this world, consider this as a temporary bond." After that she bent down and touched his feet.

10

Sohini's grand mother lived in Ambala. One day Sohini received a telegram from her. It said "Come soon if you want to see me."

Her grandmother was her only relation who was still alive. Nanda Kishore had bought Sohini from her.

Sonihi asked Nila, to accompany her.

Nila refused she said, "That is not possible"

"Why can't you come with me?"

"They are making arrangements to felicitate me."

"Who are they?"

"Members of the *Jagani* (awakening) club. Please don't worry. They are a decent lot. You will understand when I show you the list of the members. They are very selective about giving membership to people."

"What is your aim?"

"Difficult to explain. But you can make out by the name. The name has a deep meaning. Poet Naba kumar explained it to me the other day. They might come to you for donation."

"I have already donated some money; you are fully in their hands aren't you! I can't give them any more."

"Ma, but why are you getting so angry? They want to work for the country selflessly."

"Let us stop the discussion. You must have come to know from your friends that you are independent."

"Yes, I have been told."

"Your selfless friends must have also informed you that you can use can spend the money left by your husband as per your wish."

"Yes, I know."

"I've come to know that you are going to get a probate on the will. Am I right?"

"Absolutely, Mr Banku Bihari is my solicitor."

"I am sure that he must have given you some hope as well as advice."

Nila kept quiet.

Sohini continued, "I will teach your Banku *babu* (mister) a lesson if he dares to come anywhere close to the laboratory. If I can't do anything legally, I will resort to illegal means. I will come via Peshawar on my return journey I will bring some people from there. There will be Sikh sentries on twenty-four-hour duty to protect the laboratory. I will show you something before I leave…… remember I am from Punjab."

She took out her dagger and showed it to her daughter and said, "Please remember that this dagger recognizes neither the daughter nor the daughter's solicitor. I will settle the accounts when I return."

11

The laboratory was surrounded by a lot of fallow land with no buildings on it to prevent sound and vibrations from reaching the laboratory; So that the quiet environment could help the researchers to work peacefully. Rebati generally came to work in the laboratory at night.

That night too he was deep in his work. The clock down stairs struck two. For a moment he took his eyes off from his work and looked at the sky through a widow. He noticed a shadow fall on the wall. He turned back and saw Nila in the room. She was wearing her sleeping attire – a long silk shift. Rebati was about to get up from his chair when Nila sat on his lap and encircled his neck with her arms and hugged him. It made Rebati tremble. His chest heaved up and down rapidly. His voice got choked with emotion. His voice shook as he said, "Please go away from this room."

"Why?" She asked.

Rebati said, "I am finding it difficult to control myself. Why did you come to this room?"

Nila held him tightly and said, "Don't you love me?"

Rebati said, "Yes I do, but please go away from this room."

The Punjabi sentry entered the room all of a sudden and said, "Shame on you *maiji* (madam) please go out of the room."

Rebati had inadvertently pressed the calling bell.

The Punjabi sentry looked at him and said, "Babuji, the mistress trusted you please do not betray her."

Rebati pushed Nila off his lap and stood up.

The sentry asked Nila to go out of the room once again. He said, "If you do not go out of the room on your own, I will have to follow her instructions." He meant that he would use force to throw her out of the room. As she went out of the room Nila shouted, "Are you listening Sir Isaac Newton? You have been invited to a tea party at 4:45 tomorrow in the evening at our residence. Can you hear me? Or, have you lost your consciousness?" She turned back and looked at him.

He replied in a choked voice, "Yes I have heard."

Rebati watched her receding figure as she left the room. The outline of her flawless figure in her flimsy apparel was enchanting. He could not take his eyes away. After she went away Rebati put his head down on the table. What happened was beyond his power of imagination. He felt a shower of electrical spark enter his body and   flow through his entire body. He clenched his fists and tried to tell himself repeatedly, "No I will not go to the party." He wanted to take a vow, but he couldn't. He wrote on a piece of blotting paper over and over again, "I will not go, I will not go!" Suddenly he noticed a red colored handkerchief lying on his table her name 'Nila' was embroidered at one corner. He pressed it to his face and inhaled deeply, fragrance of her perfume enveloped him and he felt intoxicated.

Nila came back. She told the sentry, "I have a bit of work with him."

The sentry objected. She said, "Don't worry I have not come to steal anything. I just need his signature." She looked at Rebati and continued, "We have decided to make you the president of 'Jagani' club. The entire country knows your name."

Rebati said, "But I know nothing about your club."

"You needn't know anything just remember, that Brojendra *babu* is our chief patron."

"I don't even know who is Brojendra *babu*."

"He is the director of the Metropolitan Bank; this is all that you have to know. Please my darling just a signature." She put her right arm around his shoulder and held his hand and said, "Put your signature here."

He signed the paper as though he was dreaming.

When Nila was folding the paper, the sentry said, "Please give me the paper I have to see it."

Nila said, "You will not be able to understand. What will you do by seeing it?"

He said, "I don't have to understand." He snatched away the paper from her hand and tore it into pieces. He said, "Documents and papers that need to be signed by him, get them signed outside the laboratory not here."

Rebati breathed a sigh of relief. The sentry turned towards Nila and said, "Maiji let me take you home." And he took her out of the laboratory.

He came back after some time and said, "I keep all the doors closed. How did she get in? Did you let her in?"

Rebati found his suspicion insulting. He told him, over and over again, "Please believe me I did not open the door."

"Then how did she enter the room?" He, asked himself.

That was a mystery.

The mystery did not let him rest, he went from room to room along with the guard to find out how Nila had come in. Finally, they reached a room and found out, that the latch of a widow facing the road was undone. Someone had opened the latch of the widow during day time. The sentry was sure that it was beyond Rebati to do such a thing because he was too simple a person to indulge in such lowly activities. He struck his head and said, "Women! They can behave like devils at times!"

Rebati spent the rest of the night telling himself, come what may he would not go to the tea party. Very soon the crows started cawing and he left for home.

12

However much he tried Rebati could not skip the invitation. Rebati arrived at the venue of tea party at 4:45 sharp. He had thought that the tea party was meant for just the two of them. So, his attire was simple. He had worn freshly laundered dhoti and kurta, and had kept a folded *chadar* (shawl) on his shoulder. On arrival he realized that party was in the garden. The place was full of fashionably dressed sophisticated people. He was very disappointed by what he saw. He wanted to hide himself in a corner. But the moment he arrived he became the central figure of the party. People got up to wish him. He could not hide himself. Someone came to him and said, "I welcome you this party Doctor Battacharya your seat is there." He pointed towards a velvet covered chair right in the center. He realized that he was the main attraction. Nila came up to him and placed a garland around his neck and put a dot of sandal wood paste on his forehead –a welcoming ritual. People clapped loudly. Brojendra babu proposed Rebati's name for the post of president of 'Jagani' club. It was seconded by Bandhu babu. There was another round of loud clapping. The author Haridas babu spoke about Doctor Bhattacharya's international fame. He said the name and fame of Rebati babu was going to fill up the sail of the boat called 'Jagani club', and it would sail from one port to another long the western ocean spreading knowledge."

The organizers went to the reporters and told them to note down every metaphor mentioned in the speech.

The speakers got up one after another and spoke about Rebati. When someone said, "Doctor Battacharya has put a victory mark on our mother land's brow." Rebati's chest swelled up with pride. He visualized himself as the blazing Sun in the mid-day sky of the civilized world. He brushed aside all the unpleasant things that he had heard about the club. Haridas Babu said, "Now that the club has got the talisman called Rebati people will not have doubts about our noble aim." Haridas Babu's remarks made Rebati conscious about his fame. And he also felt responsible towards the reputation of the club. The praise showered by the speakers helped Rebati to get over his hesitation and he abandoned his shell of diffidence. The ladies crowded around his table and requested him for his autograph.

Rebati was elated, he felt as though he was in a dream all these years and now, he has emerged out of the cocoon of dreams like a butterfly.

When people started leaving, Nila held Rebati's hand and said, "Please don't go so soon."

Her touch made Rebati feel drunk with happiness.

The day was coming an end, the light was fading and a greenish shadow enveloped the garden.

They sat down on a bench close to each other. Nila took his hand in hers and said, "Doctor Bhattacharya why are you so scared of women?

Rebati replied back arrogantly, "Scared of them? Never."

"But aren't you scared of my mother?"

"No, I am not scared of her, I respect her."

"What about me?"

"I am definitely scared of you!"

"Well, that is good news. But my mother will never let me to get married to you. I will end my life if she stops me."

"I will not let anything come in between us. We will get married."

Nila put her head on his shoulder and said, "I need you desperately."

Rebati drew her head closer to his chest and said, "There is no force in this world which can take you away from me."

"But about our casts, they don't match."

"To hell with it."

"In that case we will have to send a notice to the registrar's office."

"I will definitely notify them tomorrow."

Rebati had started showing his true male spirit. Things started changing very rapidly after that.

Sohini's grandmother started showing signs of paralysis. There was very little hope for her survival and she wanted Sohini to be with her till she breathed her last. During her mother's absence there was no check on Nila's activity, she made full use of this and spend her time in pursuit of pleasure.

Rebati's charm started fading under his heavy load of erudition and Nila started losing interest in him. On the other hand, she felt getting married to Rebati would serve her well as he would not come in the way of her hedonistic life style. Moreover, she knew that a huge sum of money has been ear marked for the maintenance of the laboratory and for the projects under it. Well-wishers of the laboratory were of the opinion that Rebati was just the right person who could take over the laboratory. So, Nila did not want to lose him under any circumstances. Her friends too felt the same. Prodded by his associates who cried fie upon him for not having the courage to make a public announcement about his acceptance of presidentship of the club, Rebati got the news published in the newspapers. When Nila teased him about being scared, he would say, "I don't care." He wanted to show off his manliness to Nila desperately. He said, "I correspond with Edington regularly I will request him to come to our club someday." When the members heard him, they said, "Brilliant!"

Rebati's work got neglected. His thought process came to a standstill. He found himself waiting for Nila's arrival perpetually. She would suddenly come from behind and cover his eyes with her hands. At times she would sit on the arm rest of his chair and encircle his neck with her arm. Though his work suffered quite a bit, but he told himself that it was a passing phase once he settled down the broken threads of his work would unite automatically. But there were no signs of settling down. Nila on the other hand did not give any importance to his work. She was of the opinion that disruption of Rebati's work was in no way causing any harm to the world as there has not been any change in the functioning of this world, in other words she took the whole thing very lightly. She considered it to be a big joke. Day after day he found himself getting entangled in a net. Much to his discomfort the members of the Jagani club were getting closer to him. They were hell bent on making a man out of him. He hadn't started using using bad language as yet, but bad language did not shock him anymore. He even forced himself to laugh when someone used foul language. Rebati Battacharya was gradually becoming someone who entertained the members of the club.

But Rebati was troubled by jealousy. He would feel terrible when Nila lit her cigar from the banker's cigar, held between his lips. Try how much he may Rebati could not smoke, the smell of cigar made his head spin, but the sight of Nila lighting a cigar in this fashion was something that he could not bear. Another thing that he hated was seeing them pulling, pushing and touching each other. When he objected, she said, "But it is just my body that is being touched, we don't consider it to be important, do we? For us love is what that matters, and that is very precious I won't go around doling it out to people. After reassuring Rebati she would hold his hand tightly. It would make him happy thinking that those poor souls were happy with the outer shell where as he got the actual pulp.

The main door of the laboratory was guarded day and night. Unfinished work lay inside, no one went in.

13

Nila was lying on a sofa in the drawing room with her feet raised and her head resting on a cushion. Rebati was sitting on the floor with his back resting on the sofa next to Nila's feet. He was holding a closely written foolscap paper in his hand.

Rebati said, "The language of the speech is too flowery. It will embarrass me if I have to read it out."

"Hah you are talking as though you know a great deal about literature and style of writing. This is none of your chemical formulae. Please do not make a fuss, just mug it up. Do you know who has written it? None other than our friend Promodaranjan Babu a famous literary figure." Nila sounded irritable.

"I find mugging up those long sentences difficult. More over those words are difficult to remember. I wish he had used simple words," complained Rebati.

"How come you find those words difficult? I don't find them difficult in fact I have repeated the lecture so many times along with you that I have learnt it. 'The most auspicious moment of my life was the time when members of Jagani club honoured me by putting a garland of flowers from the gardens of......' you don't have to worry I will be sitting next to you I will prompt you whenever you get stuck."

"Look I hardly know anything about Bengali literature, but I feel this if I read out this it will sound very odd, like a mockery. Why don't you let me speak in English? I will be more comfortable. Where is the harm if I say, 'Dear friends, allow me to offer you my heartiest thanks for the honour that you have conferred upon me on behalf of the Jagani Club.... and end the speech after saying two to three similar sentences?"

"No way, the audience will be impressed to hear you speak to them in chaste Bengali specially this bit 'O the youth of Bengal the charioteers of the freedom chariot driving on a path strewn with broken fetters....' Whatever you say Bengali is the only language which can do justice to this kind of speech English will not have the same effect. And when they hear it from a scientist like you it would impress the youth of Bengal; they will dance with joy. We still have a lot of time let me help you to go through it again."

Just then the tall and hulking bank manager Brojerdra Haldar dressed in European clothes appeared on the scene after climbing a flight of stairs laboriously. He was not too happy to see Rebati over there he said, "Oh god this is unbearable whenever I come here, I find him with you, doesn't he have any work? He is like barrier of thorns which keep us away from you!"

Rebati was very embarrassed he said, "To day I had some work with her that is why I am here."

"I know you have a lot of work to do, you have invited the members of Jagani club for dinner today, that is why I came here thinking that you will be busy elsewhere. I have just half an hour before going to office I had thought of spending that time with Nila, but I find you here with Nila! And you say that you have some work with her. Funny when you don't have work you come here to spend your leisure, but when you have work even then you come here to do your work. Very difficult situation, how I can compete with such a person!"

Nila said, "You know the problem with Doctor Battacharya is that, he does not come out with the truth boldly. He is here not because he has some work to do, he is here because he could not stay away from me, that is the real truth. He occupies most of my time by his sheer will power and that is the secret of his masculinity. A rustic youth defeats a stalwart like you."

Mr. Haldar said, "Well in that case the members of Jagani Club too will exhibit masculinity, from now onwards we will practice female abduction, which was very popular during the Stone Ages."

Nila said, "Sounds very amusing. Abducting is any day more interesting that than asking for some one's hand, but how will you do it?"

Haldar said, "I can show you just now."

"Just now?"

"Yes, right now."

Haldar got up from the sofa in a flash and scooped her up in his arms. Nila did not object, she giggled loudly and put her arms around his neck.

Rebati's face darkened with anger. Try however he may Rebati did not have the strength to imitate Haldar nor he could stop him. He felt angrier with Nila for encouraging such boorish people like Halder.

Haldar said, "I have parked my car downstairs let me take you to Diamond Harbour. I will bring you before the evening. I had some work in the bank, but that can wait. Let me spend the time by doing something good. I am giving an opportunity to Doctor Bhattacharya to work in peace, he will be thankful to me to me for removing a distraction like you."

Rebati noticed that Nila was not struggling to be let off from his arms in fact she snuggled close to his chest and hugged his neck amorously. As she was going out, she said, "You have nothing to fear, my dear scientist, this is just a play acting of female abduction, he is not taking me away to *Lanka* like the demon King *Ravan,* I will be back before the party in the evening."

Rebati tore the write-up. The strength of Haldar's arms and the way he asserted his right made Rebati's erudition worthless.

The venue was a famous restaurant. Rebati Battacharya was the host. His honoured companion Nila sat next to him. A famous cine-actress had been invited to sing. Mr. Banku Bihari had got up to propose a toast. He praised Rebati to high heavens and also praised Nila. The women present were taking long drags from their cigarettes to prove that they were extra ordinary women. Middle aged women were wearing masks of youth and were trying to outdo the younger women in their gesture and loud laughter.

All of a sudden Sohini entered the room, followed by a pin-drop silence.

Sohini looked at Rebati and said, "Can't recognise you, Doctor Bhattacharya. Is that you? You had asked for some money last Friday. It is quite obvious that it has met your requirements. You will have to leave this place just now and come with me I would like to take stock of things present in the laboratory."

"Are you disbelieving me?" asked Rebati.

"I had not disbelieved you so far. But if you have any shame left in you will never talk about 'trust' again."

Rebati was getting up, Nila pulled him down.

She said, "He has invited his friends for this party. He will leave only after they go away."

There was a barb in what she said. Her mother was very fond of Rebati. She had trusted him like no one else and that is why she had handed over the laboratory to him. She wanted to hurt her mother some more so she said, "Do you know ma how many people have been invited to this party, sixty-five; this room could not accommodate all of them, so the rest are in the next room. You can hear their merry laughter. It is going to cost twenty-five rupees per person, irrespective of whether one drinks or not. Had it been someone else the bill would have shocked them, but not so with him, even the bank manager was surprised by his open-handedness. Do you know how much he paid to the singer? Four hundred rupees for one night!"

Rebati's heart was fluttering like a freshly caught fish. His lips had gone dry and he was unable to utter a single word.

"What is it that you are celebrating today?" asked Sohini.

"Oh my god, don't you know! It has been published in associated press that he has accepted the post of president of Jagani Club. The party is hosted by him to celebrate the occasion. He will pay a fee six hundred rupees for life membership as and when it is convenient for him," said Nila.

"That occasion will not arise soon," Snapped Sohini.

Rebati's was reduced to nothing as though a steam roller had gone over him Sohini asked him, "You are not a in position to come with me right now, is that so?"

Rebati looked at Nila.

Her look inspired some manliness in him, he said "How can I go now, the invitees are......

Sohini said. "In that case I am going to sit here and wait."

"Nasirullah," she addressed her Pathan body guard, "You can wait outside the door."

Nila said, "Ma we can't permit this. We are going to discuss a few confidential matters, so you must leave."

"Look Nila, you have just started playing this game of wits where as I have been at it for a very long time. You can't surpass me. Let me tell you my presence in the meeting is very important. You think I do not know what you are going to discuss in the meeting?"

"Who has told you about it I wonder."

"The source of information lies in the money bag; you need to loosen the string that's all. The three lawyers present here are going to scrutinize the documents and advise you if there is any loop hole through which you can claim the money ear marked for the laboratory. Am I right Nila?"

Nila said, "Frankly speaking, it is difficult to believe that a daughter has no share in the money left by her father. This has made people suspicious."

Sohini got up from her chair. She said, "The roots of suspicion go further back. In the first place who is your father? You are laying claim on whose money?"

Nila jumped up from her chair, she said, "What are you saying ma!"

"I am speaking the truth. I had hidden nothing from my husband. I had told him everything."

Barrister Ghosh said, "How can we believe you?"

Sohini said, "My husband knew such a situation may arise someday. So, he wrote down everything and got the document registered."

Mr. Ghosh looked at the other lawyers and said, "There is nothing for us to do in that case, so let us go."

The rest of the sixty- five guests left the place soon after that, the Peshawari guard let them go.

Mr. Chowdhury entered the scene at this point of time holding a suitcase in his hand. He looked at Sohini and said, "I received your telegram and came as early as I could." Then he looked at Rebati and said, "Hey Rebi baby what's up your face is as white as parchment, I guess you need some nourishment, where is his bowl of milk!"

Sohini pointed towards Nila and said, "She is the one who is providing that at present."

"Dear girl, are you playing the role of a milk maid (the milk maids of Vrindavan were in love with lord Krishna, they used to feed him butter and milk)?"

"Yes, and she was looking for a cow herd (Lord Krishna was a cow herd in Vrindavan). She has found him. He is sitting right there." She pointed towards Rebati.

"Who, our Rebi?" enquired Mr. Chowdhury.

"My daughter has saved the laboratory. I couldn't gauge this man. I think my daughter was a better judge, she opened my eyes, otherwise this laboratory would have become a cow shed in no time. His presence in the laboratory would have sunk the laboratory into a pit of cow dung."

The professor looked at Nila and said, "My child since this cow herd is your discovery, you will have to take full charge of him. He has everything, but what he lacks is common sense. If you are with him no one will guess that he lacks it. Moreover, it is easy to handle stupid males."

Nila said, "Sir Isaac Newton, we have already given a notice of our marriage in the Registrar's office do you want to withdraw it?"

Rebati puffed out is chest and said, "Never, not on my life."

"In that case the marriage will not be solemnized in an inauspicious moment," said the professor.

"So, what!" Cried Rebati.

The professor said, "My dear Nilu. He might be stupid, but he is not ineffective. Let him come out his trance. You will not have to worry he is quite capable of fending for himself."

"Sir Isaac you will have to get a new wardrobe in that case. Otherwise, I will have to cover my face when you are around, because of embarrassment."

Suddenly a shadow fell on the wall. Rebati's aunt appeared on the scene.

She looked at Rebati and said, "Get up and come with me."

Rebati got up from his seat like a mechanized doll and followed her obediently.

He did not look back.

Glossary

Bom Bholanath — another name for Lord Shiva. In this form he is perpetually under effect of all kinds of intoxicants like Cannabis, Datura, Ganja, bhang etc. He is oblivious about the rest of the world.

Draupadi — Draupadi was a character in Mahabarata. She had five husbands the five Pandava brothers.

Kunti — Kunti was a was the mother the three older Pandav brothers. They were fathered by three gods namely Dharma Pawan and Indra. The eldest son Karna was born when Kunti was a maiden Karna's father was Surya, the Sun God.

Sita — Sita of the epic Ramayana was a faithful and devoted wife of Lord Rama. She was abducted by the demon king Ravana. Later she was abandoned by her husband who wrongly suspected her of being unfaithful.

Savitri — Was married to Satyavaan. He was destined to live for one year after marriage. Savitri by her love, devotion and determination managed to convince the God of death, Yama to give her husband a long life.

Tandav — Dance of fury danced by Shiva. Shiva is also known as the God of destruction.

Chanakya — Also known as Kautiya. Was a famous political theorist. He was the political adviser of Chandragupta Muarya.

Lanka — The demon king Ravan abducted Sita Lord Ram's wife and took her away to his kingdom in Lanka.

Tying someone to Anchal — means tying someone to one's apron strings.

Milton Keynes UK
Ingram Content Group UK Ltd.
UKHW010630290424
441924UK00001B/159